MAY DAY MURDER

Pearl's best friend, Nathan, has persuaded local actress Faye Marlow to open the May Day festivities at Whitstable Castle and involves Pearl in his plans. Having left the town more than two decades ago, the star has been living in the South of France. Faye is nowhere to be found on the morning of May Day. Then just as the parade is about to start, the actress's dead body is discovered – tethered to the maypole on the Castle grounds ... and so it's left to Pearl and DCI Mike McGuire to unravel the mystery of the May Day murder.

MAY DAY MURDER

MAY DAY MURDER

by

Julie Wassmer

Magna Large Print Books
Long Preston, North Yorkshire,
BD23 4ND, England.

British Library Cataloguing in Publication Data.

A catalogue record of this book is
available from the British Library

ISBN 978-0-7505-4397-2

First published in Great Britain in 2016 by Constable

Cover illustration © Tom Taylor by arrangement with
Alamy Stock Photo

Published in Large Print 2017 by arrangement with
Little, Brown Book Group

Magna Large Print is an imprint of Library Magna Books Ltd.

Printed and bound in Great Britain by
T.J. (International) Ltd., Cornwall, PL28 8RW

For Kas, Sara, Caden and Tallulah

'What potent blood hath modest May.'
Ralph W. Emerson

WHITSTABLE CASTLE AND GARDENS

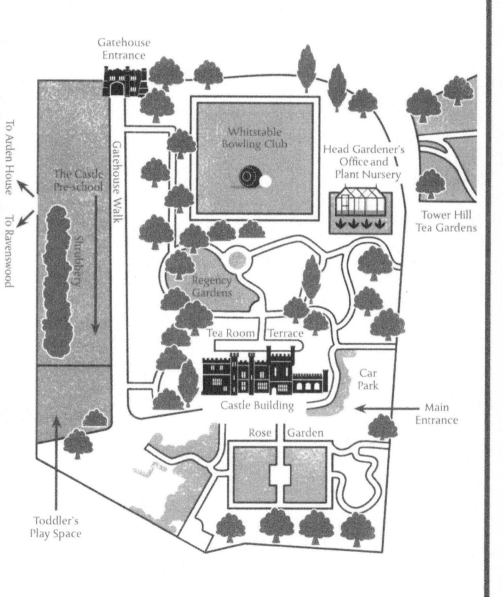

Gatehouse Entrance

To Arden House

To Ravenswood

The Castle Pre-school

Shrubbery

Gatehouse Walk

Whitstable Bowling Club

Head Gardener's Office and Plant Nursery

Tower Hill Tea Gardens

Regency Gardens

Tea Room   Terrace

Car Park

Castle Building

Main Entrance

Rose Garden

Toddler's Play Space

Chapter One

Dolly Nolan had been helping to lay a table at the rear of The Whitstable Pearl restaurant when her enthusiasm suddenly palled.

'Can someone tell me why we are going to all this trouble for just one customer?'

Pearl's mother was over sixty but at that moment she looked more like a petulant teenager, standing with her hands on her hips, waiting for her daughter to reply. In fact, it was Pearl's young waitress, Ruby Hill, who spoke up.

'Faye Marlow's not just any customer,' she insisted. 'She's special.'

Ruby then turned to her boss as if for confirmation, but Pearl replied only: 'All customers are special.'

It was a diplomatic response designed to close down further conversation and it left Ruby far from satisfied. 'But she's a film star!'

'*Was* a film star,' Dolly quickly corrected her. 'She's rather more of a has-been these days.'

A stunned silence followed this stark assessment until Pearl asked Ruby if she could fetch some bread baskets. The girl turned obediently on her heels and headed off to the kitchen, her newly bobbed fair hair bouncing above her shoulders.

Dolly remained unapologetic under her daughter's admonishing gaze. 'It's true,' she shrugged. 'I don't know why you're all so star-struck.'

'No one is star-struck.'

'No? Then why are we fussing about this table long after we should have gone home?'

Pearl refused to rise to her mother's bait. She was well aware that Dolly's irritability was due largely to her toothache, but as Dolly hated visiting the dentist she had been steadfastly refusing to make an appointment. For her own part, Pearl was frustrated because the restaurant had indeed closed after a busy lunchtime service, and by accepting this special reservation she had given up on her chance to visit the family allotment. The weather was perfect for it – set fair with uninterrupted blue skies offering a few hours of sunshine during which Pearl had hoped to plant some runner beans and chard. At this time of year, by late afternoon the sun's warmth could be chased away by a northerly breeze sharp enough to remind anyone in Whitstable not to 'cast a clout till May is out'.

In fact, the mood of the little North Kent fishing town seemed always to be determined by the weather. During the winter months Whitstable entered a period of hibernation when the shops and eateries were largely free from a veritable tsunami of DFLs (the town's acronym for Down from Londoners), who flooded the coast throughout the summer, especially during the annual Oyster Festival in July. But spring was a time of reawakening, and the first hint of blossom signalled a burst of activity during which shopfronts and beach huts were hastily repainted, and front gardens and window boxes were weeded and newly planted.

18

A competition had recently taken place to clear the many alleyways of brambles, litter and snails, with the first prize being a meal for two at The Whitstable Pearl. The winner was a resident who had not only single-handedly cleared the alley near to her home but also transformed it with seeded wallflowers and a carpet of pebbles and oyster shells. Dolly herself had even found some time to arrange a few pots at the allotment but, as ever, her efforts remained centred on aesthetics rather than hard work in the vegetable plot. That was usually contributed by Pearl and her son, Charlie, but as he was spending a year out in Berlin until September, his services were currently unavailable.

The pale spring sunshine was doing its best to chase light into dark corners and lately The Whitstable Pearl, noted for its seafood and local oysters, had become much busier, with bookings for several private functions. One of them was for the party of visitors being met at that very moment by Pearl's friend and neighbour, Nathan Roscoe, at local Manston airport. Ruby had been right in declaring that one of these was no ordinary customer: it was the actress, Faye Marlow, arriving from Nice with a small entourage consisting of her private assistant, her maid and her chauffeur. Dolly was also correct in suggesting that Pearl would never have reopened her doors for a single table of guests, but she had a good reason to do so other than being 'star-struck' – and chose now to remind Dolly of it.

'I'm doing this as a favour to Nathan,' she said, not for the first time.

'He's star-struck too,' said Dolly, not missing a beat. 'He's wanted to meet Faye for years and now he's finally seen his chance.'

There wasn't much Pearl could say to this because it was true. Having begun his working life as an advertising copywriter in his native Los Angeles, Nathan had soon tired of using his best ideas to overhype the qualities of dog biscuits and detergent and had moved on to become a free-lance journalist, contributing articles to magazines on subjects that included interior design, food and his greatest passion – film. Nathan had always been a great fan of Faye Marlow's best work: a series of films produced mainly in the mid-1990s. Together with a fellow fan, he had managed to secure this visit by inviting the actress to open a local event and, to his astonishment, Faye had accepted, leaving Nathan with the impression that he might finally gain an opportunity to interview the star.

'You know as well as I do why Faye's here,' countered Pearl. 'She's agreed to open the May Day programme – and that's got to be a good thing for Whitstable.'

Dolly remained stubbornly unimpressed. 'Oh yes? And why's that?'

Pearl gave a sigh of exasperation. 'Because Faye's so well known, of course, and she also has connections to the town.'

To this, Dolly offered only a derisive snort. Then she looked up at her daughter, reflecting for a moment on how little Pearl resembled her. Dolly's fashion sense was nothing short of flamboyant and she sported magenta highlights to mask her grey hair, with a clashing pink blouse visible today beneath her starched white Whitstable Pearl apron. She had always felt the need to scream her existence and she did so not only with her appearance but through her creative endeavours, like the paintings that lined the restaurant walls and the 'shabby chic' ceramic plates she crafted, which rarely escaped mention from Pearl's customers.

In contrast, Pearl's own style was distinctly understated. Much taller than her mother, she seldom wore jewellery – no rings or earrings that could become lost in restaurant dishes during their preparation – just a small silver locket that lay flat against her bare throat. Her modest wardrobe of clothes had been bought, for the most part, for comfort and practicality, and consisted mainly of vintage items so, with her long gypsy-dark hair tumbling around her shoulders, she could sometimes appear like a romantic heroine returned from another era – a latter-day Cathy from *Wuthering Heights.*

The fact was that Pearl looked striking whatever she wore and whatever she did to herself. A tall, dark beauty with grey eyes the colour of moonstone, some said she had the look of the 'black Irish' – the descendants of Spanish Armada sailors who had escaped death on the beaches of the west coast of Ireland to serve under rebel chiefs such as Sorley Boy McDonnell and Hugh O'Neill, Earl of Tyrone. It was true that Pearl's father, Tommy, had been able to trace his own roots back to Galway, and she had inherited the best features of both parents in her mother's spirit and her father's dark good looks.

Drawing herself up to her full height, Dolly now challenged her daughter. '"Connections"?' she repeated scornfully. 'Thirty years ago, that woman turned her back on this town and I doubt if she's ever given a moment's thought to us in all that time. There may be plenty who know the name Faye Marlow, but to me she'll always be plain Frankie Marshall – the granddaughter of a whelk merchant. If you ask me, the woman is nothing but trouble.'

Pearl was just about to inform her mother that she hadn't asked her anything at all when she noticed Ruby standing at the kitchen door, anxiously clutching three small bread baskets. It was clear the girl feared that she might be witnessing something beyond the usual small conflict of views between mother and daughter, but at that moment, a mobile sounded and Pearl went off to the seafood bar to answer it. Noting that the caller was Nathan and with Dolly's words still ringing in her ears, Pearl sensed that a problem could be looming.

'What is it?' she asked starkly.

'A hitch,' came the reply. Nathan's soft mid-Atlantic accent was still in place, but it had lost its usual relaxed tone. 'Nothing too serious, sweetie,' he added hastily, 'but...' He paused for a moment.

Ruby was busily setting the bread baskets on the table and arranging cutlery on the fresh white tablecloth, but Dolly continued doggedly to observe Pearl until the call had finally ended.

'Well?' she asked.

The restaurant table now looked immaculate

with a bowl of fresh narcissi in place – a tribute to spring as well as a reminder of Pearl's missed visit to the allotment. She took a deep breath before sharing the news she had just received from Nathan. 'It seems that Faye has changed her mind and would prefer to eat at home.'

Dolly's jaw dropped, but her expression then transformed into one of sheer triumph. Jabbing the air with her finger, she ripped off her apron, exclaiming: 'I *told* you, Pearl! That blasted woman is *nothing* but trouble!'

Half an hour later, Pearl was driving along Tower Parade with Ruby beside her; the girl was listening to some upbeat music on her headphones, judging by the tempo of her fingertips tapping on the dashboard. The boot of Pearl's Fiat was stocked with ingredients for the meal she had agreed to prepare at Arden House, where her client was staying. The house was the first in a row of grand, double-fronted Victorian and Edwardian properties that lay close to Whitstable Castle on its southern side. Pearl watched as a flock of shiny-feathered starlings swooped down to peck at the front lawns of a terrace of old almshouse dwellings, their gardens filled with mimosa, tulips and a deep blue campanula called Canterbury Bells – a fitting choice, she thought, since the city was only a twenty-minute drive away.

As they passed the western entrance of the Castle, the old flint and brick gatehouse looked at odds with a new sign that touted space for hire for weddings, functions and conferences – and Pearl couldn't help wondering how Wynn Ellis, the first owner of the Castle, also responsible for the building of the almshouses, might have felt about such brazen advertising. The road ahead forked left towards Marine Parade and the grassy slopes studded with colourful beach huts, but Pearl headed right on to Tankerton Road, turning into a driveway leading to a small parking area at the rear of two houses.

Killing her engine, she turned to her waitress with a smile and said, 'Thanks for coming, Ruby.'

The girl took out her earphones and returned the smile. 'No problem. I'm looking forward to this.' She was clearly excited at the prospect of meeting someone half-famous, while Pearl was merely grateful that her waitress had agreed to help out. Dolly herself had refused to have anything do with it and stormed off home, taking her painful pre-molar with her.

Having explained to Ruby that she'd be right back, Pearl got out of the car. She glanced around, noting that a rear access path ran along the back of the houses. A wooden fence separated it from the Castle grounds but a few panels were down so it was possible to peek through to the Castle building itself, which lay beyond some mature trees and a shrubbery that lined a walkway leading up from the gatehouse. Most local people knew that the Castle had originally been built at the end of the eighteenth century as a seaside villa owned by a businessman named Charles Pearson. Tankerton Towers, as it was then known, passed to his son, and was later taken over by Wynn Ellis and used as a country retreat – in which he promptly installed a mistress. Major improvements resulted in a summer residence in the style of a Gothic castle with the grounds extended and landscaped in a style befitting a man who was to become an MP, magistrate and county sheriff. Apart from creating the local almshouses, the Castle's former owner had also bequeathed a valuable art collection to the National Gallery in London, as well as a considerable sum to local charities.

In time, Whitstable Castle, as it became known, had been sold to the Local District Council and was now managed by a charitable trust. A £3 million restoration had resulted in a revamp – but Dolly abhorred the result, claiming that the charm of the old gardens had been destroyed and replaced with something resembling a TV garden makeover. In spite of her criticisms, the Castle was well loved by everyone. It now boasted a play area that was popular with toddlers, and a bowling green, as well as the conference space advertised on the gatehouse.

The grand houses that now surrounded the Castle had been built only after the sale of plots from a large estate had allowed for the development of a residential settlement as well as a direct route to the small town of Tankerton and its eastern neighbours of Swalecliffe and Herne Bay.

As she stepped back from the fence, Pearl noticed that a gate led directly into the rear of Arden House, but instead of making use of it she headed back on to the street.

An impressive property built on three storeys, Arden House was hedged for privacy with fragrant rosemary bushes, and though the windows of its high gables would once have offered a view for housemaids, they now provided the same for any guests who cared to rent the two holiday apartments into which the old servants' quarters had been converted. The house belonged to Tom Chandler, an actor friend of Nathan's who had offered it as accommodation to Faye while he was away touring in Dubai with a Shakespeare company.

A tall wrought-iron gate opened on to an Edwardian tiled path that led Pearl through a front garden filled with shrubs and littered with bluebells. The lower front windows were obscured by white plantation shutters and the front door was enveloped in wisteria blossom. A coach lamp swung above the front step in the breeze as Pearl rang the bell.

Pearl had expected that Nathan would greet her; instead she heard the quick patter of footsteps from inside and the door opened to reveal a petite young woman with a slim build and black hair cropped short like a pixie. Her gamine look and dark eyebrows reminded Pearl of a young Audrey Hepburn. She wore a simple black dress with a Peter Pan collar and a pair of espadrilles with ribbon tied at her ankles. In a thick French accent, she asked: 'You are ze food?' Her expression was stressed as she waited anxiously for Pearl's response.

'I am,' Pearl replied helpfully.

At this, the young woman gave a sigh of relief and stepped back, allowing Pearl to enter the black-and-white-tiled hallway. A wide central staircase wound its way to the next floor and at that moment, Nathan Roscoe appeared at the top of it.

An attractive man in his early forties with dark brown hair and a toned body, today Nathan was wearing a pale pink linen shirt and fashionably tight black trousers. He had begun to grow a short beard lately, and Pearl couldn't make up her mind whether she liked it or not, since it seemed to be flecked with ginger patches. Nathan was Pearl's closest friend and confidant in Whitstable and he might very well have been more to her – had he not been gay.

Visibly pleased to see her, he exclaimed, '*There you are!*' But as he noticed the young French woman turn to look at him, he stopped himself from commenting further and, instead, hurried down the stairs to explain quickly, in his perfect French: '*Tout va bien, Rosine. Ne t'inquiètes pas. Je vais m'en occuper.*'

Rosine nodded. '*Merci.*' And with a polite smile at them both, she headed swiftly back upstairs.

Nathan waited until he heard a door close on the upper floor before whispering, 'I'm so sorry, Pearl. She lost her nerve.'

'Faye?'

He nodded. 'She suddenly got spooked about coming to the restaurant and said she might feel ... "exposed".'

Pearl thought that Nathan might offer up some criticisms of the 'diva' that Dolly had predicted, but instead he gave an unexpected smile and said, 'She really is a darling, you know. A little sensitive perhaps, and the journey's taken it out of her, but I'm sure you'll love her.'

'Where is she?' Pearl asked.

27

'Upstairs relaxing. I know she'll be fine once she's eaten, but...' He paused before asking: 'Will it take ages?'

'No more than half an hour.'

'Parfait!'

He was about to lean forward and kiss Pearl but, before he could do so, a woman's voice rang out. 'Nathan?' It was neither loud nor harsh in tone, but compelling nonetheless – like the soft insistence of a baby's cry.

Nathan answered immediately. 'Coming, Faye!'

As he turned back again to Pearl, looking decidedly torn, she pointed towards the staircase and urged him: 'Go on. I'll be right back with Ruby and the food. We'll soon have lunch ready – a meal fit for a movie star.'

Chapter Two

It didn't take too long to prepare the meal in the kitchen of Arden House. Pearl had decided on a dish based loosely on a Florentine *panzanella* salad, though it was always her style to transform a simple recipe into something of her own. Using the recipe as a foundation, she would build on it, much as a jazz musician might use a simple tune for the basis of a complex improvisation. And so she had added to the *panzanella* her own choice of ingredients: plump black olives and anchovies. Ruby was busy laying another table, this time in a conservatory straight off the kitchen, using all

Pearl's training to make it as attractive as possible, only now with a small glass vase filled with forsythia as decoration. Pearl observed her through the kitchen window, hearing Ruby humming to herself as she worked. Then she spotted the young French girl, Rosine, hovering at the door to the conservatory, as if checking on Ruby's progress, before picking up a sewing box and disappearing back upstairs with it to fulfil her principal duties as Faye's maid.

The kitchen was impressively large – and open-plan – with a butler's sink and a butcher-block table. Root vegetables were stored in wicker baskets alongside strings of garlic and onions, while gleaming copper pots hung from an overhead rack. Pearl's own kitchen at Seaspray Cottage would have been dwarfed by comparison, and the rustic feel of Arden House's distressed cabinetry and large pieces of weathered furniture owed more to the style of a grand mountain lodge than an Edwardian house.

Nathan finally reappeared just as Pearl was taking a tray of warm sweet bell peppers from the oven. 'Faye will be down in a moment,' he announced, moving closer to plant a small kiss on her cheek. 'I really am sorry for messing you around, sweetie.'

'It's all right. You can make it up to me,' Pearl teased. 'When I finally get to the allotment you can dig a trench for my beans.'

Nathan winced. Horticulture really wasn't his thing, and though his own cottage garden was immaculately kept, the physical work was always put in by a hired hand. He opened his mouth to speak but then thought better of it.

'What is it?' asked Pearl.

He bit his lip. 'I just hope this will all work out,' he said.

'What do you mean?' Pearl was concerned he might be referring to her meal.

'The diary of events, of course,' he explained. 'There'll be so much to get through, with the press interviews, the screening of Faye's film, followed by the evening reception and her speech at the Castle on the day.'

'All perfectly planned by you and Purdy,' Pearl said confidently. She was referring to Perdita Hewett, more usually known as Purdy to her friends and family. The daughter of a local archaeologist, Oliver Hewett, and his wife, Maria, Purdy was only few years older than Pearl's son, Charlie, and she had acted as Nathan's partner in the plan to recruit Faye Marlow for the May Day celebrations.

'I guess. It's just ... well, it all seems a little too good to be true. Maybe I'm getting some last-minute nerves.' He watched Pearl efficiently peeling back the skin from the last of her peppers before she began to drizzle them with a virgin olive oil infused with herbs.

'There are two whole days before May Day,' she reminded him. 'Everything will be fine.'

'You're right,' he said, finally reassured. 'You're always right.'

She handed him the large bowl containing the *panzanella*. 'Now take this outside to Ruby for me.'

Nathan followed Pearl's order and left through

the kitchen door. A few moments later she heard a voice in the hallway, saying, 'I told you – we're not eating in the garden but in the conservatory. You won't get cold, but why not put this around your shoulders?' The voice had a crisp, businesslike tone and a Californian accent much like Nathan's.

Two figures now entered the kitchen. The speaker, a tall woman in her mid-forties, was arranging a pale blue pashmina around the shoulders of her companion, who was instantly recognisable to Pearl as Faye Marlow. In spite of the journey to Whitstable from her home in the South of France, the actress was immaculately groomed – and an icon of femininity. Her blonde, jaw-length hair was perfectly styled and feather-cut away from her face as though to frame it. Although she was now in her early fifties, she still had the figure of a young girl, as so many French women seemed able to maintain with careful diet, exercise and perhaps the help of a myriad of French creams and unguents that claimed to keep breasts and buttocks in their rightful place. Whatever method Faye employed, it seemed to be working, but in spite of the physical presence she displayed on screen, in real life she appeared somewhat diminished, a doll-like version of her cinema persona. The last thing Pearl had read about the actress was that she had recently picked up an award as one of the fifty best-dressed women over fifty years of age. It was clear that Faye deserved it. She wore a pale ivory silk blouse with a camisole top peeping above its neckline, and her dove-grey trousers were made of a fine crepe, but without a single crease, which led Pearl to suspect that

31

Rosine had been kept busy upstairs, ironing her employer's wardrobe.

Enveloped in a cloud of floral perfume, Faye moved forward to greet Pearl. 'You must be Nathan's friend,' she said, her eyes quickly scanning Pearl from top to toe. 'The chef?'

'That's right,' Pearl said warmly.

The efficient American at Faye's side offered a more accurate description. 'This is Pearl Nolan, Faye. The owner of the restaurant called The Whitstable Pearl.'

At this, Faye gave the sweetest of smiles, both childlike and sincere. 'How very nice of you to serve lunch for me here instead.' She held out a fragile but perfectly manicured hand. Her fingers were delicate – long and tapering – and adorned with rings, one of which was a stunningly large, rectangular diamond. Pearl took Faye's hand, noting that her eyes were the same pale blue as the pashmina around her shoulders.

'Now why don't you go along, Faye,' said the American gently. 'And I'll be out in a moment.'

Faye obeyed without question and no sooner had she crossed the threshold into the conservatory than Nathan could be heard greeting her. A glance through the window confirmed that he was taking good care of the star, ushering her to a comfortable seat at the head of an antique Carrara marble-topped table.

For a moment, Pearl expected the American to offer her own hand to shake, but instead she gave Pearl a warm and friendly smile. 'I'm Barbara March,' she introduced herself. 'Faye's PA.'

The woman had a slightly avian look about her,

Pearl thought. Her dark eyes were narrowly placed, like a hawk, and her nose resembled a small beak though her lips were full and softened every other feature. She wore a taupe linen dress that concealed a slim figure and she used little make-up, just a hint of pink lipstick. Her chestnut-brown hair, lightened at the temples from the sun, had been scraped into a ponytail that sat high on the back of her head. In contrast to Faye, Barbara seemed like a woman who had little time in her life for glamour, but with her employer now in someone else's care, she relaxed a little.

'I must say, it all looks delicious,' Barbara said, gesturing at the prepared dishes that lay spread on the kitchen table: the sweet red bell peppers arranged beside prawns grilled with chilli, to accompany Pearl's improvised *panzanella*. She tilted her head to one side like an inquisitive bird. 'Can I help at all?'

'Only by enjoying it,' smiled Pearl.

A phone suddenly rang out – a brutal sound, demanding instant attention – and Barbara took it from her pocket. 'Sorry about this,' she said, looking pained before stepping into the garden to announce into her phone: 'Barbara March speaking.'

Throughout the late lunch, Pearl began to wonder whether it had been Dolly's troublesome tooth that had caused her to describe Faye Marlow with such hostility, for the woman who now sat beside Nathan seemed perfectly delightful. The meal was a success, enjoyed in a convivial atmosphere as a white butterfly remained happily trapped in the conservatory, flitting between the flowers of

33

several orchids before finally settling, moving its wings slowly up and down for a moment before taking off again in the warm, fragrant air.

The only thing that bothered Pearl was the fact that Faye ate so little of her meal, choosing instead to chase the delicious food around her plate – though she was forever complimentary about the courses.

Throughout the meal Faye spoke mainly to Nathan, giving him her undivided attention as she imparted anecdotes, while he appeared captivated by both her stories and her presence. Occasionally she would glance in Pearl's direction and offer up a polite smile as she allowed Nathan to refill her wine glass, but it was left to Barbara to remain on duty, drinking only black coffee while fielding calls on her mobile phone and dictating a number of messages into a small Dictaphone she seemed to use as an aide memoire.

Noting that Pearl had been watching this, Barbara confided, 'This thing sometimes comes in far handier than a notebook.'

'I'm sure it does,' said Pearl. 'I've been considering investing in some dictation software for my computer. It would allow me to use voice commands rather than type on my keyboard – so much quicker for me when I'm writing up reports.'

'Reports? For your restaurant?' Barbara looked confused.

Nathan clarified. 'Pearl's also a private detective.' And when Barbara cast a sceptical look his way, he added, 'It's true. She runs her own agency.'

Barbara glanced back at Pearl in surprise. 'Did

34

you hear that, Faye? Apart from being an excellent cook, Nathan's friend here is also a private investigator.'

Faye summoned some mild enthusiasm. 'Fascinating,' she commented politely. 'But what on earth could you possibly find to investigate in a little town like Whitstable?' She took a long sip of wine.

'Oh, you'd be surprised,' Pearl replied. 'Wherever there are people, there are crimes.'

Barbara picked up her coffee cup. 'You're right, of course. But what would motivate you, as a chef, to solve them?'

'I trained as a police officer some time ago,' Pearl told her. 'And I always say that clues to a crime are rather like ingredients for a meal: put them together in the right way and the results can be very satisfying.'

Nathan tapped his wine glass with a spoon in appreciation. 'Well said, darling.' He was ready to expound on the cases that Pearl had solved since she had started up Nolan's Detective Agency last summer but, at that moment, Ruby entered with the dessert – a delicious fruit syllabub – which she now placed in the centre of the table.

She leaned close to Pearl and whispered, 'Shall I start serving?'

Pearl nodded and Ruby carefully filled a small bowl for Faye, who accepted it graciously. 'Raspberries,' she said. 'My favourite.'

It was clear that Ruby was thrilled to be in such close proximity to a celebrity, but under Pearl's supervision the girl quickly and efficiently served Nathan and Barbara as Faye turned her attention

35

again to Pearl. 'Do sit down and join us for dessert, and tell me more about this agency. How long has it been in operation?'

As Ruby left the room, Nathan jumped in to say his piece. 'Almost a year and she's already solved a string of murders.'

'Murder?' asked Barbara. 'Surely that's a job for the police?'

Pearl considered that if Detective Chief Inspector Mike McGuire of Canterbury CID had been present at that moment, he would certainly have agreed. All she disclosed, however, was: 'Sometimes even the police can do with a little help.'

Before anyone had time to respond to this, the doorbell sounded and Barbara immediately got to her feet, pressing a napkin to her mouth before calling out, 'Rosine?' She turned to Faye and said: 'It's probably Luc.'

'Faye's driver went to collect a hire car,' Nathan explained to Pearl.

Defying expectations, however, it was a young woman who now entered the conservatory with Rosine. 'Mademoiselle Hewett,' Faye's maid announced.

Purdy Hewett dwarfed Rosine beside her, but unlike many women of her stature, she seemed proud of her height and held herself with an upright posture, her feet planted with toes pointing outwards, almost in a ballerina's second position. Like a dancer, too, she wore flat pumps, though Purdy was often to be seen in heels – appropriate perhaps for one whom Dolly described as 'having her head in the clouds'.

'I d-do hope I'm not interrupting,' she stammered nervously.

Though Purdy was older than Charlie she seemed in many ways to be a lot younger. Having attended the best public school in Canterbury she had gone on to complete a course in Film Studies at Kent University – never seeming to venture very far from her family home in Tankerton. A warm and intelligent young woman, Purdy's passion for cinema rivalled Nathan's – though 'passion' was not a word Pearl would usually have associated with Purdy who, despite her confidence, also displayed an innocence that bordered on the naïve. Pearl suspected that this had something to do with the close relationship she enjoyed with her parents, who treated her with an almost cloying protectiveness. To Pearl, it seemed inappropriate for someone of her age – as did the way she still addressed them as 'Mummy' and 'Daddy'.

Purdy remained rooted to the threshold, awkwardly clutching a folder under her arm, and an embarrassing silence followed which Nathan was about to break when Faye suddenly breathed the following question: 'How could you possibly be interrupting, my dear?' Slowly rising to her feet, in true dramatic fashion, the actress held out both hands to welcome the girl.

Purdy's broad face broke into a smile before she moved quickly forward, and gushed, 'I can't tell you what a pleasure it is to meet you, Miss Marlow.'

For a moment, Faye studied the girl in the same way she had done with Pearl, but then she spoke. *'Enfin, mon enfant,'* she said softly. 'We finally meet.' Faye allowed the girl to kiss her on both cheeks before indicating for Purdy to take a seat beside her.

'Oh, I'm afraid I can't stop,' she protested nervously. 'I'm on my way to pick up Mummy from Canterbury, but I ... well, I just had to come by and welcome you. I mean, it's one thing to speak on the phone, as we've been doing, but to actually meet you in person – it's a dream come true.'

Purdy continued to gaze at Faye, transfixed, it seemed, by the star's blue eyes until Faye finally uttered, 'It's a great pleasure for me too.'

A moment later, Nathan introduced an element of practicality by saying: 'You and I still need to finalise those details about the screening, Purdy.'

'Of course,' the girl remembered something. 'And I've also brought the details for the press interviews.' She handed over the folder to Nathan then gave her attention once more to Faye. 'So many people will be coming to the screening. And the weather looks like it will hold too.'

'Good,' said Faye. 'I'm so looking forward to these May Day celebrations and to meeting your parents again. I can't remember how long it is since I've seen them both.'

At this, Purdy looked suddenly pained. 'Well, I ... have asked them, of course, but ... it may be a little difficult for them to come.'

'Difficult?' Faye repeated, looking confused.

'Daddy's been very busy lately. He's giving a lecture at the local library soon and–'

'Naturally,' Faye conceded, breaking in. 'He is a brilliant man and was *always* so busy, but nevertheless, he would surely like to support all the hard work you have been doing for this event, wouldn't he?'

Purdy looked down, embarrassed, before finally agreeing: 'Yes. Yes, you're right. Of course he would.'

'Then please explain to him how thrilled I will be to meet him again.' Faye smiled. 'And your mother, of course.'

'I'll ... I'll do that,' stammered Purdy. 'And I'll ... look forward to seeing you tomorrow.'

'So shall I,' said Faye. 'So shall I.'

In the pause that followed, Barbara stepped forward to Purdy. 'I'll see you out.'

She led the way from the conservatory while Nathan began talking animatedly once more to Faye. Pearl, however, noted how the actress continued to stare after Purdy Hewett. In fact, long after the girl had left the room, Faye's gaze remained fixed as though she was staring back into the past.

Chapter Three

'I'll never understand what the fascination is with Morris dancing.'

It was early on Saturday morning and The Whitstable Pearl was not yet open. Dolly was staring out of the window at a group of local dancers rehearsing on the opposite side of the High Street. A small crowd had gathered around them, attracted by the music being played on a melodeon and flute. Dressed in a regional costume of white shirts, waistcoats and black flat caps, the Morris Men were mainly locals but included a few dancers from the nearby town of Faversham. They had won acclaim at various folk festivals both locally and in Europe, but they had yet to win Dolly Nolan's favour.

'Isn't it meant to be Moorish?' asked Pearl as she straightened some tablecloths.

'More-ish?' asked Dolly.

'No. *Moor*ish. Like flamenco?'

Her mother gave a tut. 'Mimsy, more like,' she frowned now and her bad mood led Pearl to suspect that Dolly's tooth was still playing up. She continued to grumble about the dancers. 'What is it with the handkerchiefs and sticks, eh? It's nothing but a passionless tarantella.'

Pearl moved next to her mother and peered out. As if aware that they had a difficult audience to please, the dancers seemed to step up a gear. Their leader, his face painted white and green to represent the changing seasons, suddenly called out to his group, 'Come on, men, let's get airborne!' and, at this, the dancers began prancing in a tight circle, knees raised ever higher.

Unmoved, Dolly continued to observe them critically. Being a fan of dance, she herself had once belonged to a women's troupe called the Fish Slappers, who had made a bit of a name for themselves during the Oyster Festival parades. She had also taken lessons in belly dancing and flamenco – the latter with a Spanish teacher whom she had found as attractive as his dance style. For a while, the feeling had been reciprocated but, in time, Juan Pariente had returned to his native home of Cadiz – and the many phone conversations that had taken place following his departure had finally dwindled to the odd postcard.

In some ways this reminded Pearl of the progress of her own relationship with DCI Mike McGuire. Having been thrown together with Pearl during a murder case last summer, McGuire had subsequently decided against taking up his expected re-transfer to London. Instead, he had moved into a small apartment in Canterbury – though he might just as well have disappeared to the other end of the country for all that Pearl had seen or heard from him lately.

Tiring of the dancers, she suddenly asked: 'Why did you say Faye Marlow would be trouble?'

But Dolly didn't hear as she continued to stare out of the window. 'Your father didn't get it either,' she murmured.

Pearl frowned, confused by the non sequitur, until Dolly resumed: 'Morris dancing – whenever I called it traditional English folk dancing he'd always say...'

'"Give me *Riverdance* any day".'

At Pearl's words, Dolly looked back at her daughter, softening at the thought of her late husband. Tommy Nolan had been an oyster fisherman but, at heart, he had also been a true poet, and as a young man he had charmed the seafront bars with his verses set to music, wistful lines employing metaphors about life, love and the fishing of oysters – before marrying Dolly, who hated them.

'I was asking about Faye.' Pearl nudged her mother gently.

41

'What about her?'

'She seemed perfectly pleasant yesterday and not at all like you'd warned.'

'I didn't say she was "*un*pleasant", did I? I said she was trouble.' Dolly moved away from the window, leaving Pearl trailing after her as she headed to the seafood counter.

'But why?' Pearl persisted.

'Try asking Jean Wheeler.'

'Jean? What's she got to do with it?'

'Don't you remember?' Then Dolly suddenly realised. 'No, of course you wouldn't – you were far too young at the time.' She explained: 'Jean's son was well and truly taken for a ride by Faye Marlow.'

'What – Jerry Wheeler?'

Dolly nodded. 'He and Faye – or rather, Frankie as she still was then – were once an item.'

Pearl tried to summon up an image in her mind's eye of the Whitstable businessman Jerry Wheeler being 'an item' with a budding star ... but it was a challenge. Now in his late fifties, Jerry Wheeler sported a paunch and had lost almost all of his hair.

Reading her daughter's thoughts, Dolly told her, 'Thirty years ago, Jerry was a quite a looker, believe it or not, and he had prospects even then – though that didn't stop Faye Marlow running out on him. They were engaged for quite a while, but then she lost interest.' Dolly tutted again, partly in reaction to her story but also because her tooth was playing up. She put her hand to her jaw before going on.

'Jean was livid, of course, and swore that Faye

had dumped poor Jerry because she was carrying on with someone else, but I'm not sure there was ever any truth in that. Faye just enjoyed using her wiles on men. She practised on quite a few around here, like a kitten practises with a toy mouse before moving on to the real thing. No doubt she left a trail of toy mice behind in Whitstable, but the fact is, it was about that time that she got her first audition for a Hollywood role. Up until then she'd only done a bit of theatre, for which she got some good reviews – and she also had a small part in a television series set on a cruise ship.' Dolly reflected on this for a moment. 'I only saw one episode and to be fair, Faye was all right in it, but it must have cost pennies to make because you could see the scenery shaking, and it wasn't long before the audience jumped ship. But then along came this role in the States.'

'And she got the part?'

Dolly shook her head. 'She touched Jerry for the air fare and some expenses but when he planned to go out and visit her, she made some excuse about having come down with a bug and missed the audition. But she stayed on in Hollywood and the next thing he heard, she had an agent – and then a film role. She'd landed the part of Gloria in that film *The Big Time*. An apt title because that's exactly what Faye had suddenly hit. She never looked back … least of all in the direction of Jerry Wheeler.'

Pearl was taking mental note of all this when Dolly's mobile emitted a techno ringtone version of 'Guantamera'. As she answered the call, Pearl tried once more to imagine Whitstable's Jerry

43

Wheeler engaged to Hollywood film star, Faye Marlow. Though a successful property magnate, Jerry was just a big fish in a small pond and had been married for over twenty years to Annabel, a pretty woman and doyenne of the local charity circuit, but hardly someone to match Faye's glamour.

After a few brief polite words to her mobile phone, Dolly ended the call. 'That was my people,' she stated, referring in her usual way to newly arrived guests at her holiday let, Dolly's Attic, a Bohemian little flatlet situated above her shop, Dolly's Pots, from which she sold her 'shabby chic' pottery. For years Pearl had served oysters from her mother's distinctive plates and bowls, but now they were proving to be as popular with the tourists as the oysters themselves. 'They're having problems finding a parking space,' Dolly continued. 'So I'd best go and help or they'll be orbiting Harbour Street for ever.' She thrust her mobile phone deep into her crushed-velvet shoulder bag and went out, calling, 'See you in a sec.'

When, after a few moments, a tap sounded at the window, Pearl fully expected to see her mother there again, having forgotten something, but instead another face was peering through. At first glance, it was hard for Pearl to place the woman ... until she realised it was Faye's assistant, Barbara March. Unlocking the restaurant door, she welcomed her inside.

Barbara began, 'I'm sorry to disturb you so early, but I wondered if I could discuss something with you?' There was a certain urgency about her.

'Would you like a coffee first?' asked Pearl.

Barbara shook her head. 'Thanks, but I can't stay long. It's about catering,' she went on, quickly getting to the point. 'Faye loved what you served yesterday for lunch and has sent me to ask if you'd consider providing some food for to-morrow evening – at the reception after the film screening?' As if anticipating a negative response, she swiftly added, 'Faye would really like you to do so.' She smiled and Pearl faltered, thinking back to the delicious *panzanella* salad that the actress had chased around her plate.

'I thought Nathan wanted only a few simple snacks,' she said. 'Olives, pistachios, that kind of thing.' In fact, Pearl knew quite well that this was all the event's budget would stretch to.

'Faye really would prefer some fine hors d'oeuvre,' Barbara clarified. 'A light buffet of finger food. She would be *so* grateful if you could possibly oblige, Pearl?'

With just the right amount of flattery, Barbara had managed to appeal to Pearl's professional pride.

'I'll talk to Nathan,' Pearl said finally, but Barbara quickly took out a sheet of paper from her bag and pressed it into her hands. 'Some ideas.'

As she smiled warmly, Pearl found herself caught off guard. Looking down at the list of sug-gestions, she was tempted now by the challenge of putting this together in record time. 'OK,' she agreed. 'I'll do it.'

For the first time during this meeting, Barbara showed some relief as though, until now, she had been giving some kind of performance to achieve a desired outcome, but as though suddenly

45

seized by either fear or pain, she leaned forward, her hand clutching the edge of a table as if to prevent herself from falling.

'Are you all right?' Pearl asked, concerned.

Barbara looked up and Pearl saw that it was all she could do to nod her head slightly as her free hand moved to her temple.

'Here,' said Pearl, drawing a chair from beneath a table. 'Sit down for a moment.'

Barbara raised her hand in polite refusal. 'It's OK. I'm fine, but ... do you have some water?'

Quickly filling a glass from a jug, Pearl handed it to her, but rather than drinking from it, Barbara reached instead into her bag for a small bottle of tablets. Shaking two into her palm, she immediately downed them with the water, explaining afterwards, 'I suffer from migraines. Travelling really doesn't help.'

'Are you sure I can't get you something?' asked Pearl once more. 'Tea, perhaps?'

For a moment, it seemed that Barbara might accept, but before she had a chance to respond, someone else tapped on the window, heavily this time. Looking up, Pearl saw a young man waiting outside. In his early thirties, he was well built and handsome, with fair hair and a golden suntan, but he had a handkerchief in his hand and seemed troubled by a cough. Pearl allowed him into the restaurant and he offered her a polite, *'Bonjour,'* before turning his attention to Barbara as he pointed towards the street. *'Je ne peux pas laisser la voiture ici. C'est interdit.'*

Barbara took her hand away from the table and raised herself to her full height as she regained some control. *'D'accord,'* she said efficiently. *'J'arrive.'*

The young man left and Barbara said, 'Sorry. That's Luc and I'm afraid he's not in a very good mood as he's just getting over a bad cold. He's our driver and also acts as security for Faye. Rosine is his girlfriend – or I should say "partner" since they've been together for some time.'

Pearl glanced towards the window. Luc was no longer visible but two traffic wardens could be seen approaching from across the street. 'He's right,' Pearl said. 'If he parks outside any longer you're bound to get a ticket.' She looked back at Barbara. 'Are you sure you're OK?'

'I'm fine,' Barbara nodded. 'Fortunately the pills work quickly. But I'd be grateful if you didn't mention this to anyone – particularly Faye. I wouldn't want to worry her. You understand?'

'Of course.'

At this, Barbara managed a smile as though whatever pain had troubled her had finally lifted. 'Thank you, Pearl.'

A moment later, Barbara left and Pearl watched from the door of the restaurant as Luc opened the passenger door to a smart rental car. Barbara got inside, her gaze meeting Pearl's as the vehicle drove off, before Pearl suddenly remembered the list of buffet suggestions in her hand.

The upmarket store, Cornucopia, just a stone's throw across the High Street from The Whitstable Pearl, had at one time been a modest little fruit and vegetable shop known as Granny Smith's. However, on the death of its owner, the shop had passed to his son – and business had never been so good. The store's new proprietor, Marty Smith, supplied most of the fruit and vegetable requirements of The Whitstable Pearl, and having had a crush on Pearl for some considerable time, Marty always ensured that her orders were delivered personally. That was, until almost a year ago, when having witnessed something of the attraction between Pearl and DCI Mike McGuire, Marty had given up trying to win Pearl's affections and transferred his attentions to Nikki Dwyer, a local florist, new to the town. This had come as something of a relief to Pearl because although she had enjoyed a few dates with Marty, who was both attractive and hard-working, he had singularly failed to light her fire. It certainly wasn't for want of trying, but evenings spent listening to Marty's favourite topic of conversation – obscure fruit and vegetables – usually had her wishing she was at home curled up with a good book.

Entering Marty's store now, she braced herself to hear yet again about the properties of the African cucumber or the guanabana, but instead found a long snaking queue forming for the fresh fruit smoothies Marty had recently begun supplying. His exotic 'superfood' blends featured mixes with berries, rambutan and watermelon, dispensed from a selection of hi-tech machines that were whirring noisily as a young sales assistant handed beakers to those in the queue.

With no sign of Marty in the shop, Pearl asked the girl where he was. She gave a nod towards the rear of the store, indicating that her boss could be found in the back yard that he used as a storage area. During winter, the space provided a home for the numerous Christmas trees Marty sold. As Pearl stepped into the yard, it looked like one had been left behind, since a large, conical, dark-green shape blocked her path. However, on closer inspection it proved to be the traditional costume for Jack-in-the-Green – the dancing bush that stepped out of the Duke of Cumberland pub on the first Monday in May to lead a Bank Holiday procession to the Castle for the town's May Day celebrations.

The figure was said to have evolved from the use of traditional May Day flower garlands, which had become so elaborate over time that they eventually covered the entire figure that embodied the Spirit of Spring – a 'spirit' that was now raising itself up a few inches from the ground to reveal a pair of trainers. Endeavouring to make a neat 360-degree turn, 'Jack' listed dangerously to one side, before almost collapsing into a loose pile of King Edward potatoes. Then, having regained equilibrium, a small flap opened up amid the greenery to reveal Marty's beaming face, framed by leaves and spring flowers.

'What d'you think?' he asked, spitting out some blossom.

Momentarily lost for words, Pearl managed to comment, 'You're playing Jack this year?'

'Now why else would I be dressed up as a bush?' Marty asked. 'I've been chosen to lead the procession,' he said proudly, 'but it's top secret for now, so please don't let on. Everyone likes a mystery, don't they?'

He winked and Pearl was reminded of a time

when, as a teenager, she had been asked to play the part of Maid Marian in the May Day procession, only to decline on learning that Marty was to play Robin Hood. Another woman might have succumbed to what could have been construed as Fate, but over the years Pearl had remained curiously resistant to Marty's charms.

'I've been doing my homework,' he went on, 'and d'you know that aside from representing spring I'm also...' he paused for suitable effect '...a fertility symbol?'

Marty's dark eyebrows always seemed to Pearl to have a life of their own – and were capable of betraying his innermost feelings. One had become slightly arched and the gleam in his eye was unmistakable.

'Nikki must be thrilled,' Pearl said meaningfully, keen to remind him where his heart should lie.

At this, Marty's smile slowly faded and his eyebrow slumped. 'She won't be around for the parade,' he said glumly. 'She's staying with her mother up in London.' He left another pause before admitting, 'We're actually on a break.'

'I'm sorry,' said Pearl genuinely.

'No worries,' the greengrocer sighed. 'To be honest, I think me and Nikki may have gone as far as we can together. She didn't seem ready to take the next step.'

'Marriage, you mean?'

'Nope. A period of cohabitation,' he replied. 'My old dad used to say: "You never really know a woman till you've lived with her."' He gave a wise look and Pearl recognised the absurdity of having this conversation with a talking bush. As though becoming conscious of this himself, Marty asked: 'Can you give me a hand out of this, please?'

In a joint effort the light bamboo frame was duly lifted, allowing him to duck neatly from beneath it. Appearing now in his signature Cornucopia T-shirt, Marty slipped on the green baseball cap that had been folded in the rear pocket of his jeans and which matched the colour of his eyes. 'It's good to see you, Pearl.'

He took an instinctive step forward but Pearl blocked the move by telling him, 'I'm just here to see if you can meet an extra order for me.'

'Oh yeah?' He looked, in turn, disappointed then curious.

'I'm going to be catering for a small reception after the screening tomorrow,' she explained.

'Oh – the film show up at the Slopes, you mean?' Marty's eyebrows became alert once more as he brushed a few stray leaves from his T-shirt. 'That's quite something Nathan's managed, eh? A film star in Whitstable? Any chance of me getting to meet her?'

'Well,' Pearl said cagily, 'Faye will be at the screening, of course, and afterwards at the reception on the Castle grounds – but that will be by invitation only.'

Marty's brow rippled as he performed a swift calculation. 'Could you do with some of my smoothies?' A keen businessman, he had spotted a twin chance to meet a celebrity and simultaneously promote his new venture.

'Probably,' said Pearl. 'But there's a tight budget for the May Day fund.'

'Tell me about it,' he said ruefully. 'I had to

supply the ivy for my own costume.'

'Well, not to worry. Remember, it's a community event, so any contributions will be welcome. You might even get a chance to meet Faye if you were on hand to supply a few ... intermezzo drinks?'

Marty's eyebrows knitted. 'A few what?'

'Smoothies served in some small glasses. Apple and ginger might go down well as a palate cleanser?'

The eyebrows duly unknitted themselves. 'I reckon I could do that.' Another thought occurred to him. 'And you'll be there too, right?' He smiled and Pearl gave an uneasy nod, recognising that Marty was viewing this as an added bonus.

'Right,' she replied, her own smile now becoming something of a fixed rictus.

In the next moment, a shaft of sunlight escaped into the yard and it lit up Marty's green eyes. To any other woman, Marty would have appeared an attractive man with thick dark hair and a buff physique that remained honed from crate-lifting and regular visits to the gym. But to Pearl, Marty's muscles and his physical attributes could not compensate for his one, all-consuming ambition: to create an empire based on fruit and veg.

Dolly had always said that where men were concerned, Pearl was too fussy, though she herself had not welcomed her daughter's relationship with DCI McGuire – or the 'Flat Foot', as she insisted on calling him. This antipathy had not been directed specifically towards McGuire but against the police in general because, more than twenty years ago, Dolly had been shocked by Pearl's decision to join the force. This was naturally because she had feared for her daughter's safety, but also because Dolly possessed a rebellious streak and her views were somewhat anti-establishment. Having protested about all sorts of issues, from nuclear weapons to the closure of the local Visitor Information Centre, Dolly had summoned up the unwelcome image of finding herself pitted against her own daughter, armed with a truncheon, there to quell a demonstration of which Dolly might very well have been part. She had therefore done her best to try to talk Pearl out of the idea, but had been unsuccessful, since one of the few traits Pearl had inherited from her mother was a stubborn streak.

To Dolly's chagrin, Pearl had gone on to thrive within the framework of her basic police training, and during her probationary period had shown not only that she engaged well with the public but that she also possessed an instinctive understanding of people in general. This skill had singled Pearl out as a potential candidate for criminal investigation – but then a positive reading on a pregnancy test had prompted her resignation, leaving her mother to quietly celebrate – until the day that Pearl had decided to start up her own detective agency.

Dolly foresaw further problems on the horizon because she sensed that Pearl's cases might lead to increased contact with Detective Chief Inspector McGuire and so she had remained hopeful that Nolan's Detective Agency would be abandoned before too long – something that was looking vaguely possible considering the recent dearth of cases. In fact, the last had consisted of trying to track down the culprit behind the theft of a treasured bay tree from the doorway of a local Indian restaurant. The thieves had left few clues other than a trail of potting compost that had disappeared at the kerbside, suggesting that the plant and pot had been loaded into a vehicle. An unsolved case was always a disappointment for Pearl, but Dolly secretly hoped that a few more like this would seal the fate of the agency – and her daughter's association with McGuire.

In fact, DCI McGuire had been mysteriously absent from Whitstable for some time and, looking at Marty now, it crossed Pearl's mind that perhaps she might have appeared a little too keen herself and put the detective off. She knew that McGuire would be very busy with his work in Canterbury but nevertheless, in the last few months she felt he could have picked up the phone or dropped by at The Whitstable Pearl for a snack or a coffee. McGuire had always maintained that he was allergic to oysters – and Pearl was beginning to wonder if he had developed an allergy to her too.

'Here's what I need,' she said to Marty, trying to appear businesslike as she handed him her order.

He looked it over and nodded. 'Fine.' Then he tried to appear equally businesslike himself. 'I'll give it my urgent attention,' he promised, before confirming: 'I'll even make the delivery personally, how's that?' He offered another wink, but this one looked to Pearl more of a facial tic. She turned at the door, glancing back, just once, to see Marty admiring his 'fertility symbol' – the

Jack-in-the-Green costume he was looking forward to wearing at the parade.

A moment later, Pearl stepped out on to the street, surprised to find that the warm sun had brought out the locals. In fact the High Street was almost as crowded as it became during the Oyster Festival – but the Saturday crowds appeared to be drifting only in one direction. Curious, Pearl followed on, thinking that perhaps the Morris Dancers might again be the focus of some attention if they were rehearsing on another street corner – but she could hear no beating drums or bells or the distinctive sound of the melodeon that had accompanied their earlier performance. Instead, close to the Horsebridge Cultural Centre, which had housed many a local artist's exhibition, she recognised a familiar car parked in the street. In spite of the fact that it was an eye-catching 1932 Duesenberg convertible coupé, it wasn't the vehicle but its passenger that was attracting the crowds.

The car's roof was down, exposing Faye Marlow, who was looking every inch a star, wearing large, black-framed sunglasses and a wide-brimmed white hat. The puff sleeves of her polka-dot blouse were carefully slipped off her shoulders but she didn't appear to be feeling 'exposed' as she chatted to onlookers and signed autographs, while beside her, the owner of the car looked on proudly, as he must surely have done almost thirty years ago. It was the jilted Whitstable businessman, Jerry Wheeler.

Chapter Four

'How could he have done something so stupid? Twice!' Jean Wheeler looked up from the coffee Pearl had just set before her. She was a small woman but feisty, with red hair pinned up in a French pleat and an expression of barely contained fury. The Whitstable Pearl had closed its doors after its lunch service but as an old friend of Dolly, Jean had remained behind. 'Any other man would surely be full of revenge after the way that woman deserted him. Do you *know* how she broke off their engagement? Pearl shook her head and Jean paused only to take a swift gulp of coffee before exploding: 'By fax! Kept him hanging on until she finally had no use for him.'

Jean's lips pursed tight in an effort to repress further anger while Dolly came across from the bar bearing two glasses containing hefty shots of Pearl's best cognac. She handed one to Jean. 'Here. Get this down you.'

Jean shook her head. 'You know my rule, Dolly. Not a drop until after six p.m.'

'So make today an exception,' ordered Dolly, tipping the brandy into Jean's coffee. 'There. A *carajillo*. It'll do you the world of good *and* give you courage. *Corajillo!*' she exclaimed. 'That's where the name comes from.'

Jean looked between Pearl and Dolly and decided to take this advice, not least because Dolly

56

was well known for having a remedy for almost everything – usually coming in some alcoholic form or another: whisky toddies for colds, Fernet-Branca cocktails for hangovers, and *carajillos* for settling the nerves.

Picking up her cup, Jean took a sip then gave a sudden cough and a gasp. But the drink seemed to do the trick. She said, more calmly, 'Of course, poor Annabel will feel totally humiliated when she returns from Hove and finds out.' She chewed her lip for a moment. 'But why on earth she chose this time to disappear off I'll never know. It was only a Women's Institute event and she knew Faye would be in town.'

As she continued to look perplexed, Pearl asked: 'I take it she also knows about Jerry and Faye having been engaged?'

Jean looked up quickly and snapped, 'But of course! Jerry kept all of Faye's letters – and photographs. He even has some framed in his office. I don't know why Annabel puts up with that. She's far too understanding.'

Pearl and Dolly exchanged a look, each recognising that there might surely be a direct correlation between Annabel's tolerance and her husband's wealth, but Jean carried on regardless. 'She's accepted what Jerry's told her – that it's "good for business". He says the photos impress his clients. And that may be so,' Jean said sagely 'But shepherding the woman around town yesterday in such a public way – that was going too far.'

Dolly nodded. 'Whatever possessed him?' she murmured, almost to herself.

'Not what – *who?*' Jean said bitterly. 'Old

57

Frankie Marshall, that's who, though Jerry's never seen her as anything other than a goddess.' Her face set with resentment. 'You know, she actually had the gall to phone him – after all this time? And he took her out for lunch – to the Oyster Stores – for all to see!' She paused to take another sip of her *carajillo*. 'I told him straight, Dolly. I made it crystal clear what I think of all this. He's my son, my only child, and I love him dearly but the fact of the matter is ... he's always been an idiot over that woman.'

Jean looked at Pearl and Dolly as though waiting for a response and while Pearl felt unable to comment, Dolly duly reflected on Jean's last remark as she picked up her own cognac.

'Well, he's not the first and he won't be the last,' she said knowingly, before posing a question: 'Why are men like gooseberries?' Pearl and Jean exchanged a confused look until Dolly downed the rest of her cognac in one and gave her answer: 'Because women can always make fools of them!'

After leaving the restaurant, Pearl headed off to meet Nathan. He had been at the Castle for most of the day, ensuring that all plans were in place for Sunday evening, but needing a break he had suggested that they should meet at a different venue close by. The Tea Gardens at Tower Hill was one of Pearl's favourite places to visit in spring and summer. Understated, and in contrast to the Castle's Orangery Tea Rooms, which served chef's specials and a 'deluxe afternoon tea' complete with champagne, the Tea Gardens offered far more simple fare: sandwiches and homemade cakes from a servery that consisted of a clapboard hut with a thatched roof. Situated across the road from the Castle, the gardens appeared as a modest neighbour bounded by a low stone wall over which could be glimpsed a stepped-down lawn bordered with flower-beds – and the most stunning sea view – which Nathan was managing to ignore as he worked on his laptop. Sitting at a wooden picnic table, sipping a cup of tea, he was lost in concentration and failed to look up from his screen until Pearl stood right in front of him.

'Ah, you're here at last.' He beamed as she sat down.

'She's causing quite a stir, Nathan.'

'Who?' he asked, distracted.

'Who else?' Pearl began pouring herself a cup of tea from Nathan's pot. 'I do hope your interview will be worth it.'

'Oh, so do I,' he said fervently. '*If* I ever get it.' Though the gardens were populated only by a few families seated on the far lawn, Nathan lowered his voice in case anyone should hear. 'I'm sorry you got saddled with the reception, Pearl.'

'You could have phoned me instead of sending Barbara to persuade me.'

'Not guilty,' he said. 'That was Faye's idea. As soon as I found out, I was going to call to let you know how grateful I am, but...' He gave a lengthy sigh. 'Then we had the ring drama.'

'The what?'

'Faye has a diamond ring.'

'I noticed.'

'It was given to her by her late husband.' Nathan broke off a piece of ginger biscuit and nibbled it.

59

'It went missing for a while.' Noting Pearl's shock, he added, 'Precisely. I had visions of the police swooping down, maybe even your detective … what's his name?'

'McGuire. And he's not "mine",' she corrected him.

'Whatever,' shrugged Nathan. 'For a few hours yesterday morning it was *pandemonium* at Arden House.'

He took a sip of tea, while Pearl moved closer to ask: 'What happened?'

'Faye swore that she'd taken the ring off the night before and put it in her jewellery case, which she had then placed in the safe.'

'Safe?'

Nathan nodded. 'One of the conditions of her staying at Arden House was that she had to have the use of a safe for her valuables. I'm not surprised, since the ring is worth a fortune. It's a five-carat diamond, I believe, set in gold and originally bought for £50,000. Anyway, Tom *has* a safe, so no problem. Or so I thought. But yesterday I went round to speak to Barbara about tomorrow's press interviews–'

'Cut to the chase,' Pearl commanded.

'Well, Faye was getting ready to come down when suddenly we hear this piercing scream. Honestly, Pearl, you'd have thought the woman was being murdered.' He stopped to take another quick sip of tea. 'Barbara and I, and Rosine and Luc, all rushed into the hallway and realised that Faye was somewhere upstairs, wailing about the ring having disappeared.' He paused for breath. 'So, we hurry up to find her in Tom's office – eyes wide with horror and one hand pressed to her face, while she points a trembling finger towards a black velvet-covered jewellery case on the desk, which she's emptied to find ... no ring.' He fell silent.

'So what did you do?'

'Me? Nothing, sweetie. I just felt rather sick as I began to see a newspaper headline running past my eyes: MAY DAY MAYHEM, with the strapline: *Writer held on suspicion of jewellery theft.*' He closed his eyes at the thought.

'And what happened?'

'Barbara, as you might imagine, steps forward and begins to take control, examining both the case and the safe while Rosine...' He took another sip of tea.

'Rosine what?' asked Pearl impatiently.

'Gives a series of helpless squeals, looking to Luc who, in turn, looks to me. All I can do is suggest that we should call the police.'

'And did you?'

Nathan shook his head. 'No. Barbara ordered Rosine to make some coffee and started questioning Faye about the last time she'd actually seen the ring. That must have gone on for at least half an hour, with Barbara keeping it all together, as she always does, going through everything Faye told her, but...'

'But what?'

'Well, Faye was adamant that around midnight she'd put the ring in the case, and the case in the safe, and she'd then gone to bed. But now ... it was nowhere to be found.'

'Only it *was* found,' said Pearl. 'You said it went

missing "for a while".'

'That's right,' said Nathan. 'And do you know, after all that, the ring turned up under the quilt that had been lying partially on the floor beside Faye's bed. Rosine found it.'

Pearl considered this. 'So ... Faye was actually mistaken, about having put it in the safe?'

'It certainly looks that way. She must have had a few tinctures and forgotten to take it off. Maybe it slipped off her finger while she was sleeping? Anyway, it was found before the police were called so there'll be no damning headlines after all.' He gave a smile now but it quickly vanished. 'I couldn't bear it if this whole May Day – Faye Day – film fest imploded, Pearl. It's all down to me and Purdy that Faye's here at all, so if things go wrong...'

'They won't,' Pearl said. 'Everything will be fine.'

Nathan seemed to accept this, then suddenly looked suspicious. 'You said she's been "causing a stir"?'

Pearl had been planning on telling him about Faye and Jerry Wheeler but instead she merely replied, 'Just that the town is on tenterhooks. As am I.' As a distraction she suggested: 'Shall we discuss the menu instead? How does vegetable tempura and crab claws sound – with a selection of sushi and blini?'

'Perfect, but–'

'Don't worry about the cost. I'll do it as a promotion – for free – but you're going to have to find the money to pay my waitress, Ruby, OK?'

'No need, sweetie. Rosine can be waitress for the evening. She was trained in Silver Service apparently, and we'll put Luc on champagne duty – except, due to budget, it'll be champagne for Faye, prosecco for everyone else.'

'Fine,' Pearl agreed. 'That's settled.'

After finishing his tea, Nathan made a few more adjustments to the notes on his laptop and offered Pearl a lift back into town – which she refused as she had decided instead to walk, taking a route through the Castle grounds. The view she had glimpsed through the broken fence-panel close to Arden House had made her realise how long it had been since she had visited the Castle at all. As a child she had played in its grounds, as had Charlie, and it was certain that another May Day would draw a fresh generation of children here for the entertainment, which, in previous years, had included circus skills like juggling and plate-spinning alongside Punch & Judy. There had been May Day disappointments, of course, when stall-holders had been forced to pack up early after failing to hold on to their gazebos in gales, or when maypole dancing performed by local schoolchildren had to be cancelled when their teacher became stranded abroad, her flight home disrupted by a volcanic ash cloud. But, according to Nathan and Purdy, the weather was set fair for May Day and plans were now in place for a timetable of traditional events: the usual Morris Dancing, followed by a procession led by Jack-in-the-Green to the harbour, and then on to the Castle – where the May song would be sung as stallholders sold their wares.

The fresh smell of newly mown grass greeted Pearl as soon as she entered the Castle grounds;

the Head Gardener, Joy Thomson, had been busy tidying the entire area for the event. The gardens were, in fact, believed to have been Regency in their original design with trees having once been planted in avenues with curving ornamental beds. Although the restored gardens had been re-designed to reflect this, Dolly, for one, had been opposed to the uprooting of mature trees and strongly disliked the new central pagoda, which she claimed would be more suited to the garden centre of a superstore. Signs now warned that ball games were not permitted and dogs were to be kept on a lead, but for Pearl the one thing that seemed to have remained unchanged was the old bowling green, which lay spread out on the lower slope like an emerald-green carpet. A sign advised that the rinks were available to the general public and that new members were always welcome at the club. Pearl found herself heading in its direction, drawn by the sound of bowls clinking in the distance.

The white-clad players, who had appeared from a distance much like figures from a Lowry painting, now became distinct as Pearl grew nearer. She recognised one as Purdy's mother, Maria Hewett. She had been watching the players from the sidelines, which seemed appropriate for someone who had proved herself to be, in so many ways, a constant support to others. It was a role Maria performed perfectly, especially for her family. Softly spoken, she offered an opinion only when it was requested and seemed content to be one of life's spectators rather than a participant. With her pale complexion and mousy fair hair, she had managed to remain both unremarkable and un-changed – though she had grown slightly plumper over recent years. She usually wore the same comfortable items of clothing – a linen jacket or blazer over loose floral dresses or skirts – and today was no exception.

Offering a wave to Pearl, Maria moved across to the club's gate to greet her. The wind gusted and Maria's hair, inadequately secured by a few combs, fell down in loose tendrils upon her shoulders. 'How nice to see you, Pearl,' she said sincerely. 'I do hope you and Dolly are well?'

'We're all fine, thank you,' Pearl replied, as she looked back towards the green. 'I didn't know you played.'

'I don't,' Maria admitted. 'Not well, anyway, but I began recently. The members are very wel-coming, and I find it relaxing here. It's a beautiful spot, don't you think?' She was right: the bowling green was a haven from the busy town and enjoyed a stunning sea view on its northern side.

'I'm just waiting for Oliver to meet me,' Maria went on. 'I'm not sure if you know, but he's giving a lecture at the library about his studies on some rather wonderful murals in Mexico, as well as an account of the dig here on the old copperas site. He's down there right now, on the foreshore where the excavation took place. Do you know, it's almost twenty years ago now, but I don't think he'll ever forget the excitement of that project.' Her face lit up as she waved to someone approaching. It was Oliver, heading across from the direction of the Tea Gardens.

Pearl was taken aback momentarily as she hadn't

previously recognised that there was something of McGuire about Oliver Hewett, with his high cheekbones, strong jaw and bright blue eyes. A tall figure, Oliver's fair hair had thinned slightly and was now peppered with grey but he was still an attractive man, seeming as ever to Pearl as though he might have stepped out from an earlier century – an adventurer or an explorer, on a quest of some kind. He was a successful archaeologist though Pearl felt that this success had been due in part to having such a supportive wife. Oliver had been a key member of the archaeological team that had undertaken an important excavation of an area of beach below Tankerton Slopes after erosion by the sea had exposed some significant remains. A number of timber structures and a poured mortar floor had become visible along the length of the upper foreshore – evidence of the site of an important industry that had once taken place locally.

Copperas, or 'green vitriol' as it was known, had been used for many purposes: as an early dye fixative, for writing and printing ink, as well as in the tanning process for leather and the 'blacking' or antifouling for ships. Its sulphur or brimstone qualities had also made it a constituent of gunpowder, and the shores of Whitstable and Tankerton had yielded quantities of stones containing iron pyrites, or fool's gold – the basic ingredient for copperas production. As early as the 1500s, the stones had been gathered by men, women and children in the town, but over time, the early works had been abandoned due to coastal erosion and sea storms – and later copperas sites had been located further up the slopes.

At school, Pearl had learned about the traditional way of producing copperas in liquid crystal form. The gathered stones were layered in boarded beds, then left to weather for two to three years, with the resulting liquid then channelled and collected in large cisterns, before being transferred to the workhouse for boiling in lead cauldrons. The coagulated crystals were then dried and packed into wooden casks ready for shipping to dyers and clothing manufacturers in London. By the seventeenth century, the Whitstable industry had supported six separate copperas works, which had lasted a hundred years until demand had declined with new advances in industrial chemistry. The works had been abandoned, but Professor Oliver Hewett had tenaciously explored the area, working with a team from Canterbury to unearth the evidence of the first industrial-scale chemical production in England.

As Oliver came up, Maria tried to stand tall in her bowling shoes to plant a kiss on his cheek. He received it and acknowledged Pearl. 'Good to see you,' he said warmly. 'Purdy mentioned she bumped into you.'

'That's right,' said Pearl. 'I hear she's been working very hard to set up the film screening tomorrow night. She seemed very excited about it when she dropped by at Arden House to meet Faye.'

Pearl was expecting an upbeat response to this, but instead the atmosphere became somewhat strained. Maria said nothing but looked to her husband for a response, which came only after he appeared to weigh up carefully what Pearl had said.

'Yesterday, you say?' His tone was casual but his expression betrayed a keen interest, indicating to Pearl that perhaps Purdy should have been somewhere else at the time. Pearl replied. 'Yes, I'd just served a late lunch there.'

An awkward silence followed, which Pearl felt the need to fill. 'Well, I expect the whole town will be along tomorrow.'

'I expect they will.' Oliver slipped his arm around his wife's shoulder, the gesture seeming to embolden Maria.

She spoke up. 'Did Purdy stay long? At the house, I mean?' Her gaze seemed to be drawn across Gatehouse Walk, beyond the trees, to Arden House itself.

'Not long at all,' said Pearl. 'It was only a flying visit.'

Maria looked up at her husband but his expression gave nothing away. Aware that the awkward atmosphere showed no sign of lifting, Pearl said briskly, 'Well, I'd better be off. I'm sorry if I shan't see you tomorrow, Oliver. I hear you're very busy with your work.'

'Not too busy to come along,' he corrected her. He met his wife's gaze before addressing Pearl once more. 'We'll definitely be there,' he said, adding: 'For Purdy.'

With that, he and Maria said their goodbyes and went to the bowling green. Pearl watched the wrought-iron gates close after them. As she moved off towards the Castle gatehouse, something made her look back, to catch sight of Oliver and Maria Hewett, seated together, hands clasped and seemingly in silence as they watched the game taking place on the green. Pearl passed the deep boarded compost beds, reminded again of the copperas industry, although these beds were filled with grass cuttings, not stones containing fool's gold. Soon, she found herself on the Gate-house Walk where leaves and blossom had been recently swept up, but the fence-panels were still down between the shrubbery and the rear access path that adjoined Arden House. Unexpectedly, a sudden biting wind blew up as cloud blocked out the afternoon sunshine, reminding Pearl that in spite of the fair weather Nathan had predicted, it was always possible that it might yet rain on Whitstable's May Day parade.

Chapter Five

Open-air film shows had taken place in Whitstable before, though a charity screening set to raise funds for a children's hospice had once fallen foul of the local authorities when a council department had unexpectedly withdrawn its permission for the event. Those who had been looking forward to a screening of *Jaws*, suitably at a venue just a stone's throw from the sea, had had to view it instead at an alternative location that had been found hastily by the quick-thinking organiser. Although the event had gone off well, the incident was still fresh in Nathan's memory, so he had worked assiduously to ensure that nothing was likely to disrupt his planned screening of

The Chattering Classes – one of Faye's most successful films, it had won her critical acclaim and an award nomination for her role as a latter-day Emma Bovary, trapped in a loveless marriage.

It was not the merriest of choices for the May Festival but, nevertheless, Nathan felt it was the best example of Faye's work, and the film did have a happy ending. There was another happy ending too for Faye in real life, since she had gone on to marry the film's producer, Alain Severin, and left Hollywood to settle on the Continent with him. Later roles had failed to match her earlier success, however, and in spite of favourable reviews for playing the title role in a French theatre production of Racine's *Bérénice*, Faye had entered retirement – though whether from choice, or necessity, no one quite knew. What was certain was the fact that, as an actress, she was still well remembered in Whitstable, judging by the numbers of people who had turned out for the screening on Tankerton Slopes. There were many rows of seats but locals had also taken up position on the grass with picnics and camping stools. A few Police Community Support Officers were on hand to keep an eye out for troublesome teenagers, although nothing but goodwill seemed to be on offer from Whitstable's community at an event that began with a short speech from Nathan welcoming Faye back to Whitstable.

He had saved good seats for Pearl and Dolly but, acting under Barbara's orders, he had done so for Faye's special guests too, and they were all positioned in the front row. Jerry Wheeler sat beside his wife Annabel, newly returned from Hove,

70

while Purdy was flanked by her parents: Maria and Oliver Hewett. A brace of councillors had also been given prime tickets, notably because they had been known to find funding for local Arts events. Barbara sat beside Nathan with Faye at his side, followed by Rosine in close attendance, forever on hand to take care of her employer's handbag or shawl at a moment's notice. At the end of the row sat Luc, keeping a protective eye on all proceedings – and his employer.

When the film came to an end, an explosion of applause rang out. Dolly gave a few desultory thumps of her palms while Pearl clapped with all the enthusiasm she felt that the film, and Faye's performance, deserved.

Wrapped in a beautiful midnight-blue shawl studded with tiny gold stars, Faye rose to her feet and addressed those assembled with what, to Pearl, appeared lines worthy of an Oscar award acceptance speech.

'You cannot believe how wonderful it is for me to be welcomed back so warmly into the bosom of my home town,' she told them all, in a theatrical tone. Going on to thank Nathan and Purdy, Faye received more applause, along with some wolf whistles – but Dolly merely groaned.

'Is your tooth hurting?' whispered Pearl, concerned.

'No,' said Dolly. 'I've just had an overdose of Faye Marlow.'

Pearl's patience with her mother was beginning to wear thin. 'Well, whatever you think of her, you've got to admit she's a brilliant actress.'

By now Faye had returned to Nathan and was

71

acknowledging the audience's response with a serene smile and a gracious nod of her head. Dolly gave an unimpressed sniff. 'Pretending you're someone you're not is a skill that madam has perfected to a T.'

Irritated by her mother's lack of grace, Pearl argued, 'Acting isn't just about pretence, you know. A good actor has to have an understanding of people and what motivates them, as well as the ability to put themself in someone else's shoes.'

'You mean the ability to empathise,' Dolly clarified. 'If Faye Marlow's actually capable of *that*, I've yet to see it.'

As the applause finally died down, Pearl considered Dolly. 'You really do dislike her, don't you?'

Dolly looked decidedly unapologetic. 'I've no respect for her – and I'm not alone. You heard what Jean had to say. Thank heavens she isn't here tonight to watch people fawn all over that old ham. Faye humiliated Jerry.'

'Maybe,' Pearl conceded. 'But he seems to have forgiven her now. So why can't you?'

Dolly looked over towards Jerry Wheeler, who appeared to be congratulating Faye on her performance. Faye was gazing up at him with a rapt expression before she gently stroked his lapel. Dolly grimaced. 'Oh, will you look at that – and in front of Annabel too! If she really had any compassion for people, she'd show a little respect for the man's wife – *and* for Maria Hewett.'

'Maria?' asked Pearl, confused.

'Yes,' snapped Dolly. 'I told you, Jerry wasn't the only one Faye set her sights on. Purdy's father was

72

almost under her spell too.'

'Oliver Hewett?' Pearl asked suddenly, aware that this might explain the strained atmosphere between the couple when she'd met them at the bowling green.

Dolly gave a quick nod. 'I'm sure he was only saved from Faye's clutches by a long trip to Mexico.'

Pearl frowned. 'You mean ... when he went off to study those murals?'

'That's right. Bonampak. It's in the Mexican state of Chiapas on the border of Guatemala.' Dolly suddenly began musing. 'And truly fascinating,' she announced. 'Because those murals completely scotch all the early assumptions about the Maya being peaceful mystics. They show human sacrifice and battle scenes, and...'

'And what about Faye?' asked Pearl, trying to steer Dolly back to the subject.

'What about her?' asked Dolly cursorily, clearly preferring to ignore the interruption and continue on about the murals. 'You know, I'd have given anything to have seen them. I talked to Oliver about them once and he told me they were remarkably well preserved.'

'Like Faye?' Pearl said mischieveously. At this, Dolly glanced across to see Faye now talking to Nathan though she appeared to be eyeing Oliver Hewett across his shoulder.

'Yes,' Dolly agreed. 'And if I'd been Maria, I'm sure I would have done the exact same thing.'

'What do you mean?'

'Put as many miles between that harpy and my husband as possible.' She explained: 'It was

73

Maria who organised the trip and spirited him off to Mexico. Clever woman, if you ask me. Faye was all over him at the time, pretending she needed his archaeological knowledge for some film script. Archaeological knowledge my foot! With Faye, there's always another agenda – and it usually only benefits Faye Marlow.' Having had enough of the conversation, Dolly reached down for her bag beneath her chair. Oliver was now talking to his daughter. Faye, however, continued to hover nearby and Maria Hewett seemed well aware of this as she squeezed her husband's arm in a protective – but also proprietorial – way.

The crowd finally dispersed after Nathan stood up and read out the timetable of events for the following day's festivities. The invited guests retired to a private reception at the Castle where a marquee had been erected in the grounds. The maypole was set up close by, its coloured ribbons tethered to a crown that had been decorated with spring flowers. The marquee was Nathan's insurance against rain, and though the weather had remained fair, the marquee now provided some privacy for the occasion.

Dolly had gone home in a huff while Faye appeared relaxed and in her element – the centre of attention. She wore a stunning chiffon top, while the gold stars on her dark-blue shawl sparkled in the light from the lanterns that were strung from the marquee's ceiling. Luc handed her a glass of champagne, then proceeded to circulate, efficiently filling other glasses. The earlier event had gone off perfectly and the evening air remained warm, although there was now a slight heaviness to it – a prelude perhaps to the sharp downpour that was forecast to arrive overnight. Rosine meanwhile went round offering Pearl's selection of hors d'oeuvre, which were well received by all the guests.

Marty was also on hand, dispensing a special 'May Day' exotic-fruit smoothie, each glass decorated with a fine sprig of mint. He had dressed for the occasion in a smart black suit and white shirt, and his dark hair looked as if it had been sculpted. As Pearl supervised the distribution of her canapés, she noticed he reeked of a heavy musky aftershave as he leaned close to her to comment, 'Faye Marlow, eh? Who'd have thought we'd ever get this close to a real film star?'

The star in question was currently answering questions from a few members of the local press, occasionally breaking off to beam a professional smile for their cameras. Whenever she did so, it was with a pose that had clearly been perfected over the years, consisting of a slight step forward, a pouting of the lips and an upward tilt of the chin, presumably to prevent any possible signs of a sagging jawline.

'And I see all of Whitstable's "great and good" are here,' Marty observed, nodding towards Jerry Wheeler who was standing on the other side of the marquee, taking a bite of one of Pearl's mini-blinis. His wife, Annabel, was standing beside him, but their body language revealed they were miles apart. Jerry's attention was firmly fixed on Faye, while Annabel was checking an incoming text on her mobile phone. She looked trimmer than Pearl remembered, wearing a purple Thai-silk trouser suit. Her shoulder-length brown hair appeared to have had honey-coloured highlights added, leading Pearl to wonder if this more glamorous appearance was in some way meant to be competition for Faye. If so, Annabel didn't seem too perturbed by her rival as she tapped out a text on her iPhone.

At that moment, Pearl got another warning whiff of Marty's aftershave; she turned to see he was about to come close but having caught her expression he backed off slightly before commenting, 'Someone said they saw Faye out in Wheeler's Duesenberg the other day.'

'That's right,' Pearl said. 'Did you know they were once engaged?'

'Really?' Marty's look showed that he found this news as incredible as Pearl did.

'Apparently she broke it off,' Pearl informed him, aware that Jerry's eyes were following Faye's every move.

'Looks like he wouldn't mind another chance, eh? Understandable, I s'pose,' Marty sighed wistfully. 'I mean, you always hanker after the one that got away.'

Marty was still looking at Faye, but Pearl couldn't help feeling that his words were aimed at her. Not only had she, thus far, resisted his charms, but in many ways her own heart was still tied to Charlie's father, Carl, the 'one who had got away' from her.

'If you need a hand with anything in the kitchen, just shout, OK?' Marty moved off, straightening his cuffs, as Nathan took his place beside Pearl.

'What is it with you and that guy?' he asked.

'Treat 'em mean, keep 'em keen?'

'No, Nathan. I try very hard *not* to encourage him.'

'Then you must try harder, sweetie, or he'll never get the message.' Nathan shot a quick look around. 'Everything seems to be going well.' He seemed happy enough, but Pearl detected that he was still on high alert for any signs of disharmony.

'The local councillors have all shown,' he went on. 'Not that they'd ever pass up an opportunity for free food, drink and publicity.'

'And the Hewetts made it too,' Pearl pointed out, noting that Oliver and Maria were engaged in conversation with Purdy.

Nathan frowned. 'That's right – but they've looked a little awkward and out of place all evening, don't you think? I guess I should mingle and try to put them at ease. Faye will be finished with the press soon and she did mention that she was looking forward to meeting the Hewetts again. I wasn't even aware that she knew them, were you?'

'Oh, yes,' said Pearl. 'And I think she may have wanted to know Oliver rather ... better.'

'Really?' Nathan picked up the nuance and looked intrigued. 'Who told you that?'

'The Oracle,' said Pearl.

He raised a sceptical eyebrow. 'Your mother may be a mine of local information but not all of it is accurate, sweetie. I can't for one minute imagine Faye with the Prof.'

'Me neither,' said Pearl. 'Nor can I imagine her with Jerry Wheeler – but it's true.'

Nathan glanced critically at both men in turn. 'Wonders never cease,' he sighed. 'Although think-

77

ing about it, I guess of the two, Oliver and Faye would be the more natural pairing.'

'Why on earth do you say that?'

'Well, just look at them. They're two beautiful people, aren't they? Beauty always attracts, doesn't it? Even though it may not last.'

Nathan had a point. Oliver Hewett and Faye Marlow would have made a perfect couple for the cameras even now, but before Pearl could comment further, the reporters and press photographers began moving outside and this seemed to act as a spur for Nathan. 'I'll be back in a sec,' he told her, dashing off.

Pearl saw that Faye, now finally free from her interviews, was whispering a request to Barbara, who gestured to Luc to bring over the champagne. He came across instantly and refilled his employer's glass, giving her a charming smile, which Faye returned. Rosine was observing him from a distance as she offered a selection of Pearl's canapés to a group of women: councillors' wives who were huddled together as their husbands chatted amongst themselves in voices loud enough to be heard at the back of a Town Hall.

'It's all going brilliantly, isn't it?' Pearl turned to see Purdy standing before her, a canapé in hand. 'And your food is absolutely delicious – as always.' The young woman gave a broad and guileless smile. 'The journalists all turned out too.' She gestured to where Faye, champagne flute in hand, was stepping outside with some press photographers. Purdy suddenly looked rather pensive as she confided, 'You know, I really expected we might get some national press, but it wasn't to be

– and that's a dreadful shame because I'm sure that's what Faye is used to. PR for this event was my job,' she said with disappointment.

'And you managed it very well.' Pearl said gently.

'Thanks.' The girl beamed, heartened by Pearl's praise. 'Of course, it's only what Faye deserves.' She took a sip of her drink. 'Stars have to give up so much, don't they?'

'Do they?'

Purdy looked taken aback. 'Well, yes. Their privacy for one thing. That's quite a sacrifice. I mean, can you imagine what it's like to be permanently in the public eye, all your actions questioned, your mistakes under scrutiny?'

'I take your point.' Pearl said. 'But it does rather come with the territory, doesn't it? And I would think most stars consider that an acceptable exchange for fame.'

'Perhaps,' Purdy conceded before she moved off – though not before Pearl had seen how uncomfortable the girl looked with this thought.

The noise level in the marquee increased considerably after Luc had refilled people's glasses a few times. Faye hadn't been circulating so much as having been orbited by others, including Jerry Wheeler, who had spent as much time as possible engaged in conversation with her. Curiously, thought Pearl, Annabel still seemed quite indifferent to this – more interested in sampling Pearl's canapés.

The event was due to end at 10.30 with the Castle grounds cleared an hour later, and Pearl recognised that it was time for her final duty. As she set off for the kitchen, she made a point of passing Annabel. 'How are you enjoying it?' she asked, as the woman was about to take a bite of blini.

'The hors d'oeuvre or the party?' Annabel studied her blini. 'Well, this is certainly good!'

'And the event in Hove?' asked Pearl.

For a moment, Annabel looked at a loss, but she recovered quickly. 'Yes,' she said. 'That was fascinating. A talk on the Suffragette movement. Well worth the trip.' She offered no further details but raised her glass to Pearl in praise of her food and went to join the councillors' wives.

The Castle kitchen was situated on the ground floor and there, in the large catering fridge, alongside some of Marty's mangoes, Pearl found her culinary *pièce de résistance* – a large summer pudding trifle that she had prepared earlier that day. It combined the classic features of both desserts with Madeira sponge, clotted cream and raspberries, which Pearl had remembered Faye mentioning were her 'favourite'. The dessert had chilled perfectly in a large, decorative bowl that Dolly had made, and feeling pleased with her own efforts, Pearl was about to take it out when she heard footsteps and turned to see Barbara entering, drink in hand.

'If you need any help, I can send in Luc and Rosine?'

'No, it's fine, thank you,' said Pearl. 'Perhaps they can help with serving in a moment.' She set the dessert on to the kitchen table, commenting, 'They've done a fine job tonight.' It was true; the pair had worked very hard.

'Yes,' Barbara said, 'Faye and I are very grateful. Between them, they've made themselves pretty indispensable. Rosine's an excellent maid and a great help with Faye's wardrobe. She once worked in the theatre as a seamstress so she's a dab hand at repairs.' She took a sip of her drink.

'And Luc?' asked Pearl.

'He worked in Monaco, at the casino. They seem a very nice couple – on a trial period at the moment but I'm sure their next contract will be permanent.' Barbara watched Pearl dress the trifle with more cream. 'That really does look awesome,' she said.

'Well, you know what they say about the proof of the pudding...' Pearl turned to face Barbara. 'I hope your migraines are better?'

'Much,' Barbara said firmly. 'Thank you for asking. I just have to watch for stressful situations.'

'And I'd imagine there are quite a few in your job.'

Barbara smiled. 'There can be. The trick is not to let them get to you.' She set down her empty glass. 'Well, if you're sure you don't need my help, I'll see you outside.' She left, and Pearl heard her footsteps climbing the wooden staircase to the powder room upstairs.

In the next moment, Marty entered and seeing Pearl with the large dessert bowl in her arms, he rushed to her side, warning, 'You could do with a hand there. Why didn't you ask me?'

'It's fine,' she said.

But Marty chose not to listen. 'Come on – give that to me.'

He tried to wrestle the bowl from Pearl but she resisted, and for a moment or two they performed a strange sort of tango, moving back and forth in the Castle kitchen until she finally insisted: 'Marty. *I can manage!'* He finally backed off.

'OK,' he said, clearly frustrated. 'But why you have to be so stubborn, Pearl, I'll never know.'

Realising that she had rejected him yet again, Pearl came up with a compromise. 'Marty, look, I worked hard on this dessert and if anyone's going to drop it, it'll be me – not you. Now, if you could hold that door open for me on my way out, that would be a great help.'

Marty stopped sulking and did as Pearl had suggested, allowing her to exit safely with the bowl in her arms. She called back to him: 'Thank you.'

On her way to the marquee, Pearl saw that a few guests had stepped outside and were chatting together, or smoking, some pointing up to a clear night sky that was studded with stars. Maria Hewett was among them, but on noticing that Pearl had come across from the direction of the Castle, she approached to ask, 'Have you seen Oliver?'

''Fraid not,' Pearl replied. Maria looked back towards the Castle but saw only Marty bringing up the rear. She appeared vaguely troubled but then raised a polite smile and re-entered the marquee. As Pearl followed her in, a number of sighs instantly greeted the sight of the trifle. She set the bowl down in pride of place on the table and a small crowd immediately gathered to admire it. Faye was not among them. In fact, she appeared to have left the marquee; perhaps, Pearl thought, she was having some final photographs taken somewhere else in the grounds.

Rosine arrived at the table, carrying bowls, and

a selection of spoons, while Purdy, who had been talking to Nathan, looked hungrily at the trifle.

'I hope there's enough to go round!' she gushed.

At that moment, her father entered the marquee and caught his wife's eye. Pearl saw the look that passed between them; it clearly indicated that something was wrong. He quickly joined Maria and their daughter, saying starkly, 'I really think we must go now.'

Purdy looked up in confusion. 'Not now, Daddy,' she said. 'Pearl's just about to serve this wonderful pudding.'

'Is everything all right, darling?' asked Maria, unsure.

Before Oliver could utter another word, Faye swanned in. Ignoring him, she went to stand beside Jerry Wheeler while Barbara, following close behind, moved to supervise the serving of dessert.

'Daddy?' Purdy said, but Oliver failed to reply. Instead, he seemed torn as he continued staring across towards Faye. She was laughing at something Jerry Wheeler had just said, her voice sounding like the tinkling of glass. In an affectionate move, she now rested her hand on Jerry's chest, her fingers playfully stroking the club tie he wore.

Oliver Hewett's face set. 'I said we should go,' he repeated harshly.

Maria instantly put down the glass in her hand, but Purdy rebelled. 'I'm not ready,' she insisted.

Maria took control. 'You heard what Daddy said, Purdy – it's time to go.'

It was clear that the girl was about to protest further but just then, a small commotion was heard outside. Luc darted over to the marquee's entrance but he was too late to stop the woman who was now bursting in, shouting at the top of her voice: 'All right! Where is she?'

All eyes turned to see Jean Wheeler, who stood stock still while she quickly scanned the room before her gaze finally alighted on Faye. The actress was still standing with Jerry, her hand resting lightly on his chest. 'I should have known,' Jean hissed, pointing at Faye accusingly. 'How you have the nerve to return this town, after what you did!'

Luc took a firm hold of Jean Wheeler's arm. 'Please, madame?' he asked politely, trying to calm her – but it was clear Jean was having none of it.

'Get your hands off me,' she ordered. 'I shall have my say with this woman if it's the last thing I do.'

Jerry now stepped forward, and in an effort to rescue the situation, he blocked her path. 'Mother, you're making a fool of yourself,' he muttered, noting that the local councillors were all agog, watching intently.

'Oh? And you'd know all about *that,* wouldn't you, Jerry?'

The next moment, Luc lunged forward to deal with this troublesome guest, but Jerry clumsily got in his way – and Jean took advantage of the ensuing chaos to sidestep them both. She had caught sight of something ... and before anyone could stop her, she'd picked up Pearl's dessert bowl and tipped the entire contents over Faye. A collective gasp went around the marquee as Jean, bowl still in hand, looked equally shocked at what she had just done. Then she swirled a finger around the bowl, tasted it and smiled appreciatively before she

84

began to laugh – loudly and hysterically. Shoving the bowl into her son's arms, she pointed at Faye, who was smothered in raspberries, cream and jelly, and announced to her rapt audience: 'I've been wanting to do that for years!'

Barbara and Rosine rushed forward to help their employer but Faye shrugged them off. 'Get that woman out of here!' she screamed. Luc approached once more, but it was actually Annabel Wheeler who quickly took hold of Jean. She gave a pointed look back towards her husband.

'Don't worry, Jerry,' she said. '*I'll* take Jean home.' She led her mother-in-law to the door while Rosine and Barbara ministered to Faye with paper towels. Every other guest looked on, unsure whether they had really just witnessed a very public assault, or a piece of theatre. It was Marty, however, who had the last word. Leaning in to Pearl he whispered: 'Is that what you call "getting your just desserts"?'

The reception was swiftly wound up after Jean's assault on Faye but it was almost 11.30 before Pearl had packed away her dishes into the car. She stood in the Castle car park, taking a deep breath of night air, seeing that the moon had risen but was now streaked with skeins of cloud. She had just taken out her mobile and was checking it for messages when Marty came up beside her.

'Why don't you leave your car and let me give you a lift home?' he said. 'If we hurry, we could catch a late-night drink at the Conti'. I reckon we could do with one after the shenanigans here tonight. It's a wonder no one called the police, eh?'

85

'Thanks,' said Pearl, 'but I said I'd wait for Nathan and he shouldn't be much longer.'

'I wouldn't count on that,' scoffed Marty. 'I bet all hell's breaking loose back at that house after what Jean Wheeler did tonight.' He paused before suggesting: 'Why don't I wait with you?'

'No, I'm fine, Marty. Please go.'

Marty gave a shrug, knowing all too well how it felt to receive a polite brush-off from Pearl. Equally, Pearl knew how to give one. With a mixture of disappointment and resignation, he shuffled over to his Cornucopia van and got in, offering a wave and a tired smile before he drove out of the car park and on to Tower Hill. Pearl looked down again at her mobile phone. Nathan's first text to her had come through more than half an hour ago, explaining that, although he was still with Faye at Arden House, he was hoping to leave shortly. Before Pearl had a chance to reread it, another text arrived from him. It read: *Can you pick me up?*

She quickly texted back: *OK* – and less than five minutes later, she had just parked her car outside Arden House when she saw Nathan closing the front gate and stepping out on to the pavement. She flashed her headlights and he came straight over. As soon as he had climbed into the passenger seat, Pearl asked: 'How is she?'

Nathan looked at her. 'Utterly humiliated, of course. But she's nothing if not a trouper and insists she's going ahead with the event tomorrow. If I were in her place I'd probably be filing assault charges against that lunatic.'

'I don't think Faye will do that,' said Pearl. 'I

can't imagine she would possibly want to draw any more attention to what happened tonight.'

'Maybe not,' Nathan sighed, 'but thank heaven the press had already left. What on earth possessed Jean Wheeler to attack Faye like that?'

Pearl looked at him. 'I think it's called "mother's love".'

Starting up her Fiat, she drove off towards town and in no time had dropped Nathan outside his cottage. He got out and said awkwardly, 'I'd ask you in, sweetie, but...'

'I understand,' said Pearl. 'It's been quite a night.'

'Yes,' said Nathan, raising a tired smile now. 'But thanks for being there. I guess the one consolation in all this is that nothing worse could possibly happen now.'

'I'm sure you're right, Nathan.'

He leaned down and gave her a quick kiss on the cheek through the open car window, then crunched up the gravel path to his home.

When Pearl arrived back at Seaspray Cottage, she found her cats, three-legged Pilchard and his brother, Sprat, curled up together on her duvet, fast asleep. The house was quiet and peaceful, with only the gentle sound of waves lapping on the beach outside ... but Nathan's words still echoed in her mind. Could the worst thing that might happen really be out of the way? Pearl had agreed with Nathan, but she'd failed to convince herself, not just because of all that she had witnessed tonight but because, outside her window, she could see a long black stripe of cloud drifting ominously in on the horizon.

Chapter Six

'You have to help, Pearl. I need you!' Nathan's voice on Pearl's bedroom phone was panicked but she had only just woken, and the narrow shaft of sunlight that was streaming into the room through a crack in the curtains was the only sign that it was morning.

'Calm down,' she ordered, 'and just tell me what's happened.'

A moment's silence followed as Nathan took a deep breath. Then: 'She's done a runner,' he said bleakly.

'Faye?'

'Who else?'

For an instant, Pearl wondered if she might still be dreaming, but the bells of St Alfred's suddenly chimed the quarter hour and brought her fully awake.

'Come round and I'll explain everything,' he said, in a tone that told Pearl she had no other choice.

In no time, Pearl had thrown on some clothes and found herself in Nathan's car en route to Arden House. He used the journey to relate what he had learned that morning from Barbara: that Faye was literally nowhere to be found. She had disappeared and no one had a clue where she could be. Barbara had asked him to come straight away, but had suggested that he should also bring Pearl. As they approached the house in Nathan's Volkswagen, rain began to splatter on the car's windscreen and he put on his wipers. 'I don't believe this,' he lamented. 'What else can possibly go wrong?'

They soon found themselves seated at the table in the conservatory of Arden House with Barbara, Luc and Rosine. As Pearl might have expected, Barbara had risen to the occasion and appeared to have taken complete control. She explained that she had asked for Pearl to come along so that she could seek her professional advice.

'I haven't called the police,' she told Pearl, 'because I don't want to raise an unnecessary alarm.' She paused to sip some strong black coffee. 'Faye was understandably upset last night, after everything that happened, so it's possible she's reacted to that and taken herself off somewhere.'

'Is that likely?' frowned Pearl. 'I mean, has she ever done something like that before?'

Barbara looked hesitant, as though the question had put her on the spot, but she made a decision and finally admitted, 'She did once run out on a theatre first-night performance.'

Nathan gave an audible sigh.

'But it was quite out of character,' she added hastily. 'Faye has always been a consummate professional. I can absolutely vouch for that because I've worked for her for twenty years and my father was her agent until his death.'

Pearl glanced around the table. 'Who was the last person to have seen her?'

Barbara immediately looked to Luc and everyone else's gaze followed.

'I saw her.' he said. In perfect English, he explained: 'Late last night, some time just after midnight? Rosine was asleep but I came down to check that everything was locked and I heard something.'

'Where?' asked Pearl.

'Here, in the conservatory,' he replied. 'I came in and Madame Marlow was here.'

'Alone?' asked Pearl.

Luc nodded. 'She said she couldn't sleep.' He shrugged. 'That was it. Nothing more. I said good night and returned to bed. Rosine was still asleep.'

Pearl asked Barbara, 'Did Faye ever have trouble sleeping?'

'Not that I know of. But, as I say, she was badly shaken up by what had happened.'

Pearl addressed Luc again. 'Did she say anything else?'

'Nothing. *Rien du tout.* And then this morning...' He looked at Rosine and she gave a small nod of her head.

'I took coffee to Madame Faye. Always I do,' she explained. 'I knock,' she mimed a rap upon a door, 'nothing. *Silence.* Again, I knock. *Rien.* Nothing. So I leave.'

Barbara took up the story. 'I told Rosine to try to wake Faye again by eight-thirty. This time when she knocked and there was no response, she opened the door.'

Rosine took up the story once more. 'Ze room – empty. Ze bed – empty. Like magic – *elle a disparu.* Gone!'

Nathan sank his head into his hands. 'Oh my God,' he said. 'Where on earth could she be?'

But Pearl ignored him, and continued to question Luc. 'And when you saw Faye last night, how was she dressed?'

'In a *chemise de nuit*,' he replied. 'With a white ribbon – here, at the neck.'

'A nightdress?' asked Pearl.

Barbara nodded. Luc continued. 'And a dressing gown.'

'What was she doing?' Pearl asked.

'Nothing,' the young man replied. 'I came in here. I saw her. She was standing by the door, looking out.'

'Towards the garden?'

He began coughing a little then nodded.

'Thank you,' said Pearl. 'And did any of you hear anything more? A door opening or closing, perhaps?'

Rosine and Luc shook their heads but Barbara said, 'I did wake up at some point. I heard a dog barking. It went on for quite a while but I'm not sure what time it was and when it stopped I went straight back to sleep.'

'And Faye left no note?' asked Pearl.

'Nothing,' said Barbara, anxious. 'She doesn't seem to have taken anything with her. Her bag is still upstairs – and her suitcase.'

'And her coat?' asked Pearl. 'Would you be able to see what clothes of hers may be missing?'

'Rosine looks after Faye's wardrobe. She'll know exactly what, if anything, is missing.'

'Good,' Pearl nodded. 'That's something the police will want to know.'

'Police?' asked Nathan. He looked at Barbara, who took her cue.

'Pearl, I've just explained, I'm reluctant to involve the police quite yet – if at all. That's why I asked for you to come. I promise you, when Faye returns, she won't thank us for a scandal.'

'And if she doesn't return?' asked Pearl. 'In just over an hour's time, the town will be gearing up for May Day. Everyone will be expecting to see Faye open the day's events. If she's not here...'

'Pearl's right,' Nathan interrupted fretfully. 'What on earth are we going to say?'

In the pause that followed, Pearl thought of at least one large talking bush – Whitstable's Jack-in-the-Green – who would be extremely disappointed if May Day was suddenly cancelled.

'Surely she couldn't have run out on us?' said Nathan. 'But if she has, there must be a good reason why. She said last night that she would see me and Purdy at the Castle today at nine-thirty. I can't believe she would just disappear like this when everyone's expecting to see her.'

'Faye's a star,' Barbara said. 'I assure you, she knows she has a special responsibility to her fans. But you're right. I'll take your advice, Pearl, and I'll call the police.' She had got to her feet when Nathan suddenly turned to Pearl.

'Is there any way you could talk to that detective friend of yours? Maybe he could keep things under wraps.'

'I don't think so, Nathan.' Pearl was just about to explain that McGuire would be the last person to hold back on police procedure when a loud and piercing scream sounded outside.

'What on earth was that?' asked Nathan, unnerved.

Luc jumped immediately to his feet and looked out of the conservatory door towards the garden. He pointed to the Castle grounds. 'It came from over there.' He moved quickly outside and everyone followed.

Hurrying to the end of the garden, they soon reached the path beyond Arden House, where Pearl led them through the broken fencing and on to Gatehouse Walk. A clap of thunder sounded and the rain grew suddenly heavier as they rounded the boarded compost bed near the bowling green.

Barbara looked around, calling out loudly, 'Faye? Where are you?' But there was no reply.

Moving on, they hastened towards the marquee, which was still in place, obscuring the view of the Castle Tea Room terrace. As they passed the central pagoda, a figure became visible, standing motionless in front of the maypole on the lawn. Dressed in khaki and wellington boots, she was instantly identifiable to Pearl as the Castle's head gardener, Joy Thomson.

'Joy!' she called, but closer to, she saw that the woman was staring transfixed at something directly before her. Her whole body was trembling and just as Pearl reached her, the small trowel she had been holding in her left hand dropped to the ground as though all strength had gone out of her. Pearl took another step forward, about to say something, but finally saw what Joy Thomson was looking at, and the words died on her lips.

Faye Marlow's body was tethered to the maypole by the brightly coloured ribbons that flowed from its floral crown. The dressing gown she wore gaped, revealing the nightdress Luc had described, except it was no longer white, but stained red from the blood that had seeped from a knife plunged to the hilt into the actress's chest. Rain dripped from Faye's soaked blonde hair and her make-up was streaked, mascara running down her cheeks like the tears Dolly doubted the actress could shed.

Barbara stepped forward to stand beside Pearl – and was confronted by the same shocking image. 'Oh my God,' she breathed, while Rosine collapsed into Luc's arms, burying her face in his chest.

Nathan's hand moved to his mouth as if to silence his anguish, but it was the young woman approaching from the Castle car park whose plaintive cry gave voice to what everyone felt on coming across such a terrible scene. On seeing Faye's body, Purdy's legs failed her and she fell to her knees on the wet earth of a flowerbed that had been freshly weeded for a May Day celebration that now would never happen.

Chapter Seven

When the call came in to Canterbury CID on Monday morning, Detective Chief Inspector Mike McGuire assumed there had been some mistake. He was tired and about to go off duty, and on hearing that a body had been found in the grounds of Whitstable Castle he allowed himself to think for a moment that this might simply be a report about someone having been discovered sleeping on the lawn or perhaps in a wheelie bin as happened more frequently around the city these days. It wasn't just the homeless who took refuge in bins these days, it was the drunks, too, who were climbing into large communal recycling bins, unaware that they risked being crushed to death once the lorries picked up their loads.

There had been several such near-misses recently. Two men in their fifties, sleeping it off on a comfortable bed of recycled paper, had actually been tipped into a collection lorry only for staff to hear their screams just in time. Emergency buttons had been hit, cancelling the crusher at the very last moment – proving that it was possible for even a homeless drunk, with nowhere to sleep other than a rubbish bin, to consider himself lucky.

As more details came through of the discovery at the Castle, however, McGuire recognised that he had more than a skip incident on his hands.

McGuire hadn't set foot in Whitstable since February, when a bitterly cold north-easterly wind was still blowing on to the town's shore. With holiday leave to take, he had decided to turn up, without first notifying Pearl, his plan being to drop by The Whitstable Pearl after the lunchtime service had ended, and invite her for a meal at Jo-Jo's. He could have booked a table at any one of a number of expensive eateries in Whitstable, but the centre of town was Pearl's territory and he had always hankered after spending time with her on neutral ground. The restaurants in Canterbury were filled with year-round visitors and felt, for the most part, like busy waiting rooms, but having driven past Jo-Jo's in Tankerton several times last summer, he had always sensed this might be the perfect place for a date – especially since he remembered Pearl telling him that the chef's calamari rivalled her own.

He had almost managed to get her there before Christmas but something had got in the way – namely, the discovery of a dead body. He had then taken up an invitation from Pearl to join her for Christmas lunch at Seaspray Cottage, but it had been a family affair with Dolly present and Pearl's son home for the holidays, causing McGuire to feel, as he so often felt in family environments, like an intruder – a cuckoo in the nest. Once Charlie had flown back to Berlin, McGuire had returned to Whitstable to take a second chance at spiriting Pearl away for lunch at the restaurant, only to find a bold notice on the door of The Whitstable Pearl – *Closed for Redecoration*. He could still feel the dull thud of disappointment he had experienced on seeing this, and though he could quite easily have selected the number stored for Pearl on his mobile, and sought her out, either at home or at her office at Nolan's Detective Agency, instead he had chosen to accept this as a clear sign that he would be better placed planning ahead for the next opportunity.

That day, instead of sitting at a table with Pearl, watching the fishing boats return to Whitstable harbour, he had driven on to Broadstairs to eat Dover sole alone, staring out from the Albion Hotel at a deserted sweep of sandy beach at

Viking Bay while reflecting how, in so many ways, he and Pearl were opposites. In his job and in his life, McGuire had come to rely on the certainties of procedure, while Pearl always trusted her instincts. McGuire was a sociable loner whereas Pearl was so obviously a 'people person'. They even looked as though they might have sprung from different tribes, for McGuire was fair and could easily pass for a Scandinavian tourist in the anonymous crowds in Canterbury, while Pearl was a dark beauty deeply rooted to her home town. Only one thing had brought them together – murder. Now, thought McGuire, it was surely about to do the same again.

Further details from the crime scene at the Castle reminded McGuire that it was a Bank Holiday – May Day – and he now asked himself what it was about small towns like Whitstable, where he had previously imagined nothing much might ever happen in the way of crime other than the theft of a bicycle or the arrival of a few poison-pen-letters, that might warrant the attention of his department. Nothing seemed to occur from one festival date to another, until a pebble was thrown into the ostensibly calm waters from which all manner of ripples emerged. That pebble was murder – and twice over, McGuire had come together with Pearl to track down the person responsible. Twice over, they had succeeded.

But McGuire's association with Pearl was proving to be problematic, not just in the prickly nature of their own relationship – though that was challenging enough – for while Pearl was feisty, competitive and stubborn, McGuire was smart

97

enough to recognise that these were all pejorative terms for what might, in other scenarios, be considered as admirable traits. Pearl was also brave, challenging and persistent, and placed in the context of a police career the detective had to admit that she would certainly have made an excellent police officer, not least because most murders were solved by using dogged perseverance in following up every lead until a prime suspect was identified. Nevertheless, if it had been down to McGuire he would have preferred to see Pearl in the role of detective sergeant – someone who would report to him and not dominate him. Instead, it was clear that while she might consider herself McGuire's equal, Pearl Nolan would never be his inferior.

As a young woman she had gone through police training and though she still hankered after satisfying an early dream, at the end of the day she was simply a restaurant-owner who ran a small local detective agency. For that reason alone, any connection to a senior officer involved in the investigation of a serious crime would have come under scrutiny from McGuire's superiors. Using any local knowledge from Pearl had to be handled carefully since the relationships between officers and informants had always to be strictly regulated and monitored – in theory at least. McGuire's own superior, Detective Superintendent Welch, had already shown himself to favour his own local officers over a Londoner like McGuire, in spite of the fact that McGuire had spent almost two decades in the force. Ultimately, Welch was no more than a big fish in a small pond and he had no wish to be reminded of it – especially by McGuire. Welch found McGuire's mere presence at the station to be irksome, let alone the fact that the new officer had solved two homicide cases. But an officer's successes still reflected positively on Welch, so McGuire recognised that he had to walk a tightrope in his new position. Welch might be happy to see this DFL detective gone but the truth was McGuire really had nowhere else to go. Since the death of his fiancée, Donna, two years ago, in a random hit-and-run incident in London, only one thing had supported him through the resulting emotional turmoil – his job – and he was not about to risk it without good cause. As a fresh investigation began, he knew he would have to tread carefully, particularly in his relationship with Pearl Nolan.

After the initial discovery of Faye Marlow's body, the first person on the scene had been a local Police Community Support Officer – not ideal, Pearl considered, since the PCSOs did not have the same kind of mindset or training as police officers themselves and there was always a chance of some mismanagement of a crime scene – especially with one such as this. It was fortunate therefore that a sergeant who had been in the area investigating a minor traffic incident had quickly arrived to supervise the securing of the crime scene. In practical terms this was always done to prevent the destruction of potential clues or evidence and it wasn't long before a boundary of police tape had gone up around the Castle's Regency Gardens with an ambulance crew arriving to confirm that all life was extinct, although it was clear to anyone who had come upon the body that morning that there could be little doubt about that.

Within an hour of the gruesome discovery, police procedure had moved at an impressively efficient speed. The murder scene and body had been photographed and videoed, and an inflatable tent was now in place beside the marquee, which had been left erect to protect any vital clues. Local officers had taken voluntary statements from all the witnesses within the Castle itself, and the Mallandain Room – named after a latter-day owner of the Castle – soon became the setting of a temporary incident room, though it was more usually employed for council meetings and wedding receptions. Pearl knew from her police training that the first few days of any murder investigation were crucial, not least because it was at this time that witnesses' recollections were still fresh in the mind – but also because the perpetrator of the crime had little time to plot an alibi or make a getaway.

Pearl's interview had taken place upstairs in the Holmes Room, conducted by Sergeant Rita Barrows – a pretty woman in her mid-forties, with a firm but considerate manner. While following strict procedure, Barrows treated Pearl courteously, and with every attempt to put her at ease, explaining that the primary aim of the interview was to obtain a clear statement, from Pearl's unique point of view, of what exactly had occurred. She emphasised that Pearl was being treated only as a witness – and not a suspect – though Pearl knew full well that this could easily change.

Pearl relived the morning, relaying to the sergeant all that she had seen and heard, recognising the importance of such a statement being taken as soon as possible before she or any of the others could have a chance to discuss their own recollections and by doing so, influence any of the other witnesses.

As she described coming upon the body, her attention was continually drawn to the window, looking out towards the road on which she felt sure McGuire's car would arrive. But the rain grew heavy, beating down on the leaded panes of the windows while a sudden cold rush of air found its way into the room – along with the smell of death. Whatever efforts were being made by the police forensics to secure the integrity of the scene below, Pearl knew that vital evidence would surely have been lost by now, washed away with the driving rain.

Sergeant Barrows read out Pearl's statement to her, recounting in a strangely prosaic tone the grim discovery of Faye's body, before she finally asked Pearl to sign her name. As she did so, Pearl realised that her hand was shaking and wondered how the Castle's Head Gardener, Joy Thomson, would be bearing up after the shock of being the first person to have arrived on the scene.

Once the interview was over, Pearl was led out of the Castle by a rear exit through the kitchen, where plates and pans had been washed and restored to order. It now seemed impossible to believe that less than twenty-four hours earlier, she had actually been preparing food for Faye Marlow's reception. Staring around for signs of

101

Nathan, Purdy or any of Faye's staff, Pearl saw only police officers pursuing their respective duties like ants in a busy colony.

Before long, she knew, everything would be in place for a full murder investigation, with police staff transferred from other duties, an exhibits officer collating all the objects that might possibly be used as evidence in court, and squads sent out to conduct house-to-house investigations, seeking statements as to what might have been seen or heard by residents overnight. If the facts of Luc's story were accurate, Faye's death had occurred between shortly after midnight and the discovery of her body at 9.27 a.m., and as far as the police were concerned there would be two important times associated with such a violent death: the legal time, determined by confirmation from a medical professional that death had actually occurred, and the estimated time of death, which was precisely that. Pearl knew the procedures by which a pathologist would produce an estimate of the number of hours since death. She had avidly learned about this during her time spent in the world in which she felt she belonged – but from which she was now excluded. Her role seemed destined to be merely that of witness – while McGuire, as Senior Investigating Officer, remained firmly in his element.

Outside on the street at Tower Hill a crowd had formed, held back by a brace of PCSOs. Pearl recognised one of them as Clyde Atkins, a former lifeboat volunteer. Clyde was in his early thirties, an attractive man with a pretty wife and a young family who would no doubt have been looking forward to enjoying the May Day celebrations, had this brutal murder not taken place. It seemed impossible to believe that the person at the centre of the festivities, the famous star due to open the May Day festival, was no longer destined for applause but for a drawer in a police morgue. It was almost too horrific to be true, and yet the sight Pearl had encountered that morning, of beautiful Faye Marlow strung up on the very symbol of the festival itself, had been real enough – so much so that the image was now branded on her memory for all time.

Glancing at her watch, she saw that almost two hours had passed since she had stood on the lawn of the Regency Gardens and been confronted by Faye's corpse. She couldn't be sure what had happened to Nathan or Purdy or any of Faye's staff, but she was certain that the first person to have found Faye's body and to have alerted the neighbourhood with her piercing scream would have been taken to Canterbury CID to give a detailed witness statement under a formalised procedure on audio tape.

McGuire, as Senior Investigating Officer, would surely be taking that statement from Joy in the room in which he had once questioned Pearl about the death of an oyster fisherman last summer. From Tower Hill, where Pearl now stood, it was only 200 metres to the sea. The offshore breeze that blew in at this time of year was usually fresh and welcome, but today it had been replaced by a cold wind that stirred the white-capped waves in a grey sea that owed nothing at all to the promise of the season, and instead reminded Pearl of the pallor of Faye Marshall's lifeless complexion.

On her way back to town, Pearl could hear bells and drums faintly pulsing in the distance, but the usual merry sound of May Day had, to her, struck a funereal tone. The sound that suddenly joined it seemed disconnected for a moment before she realised it was the ring tone of her mobile phone, which was barely holding the last of its battery. She quickly answered the call as she registered the identity of the caller.

'Are you OK?' McGuire's tone was cautious but concerned.

'I think so,' she heard herself reply. 'I've just given a detailed statement and told the officer everything I saw.' She paused. 'But not quite everything I know.'

McGuire asked, 'What do you mean?'

'I mean that I haven't been able to make sense of it yet, but in the last few days I've become aware that a number of people would have liked to have seen the back of Faye Marlow – though whether they were actually capable of murder is quite another thing.'

McGuire considered this but, at that moment, a young WPC put her head around his door and gave a nod to signal that the Castle's Head Gardener, Joy Thomson, was ready for questioning. 'I'll be right there,' he told her.

'What did you say?' asked Pearl, confused, on the other end of the line.

'I'll be in touch,' McGuire told her. 'Tomorrow.'

As he ended the call, Pearl replaced her phone in her pocket and from somewhere deep in her memory the lines of a poem, learned at school, began to sound in her mind, echoing with her footsteps as she continued on into town: *They call me cruel-hearted, but I care not what they say, For I'm to be Queen o' the May, Mother. I'm to be Queen o' the May.*

Chapter Eight

Nathan spoke slowly and deliberately. 'A nightmare,' he shuddered. 'An absolute nightmare. That was surely the most dreadful thing I have ever seen in my entire life.' He moved to offer Pearl a coffee before joining her on the sofa in his Island Wall cottage. 'I didn't sleep a wink last night, did you?'

Pearl shook her head, recalling how the storm that followed the discovery of Faye's body the day before had blown long into the night, lashing rain against her seaward-facing bedroom window. At various times she had managed to drift into a shallow sleep, only to be woken by another powerful gust – seemingly a reminder of the brutal nature of this crime.

'I take it you've heard from your detective?' Nathan asked.

Usually Pearl would have taken issue with his description of McGuire as such, but today she didn't feel the will to do so. He continued, 'So where was he yesterday?'

'At the police station,' Pearl said. 'Interviewing Joy, the Castle's Head Gardener. She was in such a state of shock that she needed medical attention.'

'I'm not surprised,' Nathan said. 'Imagine coming across a body like that all on your own. Poor, dear Faye. Why on earth would someone want to kill her? And in such a terrible way – strung up like that for all to see. It was almost like a ... crucifixion.'

'Yes,' Pearl said. Nathan was right. Though it would have been a quick death, she considered, stabbed through the heart – which was perhaps some consolation. She went on, 'Whoever murdered her chose to display her body in the most public way. But why?'

'I've no idea. But don't tell me it was because she ruffled a few feathers in this town when she was younger. Whoever it was had almost thirty years to get over it, and if they believe murder's the only way to redress the balance they're clearly psychotic.' Nathan sipped his coffee and calmed himself with a deep breath. 'So what now?'

'The police have begun a murder investigation.'

'Thanks for stating the obvious, sweetie.' He stopped suddenly. 'You don't think they suspect that either of *us* could be the murderer, do you?'

'Do you have an alibi?'

Nathan looked shocked. 'Well, actually, yes I do – up to midnight at least. I was with Purdy, going through the charity donations until her father picked her up.'

'And after that?'

He looked at her, his eyebrows raised.

'I'm just asking,' said Pearl.

He pointed to his laptop. 'I was on that for a while longer, then had a glass of Rioja and passed out on the sofa. No witnesses, I'm afraid, apart from Biggy.' He indicated the ginger tom cat, who lay sleeping peacefully on a leopard-print fleece blanket on the sofa.

'And did Oliver and Purdy go straight home?

'How should *I* know?' Nathan frowned. 'I'd imagine so, since there's hardly anywhere open at that time, apart from the local kebab shop – which I don't think is quite the Hewetts' style.'

'Have you talked to Barbara?'

Nathan nodded. 'On the phone, but not for long. The press are all over her like a rash. And not just the local rags. Some of the nationals have been calling too, so she's had to issue a media release.'

'I haven't opened the restaurant today,' Pearl told him. 'Partly out of respect but also because the papers are bound to pursue us for stories until the initial stampede for information subsides. Best to simply offer up a "no comment",' she advised.

'Don't worry, sweetie, I shall. I'm not picking up any unidentified calls on my mobile and I've left the answering machine on.' He looked at her. 'What do you think?'

'About?'

'You know very well. Do you have any idea who might have done this?'

'How could I?'

'Because you're you – and I'd imagine you have the edge on your detective because you've been with me for the last few days, you met Faye and you were at the reception...' He broke off. 'Oh God, you don't think it could have been Jean Wheeler, do you?'

'Why should I?'

'You saw the state she was in that night. She gate-crashed the reception and assaulted Faye.'

'With a summer pudding trifle, Nathan. Do you really think if Jean had had murder in mind, she would have turned up at the reception like that and incriminated herself?'

'Double bluff?' he suggested. 'Making herself the obvious suspect doesn't mean she's off the hook, does it?' He then reached over and stroked Biggy as though for comfort. 'Poor Faye. I'll never get my interview now.'

Over in Cornucopia, Marty Smith placed a business cheque in his till and closed the drawer. 'So, we finally get a real guest of honour in town – a celebrity to do us proud on May Day – and someone goes and does her in.' He shook his head at the thought then glanced at the Jack-in-the-Green costume that stood in view at the back of the shop, its leaves curling. 'I'd just put that on when the news came through,' he recalled. 'I hadn't even got as far as the pub.'

He took off his baseball cap, scratching his head, before he remembered something and showed the cap to Pearl. 'At least I got her autograph,' he said, and Pearl saw Faye's name scribbled in biro on Marty's cap. 'Can you believe she actually signed this for me and just a few hours later she was murdered?'

He stared at the cap and then, rather than place it back on his head, folded it respectfully and put it into a drawer. 'May Day,' he said. 'Cancelled.'

As he looked at her with sorrowful green eyes, for a moment Pearl felt some affinity with him ...

then she noticed his expression flatten as he looked directly behind her. 'Well, well...' Marty said, slowly. 'If it's not Detective McGinty.'

'McGuire,' the detective corrected him, giving Marty a withering glance before turning to Pearl. 'Could I have a word?'

Pearl saw Marty offer a vengeful look at McGuire. 'Of course,' she said, keen to get McGuire off Marty's territory.

As she moved off with the detective, she could still feel Marty's eyes boring into her. When they reached the door, he called out suddenly, 'Hey, Pearl! He's meant to read you your rights first, you know.'

Looking back, she saw Marty was standing with his arms folded high up on his chest, but she said nothing – not wishing to fuel his resentment.

Once out on the street, the detective asked her, 'What's *his* problem?'

'You,' she said simply. They could see that Marty was now eyeing them through his front window, apparently unaware that his head was positioned at the top of the banana painted on the glass exterior.

'Very apt,' commented McGuire, opening the passenger door of his car for Pearl. Through the windscreen, she could see that a banner was still in place, slung across the road between two tall buildings, advertising *Fun at May Day.*

'Is there somewhere private we can talk?' McGuire asked.

Pearl fastened her seatbelt. 'I know just the place.'

There were only three sets of allotments in the whole of the Whitstable area and, at any one time, more than fifty people were waiting on a list for a plot to become available. Pearl's family allotment was precious to her because Dolly had long surrendered most of her own garden to the extension she had built in order to add more space to her holiday let, Dolly's Attic. Pearl's own garden at Seaspray Cottage was attractive, with a sea-facing view, but it was tiny and further en-croached upon by the former beach hut that now stood on her lawn and that she used as the office for Nolan's Detective Agency.

The allotment provided a valued location for Pearl to grow not only her own fruit and vege-tables but flowers too – like the seemingly un-ending supply of sweet peas she used throughout the summer in her restaurant. A few neighbouring plots had been known to change hands after their holders had given up on them, shocked by the hard work they had encountered, compared to the relative ease displayed in garden makeover shows. But Pearl had held on to hers not only because she respected its family history – having been handed down from Dolly's grandparents – but also be-cause she appreciated a wider sense of history, having learned how early allotments had grown out of the theft, for want of a better word, of common land that had been lost to the enclosures.

The idea of allotting a piece of land to poor labourers, on which they could grow their own food, had taken root during the Enlightenment, when the ruling classes had deemed it more favourable for peasants to be occupied in planting root crops than with any other wayward habits. But once the Industrial Revolution had forced people off the land and into mills and factories, it became clear to the same ruling classes that a large proportion of the population could no longer feed itself. Allocated allotments of land became an insurance against starvation for families, and after the First World War, the provision of allotments to returning soldiers was extended, with local authorities providing such land according to demand. As Dolly's grandmother had always said, 'As long as you have a piece of land to put a spade into, you'll never go hungry.'

Pearl had no fear of starvation, merely a will to make good use of the plot while taking time to relax from the demands of The Whitstable Pearl. It was true that her presence in the restaurant was not always required, since the menu was of such simplicity that her staff could manage well without her, and though she was always busy, she still felt the need to find time to plant in spring, even if the resulting crops were not always a success. What was important for Pearl was to feel connected to the earth: to turn it, to feed it and to make use of it in a positive way – so that sometimes, on a hot summer night, after watering her crops and flowers, a stillness would fall during which she liked to think that the earth itself was giving up thanks.

At other times, she might be digging deep into the earth when she came upon a piece of buried treasure – an old Roman coin or perhaps nothing more than part of an old gardening tool. Nevertheless, this allowed her to feel something of the greater thrill she imagined was enjoyed by archaeologists like Oliver Hewett when he had excavated the old copperas works on the beach or studied the Maya murals of Bonampak. It had been said that angels talk to a man when he's walking but Pearl knew that answers came to her when she was either out on the sea or working this small rectangle of land beneath which layers of history existed – clues to the greater mystery of life itself. It was for that reason that she had directed McGuire on to Joy Lane at Borstal Hill and then on to a narrow dirt track that led to a strip of land bathed yellow with buttercups.

McGuire parked his car in a clearing and looked at her. 'So where are we?'

'Come and see,' she said. Getting out of the car, she explained: 'This track leads to Prospect Field, which is almost four acres of scrub and grassland that run along the railway line. A group of volunteers preserve it for wildlife and the local community. If you think about it, apart from the golf course, the grounds of the Castle and the railway embankment, there are few habitats left in the town for wildlife, but this is a haven for hedgehogs, butterflies, woodpeckers – even grass snakes and lizards.' She pointed out towards the coast. 'There are great views from here too across the Swale Estuary.' She smiled. 'On a good clear day you can even smell the candyfloss from Southend.'

McGuire stood close beside her and looked at the view. It was cloudy and hardly the Caribbean, but the area was certainly peaceful and clearly home to many wild rabbits that were scampering across the embankment. Beyond the railway lines lay only a caravan site, but the bells of St Alfred's could still be heard chiming – a reminder that the centre of town wasn't far away.

'You said you wanted somewhere quiet?' said Pearl. 'Come on.' She led him back towards the car but then on, up to some rusty metal gates. The path was still damp from last night's heavy rain, prompting her to think of the wet earth at the Castle grounds upon which Purdy had sunk to her knees after catching sight of Faye's body. Looking up, Pearl could see that the sun was now trying to shine through hazy cloud.

After opening the gates, she and McGuire entered a local allotment site. The detective took a cursory look around the patchwork of plots that were studded with sheds and bamboo wigwams. Only one other seemed to be occupied – on the far side, a man in his sixties, wearing a flat cap, was busily painting a fence. Pearl's plot was easily identified by the large decorative panel that was attached to the side of a shed. It was Dolly's work and featured an oyster and a totem pole with the sun shining down on a burgeoning crop – wishful thinking perhaps, since the plot itself contained little other than a wheelbarrow of topsoil and a snazzily dressed scarecrow wearing an old striped blazer and a Panama hat. A brightly painted yellow bench stood outside the shed, along with terra-cotta pots that had been artificially 'aged' by Dolly using yoghurt. A brazier seemed to be filled with damp cardboard.

McGuire noted that the shed itself was rather more of a cabin for which Pearl was struggling to find the right key. 'This is yours?' he asked.

113

'My family's.' She finally managed to find the key and unlocked the door, saying, 'Come in.' In a few swift moves she had lifted the wooden shutters from a pair of windows, allowing light to fall upon a small French wood-burning stove with an Art Nouveau motif on its grille. Dolly had bought it from a junk shop long ago, but now it was to be put to good use. Pearl efficiently stacked it with paper and kindling before striking a match while McGuire offered a log from a basket. She took it from him and loaded it into the burner before closing the stove's door. Picking up a cushion from Dolly's rocking chair, she tossed it to McGuire, indicating for him to take a seat by the fire. 'It's still a bit damp in here from last night's rain, but it should dry out soon.'

McGuire felt vaguely uncomfortable, not because of his seat, but from finding himself in unexpected surroundings. The hut was filled with strange ornaments: enamel mugs, old scythes and a kitchen cabinet with dimpled glass doors that had surely survived the Blitz.

As Pearl scooped up her long, dark hair and secured it with a comb from her pocket, she completed the picture by looking much like a wartime pin-up. 'I'd make you a cup of tea but I haven't got properly settled in yet for the spring.'

'It's fine.' He said nothing more but Pearl recognised she was under his scrutiny.

'What are you thinking?' she asked.

McGuire had left his office planning to ask numerous questions, but now he found himself asking the one that had only just sprung to mind. 'Why is it that whenever a murder takes place,

114

you're never far away?'

Pearl gave a shrug. 'It does rather seem that way, doesn't it?' As she smiled, all thoughts of Superintendent Welch suddenly disappeared for McGuire.

Pearl went on: 'Nathan asked me to go to the house with him.'

'House?'

'Arden House. It's where Faye had been staying since her arrival. I served late lunch for her there on Friday afternoon. Afterwards, her assistant, Barbara, asked me to cater for the reception at the Castle. Everything was set for the May Day parade and events when Nathan called yesterday morning to break the news that Faye had disappeared. I'm sure you've established that Luc seems to be the last person to have seen her, just after midnight.'

'He told you that?'

'Yes. Nathan was worried that Faye might have lost her nerve about the May Day event, so he asked me to go with him up to the house.'

'Why you?'

'Why not? I'm his friend – and a detective, remember?' She gave McGuire a pointed look then admitted, 'But I didn't actually get very far with questioning. Luc said he'd last seen Faye in the conservatory – and that she was wearing her nightdress. I presume that's the one she was found in? He mentioned it had white ribbon at the neck.'

'And?' prompted McGuire.

'And he said he saw her looking from the conservatory towards the grounds. As I say, I hadn't got very far when we suddenly heard the scream. I can still hear it. It was an unearthly

115

sound. Piercing... That's exactly how it felt, as if it was piercing your soul. At the time I'm sure we all thought it might be Faye, but it was actually Joy reacting to the sight of Faye's body.' Pearl looked down as though trying to make sense of something before finally giving her attention once more to McGuire. 'I know you'll need to wait for an autopsy report to confirm the cause of death, but it looked pretty conclusive to me.' She paused for a moment. Then: 'You must have been very busy.'

'True.' McGuire replied. 'Apart from the investigation, there's a lot of media attention to field.'

'I wasn't talking about the murder.' She held his look. 'I meant since Christmas.' Her tone was admonishing but just in case he still hadn't got it, she said, 'You could have stopped by – at the restaurant?'

McGuire weighed up the pros and cons of whether he should let her know all the details of his abortive visit in February. In the end, he said only: 'I did. You were closed. For redecoration.'

She eyed him, unimpressed. 'Well, you could have come back, couldn't you? It was finished in two weeks. I'd gone to see Charlie in Berlin. For my birthday.' She chose not to explain that it had actually been a significant birthday – her fortieth – which she hadn't cared to spend on the North Kent coast during the coldest month of winter. Instead, she asked: 'Why didn't you phone me?'

'Why didn't you?'

'I've been busy.'

'Snap.'

She gave an unexpected smile and McGuire relaxed under her gaze.

116

'I suppose you heard about the incident at the reception?' she asked.

McGuire nodded slowly. 'Mrs Wheeler. What can you tell me?'

'I'd suggest you're better off talking to my mother as they've been friends for a very long time. But there again...'

'Your mother doesn't much like talking to policemen.'

'You noticed.' She pondered. 'All right. Here's what I've learned: Jean's angry with her son Jerry but chose to take that out instead on Faye Marlow.'

'Real name Frances Severin,' said McGuire. 'Née Marshall.'

Pearl went on, 'Who broke off her engagement to Jerry more than twenty years ago. Jean was in the restaurant just the other day, furious that Jerry had been shepherding Faye around town in a very conspicuous way, while his wife, Annabel, was away in Hove. To be honest, I think Jean was frustrated that Annabel hadn't been on hand to prevent this, although judging by the way Faye was flirting with Jerry at the reception, I'm not sure that even Annabel could have stopped her. Jean hadn't been invited to the reception but she came anyway. What she saw on her arrival tipped her over the edge.'

'And what did she see?'

'It was bad timing. Jerry was clearly captivated by Faye and she was playing up to him. I'd just brought the dessert to table.' She sighed ruefully, as she remembered. 'A delicious raspberry summer pudding trifle which nobody got to try because Jean used it instead to assault Faye. I'm sure it damaged nothing but Faye's pride – and her outfit. I'm equally sure that if Jean really *had* intended to harm Faye, she'd have used something more lethal than my dessert.'

'Like a knife,' McGuire said starkly.

'That's what Nathan suggested this morning, but if she was planning to murder Faye, why would she have gone and made herself prime suspect with the trifle attack?'

'Because she wanted you to ask that same question?'

'Nathan said that too,' Pearl repeated pensively, before she changed the subject. 'So, this time you've been made Senior Investigating Officer and not Shipley?'

McGuire stiffened at the mention of DI Tony Shipley, the former sergeant who, in spite of all his inadequacies, had been promoted by Welch and then handed the last murder investigation at Canterbury CID. Admittedly, procedure had prevented McGuire from taking charge of that case because, technically, he had been a witness to the crime, but in partnership with Pearl, the murder had been solved and it had been McGuire, and not Shipley, who had made the formal arrest – something that still rankled for Welch.

'Yes,' McGuire said finally. 'It's my case – and while any information you can give me will be welcome, if you're thinking of running another parallel investigation, you had better think again, because this time we do it by the book.' He had surprised himself by managing to express as much without Pearl having once interrupted him but, in fact, she was staring at him now in all innocence.

'But of course,' she agreed. 'The previous cases were all quite different.'

'How?'

'Well, in the first, I happened to find two bodies which you were willing to accept weren't the result of foul play, and during the last, you and I were trying to make up for Shipley's inefficiency. But this murder investigation looks to be a straight-forward case for CID. I'm sure you'll be able to solve it.'

McGuire noted her disingenuous smile and stated boldly, 'I'm sure I will.'

'Then, for once, we agree.'

At that moment, McGuire's mobile sounded. He answered it, initially speaking in mono-syllables to the caller. 'When?' Then: 'Did he say how?' And: 'How long before it's ready?' Finally, he nodded to himself 'OK, I'll be right there.' Brooding on the call, he slipped his phone into his jacket pocket.

'Forensics?' Pearl asked. Before he could speak she hurried on: 'I imagine they wouldn't have found much at the scene due to the heavy rain. And I'm sure you've considered how Faye and the murderer might have found their way into the grounds? There are metal railings surrounding them although they could be climbed over, by someone agile, after the gate is locked. The walls are floodlit at night – multicoloured.' She winced at the thought. 'A bit too Disney for my mother's liking, but–'

'What are you trying to tell me, Pearl?'

'Well, I'm sure it's already been noted, but there

119

are a few fence-panels down near the shrubbery on the Gatehouse Walk, which would actually make it rather easy for *anyone* to enter – and to leave.'

McGuire considered this but decided against offering any comment. Instead, he got to his feet. 'Come on. I'll give you a lift home.'

Pearl remained seated. 'Thanks. But if you don't mind, I'm going to stay here for a while. In fact, I'm going to do some digging.' She gave him a mischievous look.

McGuire pointed at her. 'I'm going to keep my eye on you.'

She nodded. 'I hope you do.'

McGuire turned for the door then suddenly turned back again. He decided he would plunge in, as with a cold swimming pool, rather than hover around the steps, dipping in a toe. 'How about supper Thursday night?' As her jaw dropped open a little, he saw he had taken her by surprise. Deciding to capitalise on this, he added in a little more temptation. 'A long time ago, I promised to take you to Jo-Jo's, remember?'

'So you did.'

'So how about it – Thursday night at seven-thirty?'

'Yes.' She smiled now. 'I'll see you there.'

For a moment, McGuire couldn't believe it had really been that easy. As he left the cabin, he allowed himself to smile too. Perhaps he was finally getting somewhere.

Chapter Nine

The next day, Wednesday, Pearl headed east on foot from the Tea Gardens at Tower Hill, where the long sweep of Marine Parade offered a clear sea view for the properties that overlooked Tankerton Slopes. They were built in a variety of architectural styles, with the much-loved Tankerton Arms pub having been converted long ago into desirable apartments. Over the years, bungalows had been extended and further developments had sprung up, offering stylish second homes to DFLs.

Set amongst its more contemporary neighbours, one residence in particular was all the more conspicuous for its traditional construction and appearance. Haversham House had been occupied by Oliver Hewett's family since the First World War. It was set back from the pavement with a front and side lawn bordered by a picket fence; its herringbone brickwork was of a Jacobean-revival style and its roof was thatched. An old crab apple tree stood on the front lawn, much of its blossom having remained intact apart from that dislodged by the heavy rain, which now lay strewn at Pearl's feet like pink confetti. The tree's fruit was used every year by Maria Hewett to make the crab-apple jelly she always donated for charity sales at St Alfred's Church. A feisty robin sat on a spade that rested against an old wheelbarrow, until chased away by the arrival of a black crow. Eyeing the crow, which stared back at her, unmoved, Pearl rang the doorbell. The door opened to reveal Maria Hewett – clearly surprised to see her unexpected visitor.

'I don't want to trouble you,' Pearl began. 'I just wondered how Purdy is.'

Maria looked beyond Pearl, as if to check that she was alone, and then beckoned her inside. 'Come in,' she said softly. Closing the front door, she shot a quick glance upstairs then gestured for Pearl to follow her to the back of the house and into a warm kitchen, where a strong smell of sweet cinnamon rose from the cooker.

Maria took off the apron she wore and tucked loose strands of her poker-straight hair back into the ponytail from which they had escaped. 'Can I offer you some tea?' she asked. 'I was just about to make some.'

'That would be nice.' As Maria busied herself filling the kettle and taking down mugs from a stand, Pearl glanced around, noting evidence of academic study everywhere. Books lined each wall – tomes and reports from various archaeological societies. Seeming to read her guest's thoughts, Maria commented, 'You'll have to excuse the mess but I'm afraid living with Oliver means putting up with lots of literature about the place.' She raised a sad smile. 'It's kind of you to drop by, Pearl. It's been a dreadful shock for Purdy – well, for all of us – including you yourself, I'm sure.' Pearl nodded mutely and Maria sighed. 'Purdy was brought home by the police, you know. She was quite inconsolable.' She then turned her attention to the boiling kettle.

'Of course,' Pearl said gently. 'She had got to know Faye.' At this, Maria glanced back at Pearl, who continued, 'They'd been corresponding for some time, I believe – about the event. Nathan's been very grateful for Purdy's help. The two of them were both such fans of Faye.'

'Yes,' Maria said a little stiffly. 'But it wouldn't be correct to think that Purdy knew Faye well. After all, she was a film star and Purdy – well, as you say, my daughter's just a fan.' She handed a mug of tea to Pearl, who thanked her.

'Is she home?' Pearl asked.

'Yes, but...' Maria broke off, looking torn. 'I really think it might be best if you didn't see her today.' Explaining this seemed to pain Maria, as though she was more accustomed to satisfying, rather than disappointing, the expectations of others. 'The thing is,' she went on, 'Purdy hasn't been herself since all this happened. She can't sleep properly. At night I hear her pacing around in her room.'

'So you're unable to sleep too,' Pearl reasoned.

Realising what she had just said, Maria nodded a tame admission. 'The whole thing is really too macabre to contemplate, but ... nevertheless it's difficult to do anything else.' An alarm sounded and Maria flinched for a moment before heading across to check the progress of her baking. She proceeded to take a tray from the oven. 'I'm only trying to keep busy,' she said helplessly. 'I realise cakes are mainly for celebrations, aren't they?' Defeated, she set two sponge layers on a stand to cool.

'Don't worry,' said Pearl. 'Please just tell Purdy

I called by.'

She had finished her tea and was about to stand up and take her leave when the door suddenly opened and Purdy entered, her dark eyes looking deep with sorrow against her pale complexion. Startled at seeing Pearl, she faltered for a moment. 'I heard the doorbell go but I didn't know it was you, Pearl.' She looked at her mother, as if for an explanation.

'You can talk to Pearl another time, my love,' said Maria. 'You need to rest.'

But Purdy shook her head and asserted, 'No, I'm fine. In fact, I'd like to talk to you, Pearl, if I may?'

Maria stepped forward. 'Purdy, I really think–'

'Mummy, I said I'm fine!' The girl's frustration was clear, though she was trying to keep it under control.

Maria was visibly stung by the response but she gave in straight away, replying: 'All right. I'll be upstairs if you need me.' She left the room and as soon as the door had closed after her, Purdy gazed towards the French windows where two small terriers were play-fighting on the lawn.

'I'd suggest we go into the garden,' she began, 'but being there only reminds me of...' Unable to complete the sentence, she took a deep breath and simply stated, 'It was a terrible mistake, wasn't it?' She seemed slightly dazed and as though she was speaking to herself.

'What was?' asked Pearl.

'Inviting Faye here. To Whitstable.' She looked at Pearl as though she was in fact looking straight through her. 'If we hadn't done that, Faye would still be alive.' She hung her head.

'Purdy, there's no point in thinking that way.'

'But it is true,' the girl insisted. 'It's all my fault.'

'How can you say that? It was Nathan who invited her.'

'But I was the one who persuaded her to come. I wanted to meet her so badly, and now look what's happened.' Purdy's face crumpled in sorrow but she managed to hold back tears. 'I've never seen a dead body before,' she admitted. 'But finding her like that – tied up, murdered – how could anybody do that to another human being? Let alone to Faye?'

'I don't know,' Pearl replied honestly.

The girl seized her hand. 'Pearl, you're a detective. You'll be able to find out, won't you? You must have an idea!'

Pearl was about to respond to placate her when there was the sound of the front door closing. Footsteps approached the kitchen and Oliver walked in. Wearing a tweed jacket and carrying a briefcase, it was clear he had just arrived home. He saw his daughter's feverish expression and asked with some suspicion, 'What's going on?'

'Nothing,' said Purdy, instantly getting to her feet.

'Pearl?' demanded Oliver, waiting for her reply, but it was Purdy who spoke again.

'We were just talking,' she told her father quietly. 'About what happened.'

Oliver's gaze shifted to Pearl. He set his brief-case down and said, 'My daughter's very upset.' His expression showed that, in his opinion, this simple statement was all that was required.

'Of course,' said Pearl. 'I'm sorry.' She made a

move to leave but Purdy protested.

'No, Pearl. I'm perfectly all right. And I do need to talk about this.' She looked directly at her father. 'Do you understand, Daddy?'

Oliver had no time to respond because just then, having heard raised voices, Maria entered. She made a quick assessment of the situation and seeing Pearl on her feet said, 'I'll see you out.'

But then Purdy spoke again, a cry of frustration this time, as she implored: 'Why doesn't anyone ever *listen* to me?'

Concerned by his daughter's outburst, Oliver tried to comfort her, but she shrugged him off and stormed from the room, her footsteps thumping on the stairs before a door slammed loudly above them.

Oliver looked both embarrassed and defeated. 'I'm sorry,' he apologised to Pearl, for want of something else to say.

'No, I shouldn't have come,' Pearl decided. 'It was a bad idea.' She joined Maria at the door who led the way back into the hall.

'We're ... finding this very difficult to come to terms with,' Maria said softly. 'If only Purdy had...' She broke off suddenly, as if she was looking at something only she could see: a ghost, a memory perhaps, thought Pearl – but finally she pulled herself together and opened the front door.

'Let's talk another time,' Pearl suggested. Maria smiled weakly and Pearl stepped outside, back into the daylight while the door to Haversham House closed after her. Walking back up the garden path towards the pavement, Pearl sensed that she was being watched. She turned but saw only that there were now two black crows perched on the front gable of the house, as though protecting their territory.

That afternoon, at The Whitstable Pearl, Dolly hung up her apron after the lunchtime service had ended and checked her appearance in a small mirror near the door.

'Poor Jean, of course, is distraught,' she said.

'About Faye's death?' asked Pearl, confused.

'No. About having been treated like a murder suspect.' Dolly slipped into a light summer jacket.

'We were all questioned,' argued Pearl.

'Maybe so, but Jean was taken to the station. They cautioned her too. The ignominy. Picked her up in a police car and carted her off in it. Every curtain in the street was twitching.'

'But she was released again.'

'Of course she was!' Dolly exclaimed. 'Habeas corpus and all that. 'They've nothing on Jean. She couldn't hurt a fly.'

'Oh really? She certainly did some damage to my dessert – and Faye's pride,' said Pearl.

'What happened up at the Castle was merely a … custard-pie moment,' Dolly argued. 'And nothing less than Faye deserved, by the sound of it. I would never have wished the woman dead, but we can't let a grisly murder mask the truth – that Faye Marlow was a minx of the first order. Like I said – trouble.'

'And if that's true, it might suggest a number of potential suspects,' mused Pearl.

'There you go again!' said Dolly. 'Talking like a Flat Foot. And I presume *he's* back on the scene?'

'McGuire's in charge of the case, yes, if that's what you mean. He's SIO.'

'DFL,' Dolly interrupted. 'And a PIA: pain in the...'

'Please,' sighed Pearl. 'Let's try and keep this civilised.'

'And in what way is murder civilised?' Dolly eyed her daughter then picked up her bag. She was just about to head out when she hesitated. 'Pearl, promise me you're not going to get involved in all this, are you?'

Pearl said nothing and Dolly took her silence as the response she most feared. 'Well, if you *must* snoop, can't you at least stick to lost dogs, cheating partners and ... missing bay trees? Murder's something else entirely.'

'Don't you think I know that?'

'No, I don't, quite frankly,' argued Dolly. 'Maybe it's my fault. I let you watch too many television shows as a child – but you're not Cagney. Or Lacey. And that Flat Foot friend of yours is certainly not Columbo.'

'I'm sure he'll be pleased to hear that,' said Pearl. 'He's certainly better dressed.' She eyed her mother.

'This is no joke,' warned Dolly. 'There's a psychopath out there. *Don't* get in his way.' She marched to the door.

'What makes you think it's a man?' Pearl called after her.

Dolly turned to her daughter. 'Leave it to the Flat Foot,' she said determinedly. And with that she was gone.

Later that afternoon, Pearl was in her office in the garden. She hadn't set foot in there since before Faye's murder, but now as she sat down at her desk, she eyed the plastic holder containing the business cards that Charlie had designed for her when she had first started up the agency last summer. Full of hope and expectations for her new business, she had also invested in a few specialist computer programs. As she had mentioned over lunch at Arden House, technology could play a key role in the business of a private detective, and the use of new apps and online search tools could provide important checks on criminal histories, details of divorce and driving records.

Software technology companies were building programs to run on smartphones and tablets, and it wasn't too long ago that Pearl had been approached by a sales rep, on a cold call, who had tried to impress upon her the need to keep up with the latest trends and the importance of learning how to 'integrate technology' into her operations. He had spent more than an hour trying to sell Pearl some genealogy software with which she could research family histories, along with some Face Reading technology by which he claimed a personality evaluation could be created simply from facial characteristics. He had done his best with a hard sell, but he had left empty-handed apart from the impression he had gained that Pearl's methods were somewhat prehistoric.

Nevertheless, the important thing for any detective was simply to get results and while Pearl was hampered by not having access to police forensic results, she still recognised that working as a private detective had its advantages. Being a member of the police could be a hindrance to investigations since most officers stated their presence with flashing lights, badges and sirens – but a private detective could work in a much more subtle and stealthy way. That was one reason why many retired police officers found it so difficult to make a switch to private investigation and ended up working in security.

Thinking back to when she had started up the agency, Pearl remembered assuming that perhaps six months would be all it would take for Nolan's Detective Agency to become established locally with some challenging jobs coming in to test her skills. She had longed for a missing person's case, something that might stretch her talents or even take her on a trail beyond Whitstable, but Dolly was partly right: it was true that Pearl seemed to be piggybacking McGuire's cases – and although she had succeeded in solving them so far, this wasn't how she had expected things to be. The same could be said of her relationship with McGuire. After a long absence, he had arrived back on the scene, appearing decidedly frosty, though he had, at least, invited her out for dinner the next evening. She tried not to form any expectations of the date, aware that, yet again, he might be interested only in gleaning more information for his case.

Leaning forward, Pearl switched on her computer – idly putting in a search for Faye Marlow. A number of links became instantly available, including one for the Best-Dressed Woman Over Fifty award. Selecting the article, Pearl began to read it and then studied the photo of Faye looking stylish and vital at the awards ceremony, dressed in a chic black tailored dress that exposed her shoulders. Pearl was sure that both Barbara and Rosine had been kept busy regarding this occasion, not least with having to answer the obvious question of what to wear for a best-dressed awards ceremony. It now occurred to Pearl that there would have been no shortage of fashion designers keen to offer outfits for Faye to borrow, because just as planets orbit a solar system, so lesser beings orbit Hollywood stars, hoping to collect some sparkle for themselves.

Dolly was right that Nathan had been seeking an interview with Faye Marlow, and for Purdy, the attraction had surely been that of a tame fan drawn to a star, like a butterfly to an orchid. But Purdy had confirmed that it was *she* who had ultimately persuaded Faye to make the trip – and the girl had clearly charmed the actress, judging from Faye's warm reaction to meeting her for the first time at Arden House. It was clear to Pearl that Faye was a man's woman and as such she might need to size up other women as potential rivals, but it was also true that she had seemed genuinely captivated by Purdy Hewett at the meeting – a fact that was leading Pearl to suspect that, away from her clinging parents, the girl might not be as gauche or immature as she appeared.

Among the images on Pearl's computer screen she now focused on a shot of Faye with her husband, the film producer, Alain Severin, taken at a Cannes Film Festival almost a decade ago. They made for a glamorous couple, Faye wearing the diamond ring he had bought for her, but Pearl's attention was suddenly distracted by a small spider that had just dropped on to the desk in front of her. It was still attached by a thread to a web spun in the corner of her window, in which the relics of several winged creatures were still bound. The office needed a good spring-clean to rid it of the garden insects that would surely take it over, given half a chance. Pearl picked up her phone, intent on calling the agency that supplied her restaurant cleaner, when she suddenly noticed the red flashing light of her answerphone. She pressed Play and a voice filled the silent room.

'Pearl, it's Jerry Wheeler here. I wonder if you would kindly give me a call when you get this message? I'd like to talk to you, if that possible – in the privacy of my office.' The usual beep now sounded and the light on the machine was extinguished as Pearl told herself that she really should check her calls more frequently.

Chapter Ten

The offices of JW Holdings were situated on a large commercial estate on the outskirts of town. The company owned the land and leased the units to at least another twenty businesses. Pearl was aware that Jerry Wheeler had made most of his money from lucrative property deals in the 1980s but he now had a portfolio that extended to a considerable number of commercial and storage premises. JW Holdings was a force to be reckoned with and its offices sought to reflect this.

Having left her Fiat in the large company car park, Pearl waited in a reception that felt strangely like a cross between a gentleman's club and a showroom for Chesterfield sofas. The walls were hung with some large antique maps of Kent and watercolours that featured rustic scenes of cottages and barns. A model schooner sat beached on a mahogany plinth by the window, its sails drooping. It wasn't long before a panelled door opened and a young blonde appeared, offering a professional smile for Pearl as she announced, 'Mr Wheeler will see you now, Ms Nolan.'

Jerry Wheeler's secretary was in her mid-twenties, dressed in a figure-hugging blue sweater and a black skirt that showed off her slender tanned legs. Her efficient manner was tempered by her pretty features and a childlike voice. 'This way.' Wearing flesh-coloured high heels, she minced the way towards another panelled door on which she rapped gently as gold bracelets jangled at her wrist.

A familiar voice called out: 'Come in,' and the girl opened the door, allowing Pearl to enter before asking, 'Can I get you some tea or coffee?'

'Thank you,' Pearl replied. 'But I'm fine.'

The young woman offered another smile, this time for her boss – who rewarded it with a nod. 'Thank you, Mandy.'

As Mandy turned on her heels and left the room, Jerry stared after her for a moment before giving his full attention to Pearl.

'Thank you for coming,' he said, shaking her

133

hand and indicating a seat facing his desk while he took the one behind it – a leather button-back Captain's chair that matched the dark red of the sofas in the reception. Before going on, Jerry passed his palms across the side of his head in an effort to smooth down a few stray hairs at his temples, then said, 'I suppose you can guess why I've asked to see you, Pearl.' Straightening the knot of his striped tie, he gave her the distinct impression that although he had instigated this meeting, he was nervous about it.

'I presumed it's about Faye Marlow.'

'Yes,' he admitted, his gaze moving automatically towards a bookcase near the window.

Pearl saw that it contained a large number of reference books but, on one shelf, two framed photographs showed a young man with dark hair beside Faye Marlow. If Pearl had not been told about the photos she would never have recognised Jerry Wheeler, although Faye was unmistakable. One image featured the couple at the bar of a night club, posing with champagne glasses in hand, while the other showed them in a convertible car on Tankerton Slopes with Faye wearing Rayban sunglasses. In both, Jerry looked on as proudly at Faye as he had done in his car at the Horsebridge, his arm circling her shoulder in a protective embrace. Studying the photos and the adoring look on Jerry's face, it became abundantly clear to Pearl that Faye's desertion of her fiancé must have dealt him a devastating blow.

Jerry got to his feet and moved to the window where sunlight was just beginning to peep through, but he angled the vertical blinds so that it was deflected. Stepping back to his desk, he sat down again.

'I've asked you here, Pearl, because...' He paused for a moment, searching for the right words. 'Not only is Dolly a very good friend to my mother but I know you run a detective agency. I'm therefore quite sure I can trust your confidentiality.'

'Concerning?' asked Pearl.

'I'd like some advice if you are able to offer it – from a professional point of view. You see, it's rather unfortunate that my mother reacted so badly at the reception the other evening.' He began tapping his pen nervously on the desk before him. 'She's been interviewed by the police.'

'I know,' Pearl nodded.

Jerry stopped tapping his pen, and went on hurriedly, 'Well, it's occurred to me that with your agency work, you may have dealings with the police yourself – and while I'm aware they have a very important job to do, I'm sure you'll agree that it would be ... wholly wrong for them to believe that my mother had anything to do with Faye's death.'

He waited for a response from Pearl and when it failed to come, he appealed: 'What I'm asking is, do you think the police could possibly consider her to be a suspect?'

'Is that the impression they've given you?' asked Pearl, side-stepping the question.

Jerry shook his head in frustration. 'I honestly don't know what to think. I can hardly believe any of this has happened at all. I mean, there she was the other evening – so beautiful, so alive – and now she's...' He broke off and cleared his throat, looking once more towards the photographs in the bookcase before coming to his senses. 'My mother never liked Faye but then she didn't know her as I did. I'm sure you've heard that Faye and I were once engaged and ... though things didn't work out as planned, I never blamed her. I would have found it impossible to do that.'

'Why?'

At this, Jerry looked up in some surprise. 'Well, because she was Faye, of course. It was easy to forgive her – for anything – but we're talking about something that happened nearly thirty years ago. That's when Faye and I first started seeing one another. There's been a lot of water under the bridge since then and I'm very happily married to Annabel, as you know, but ... perhaps I was a bit foolish the other evening.'

'At the reception?' asked Pearl.

Jerry nodded slowly. 'I had drunk a little too much and I got carried away.' He looked at Pearl, defensively now. 'God knows, I work hard enough, I should be able to enjoy a few drinks from time to time but–' He put a brake on himself. 'It was unfortunate my mother should have chosen to come along. She's been brooding ever since Faye's arrival. But that doesn't mean to say she murdered her,' he added pointedly. 'If she had been able to tip a trifle over Faye all those years ago, she would have done so and no doubt would have felt better for it – but as it was, she had to wait a long time.' As he looked sadly at her, Pearl recalled the old saying: 'Revenge is a dish best served cold' – like her beautiful, but entirely wasted, raspberry summer pudding trifle.

136

'That's all, Pearl. My mother isn't capable of murder. You and Dolly must know that.'

Pearl nodded to acknowledge this. 'Do you have any idea at all who might have wanted her dead?' she asked.

Jerry looked suitably horrified at the thought. 'No, of course not. She may have made enemies for herself in Hollywood – rivals perhaps? But not here, no, not in Whitstable. That screening showed just how much people thought of her, surely? They were in awe of Faye. She was so successful.'

'As are you,' Pearl reminded him.

At this, Jerry heaved a long sigh. 'I have a successful business,' he conceded, 'and that means I've made a lot of money, but property can be remarkably dull, you know. Faye actually managed to become a success at something she really enjoyed. And she did it well. She came from nothing and she became something. I admired her. I was fascinated by her. Perhaps I was even a little envious of her?' He then stated fiercely: 'But I had no reason to kill her – *and neither did my mother.*'

His phone rang suddenly, seeming almost to signal the end of the conversation. Jerry picked up the receiver in an automatic reflex, appearing to relax only when he realised who the caller was. 'Annabel,' he said. 'No, I'm not planning on staying late.' He listened to his wife on the other end of the line. 'That'll be fine,' he went on. 'I'll be home well before then.' His eyes met Pearl's as he replaced the receiver, and he apologised. 'Sorry about that.'

'It's fine.' Pearl then asked a question. 'Does your mother have an alibi for the other evening?'

137

Before Jerry could respond, she added quickly, 'I ask because if she did have one, it would obviously help to exclude her as a suspect.'

Jerry gave this some careful thought, before he finally declared, 'No. Annabel took her home but she left her about an hour later. My mother lives alone, as you know.' He looked contrite. 'I should have gone too but ... well, to be honest, I was angry with her and I felt I owed it to Faye to stay. We got her home, as you know.'

'We?'

'Her staff, Purdy Hewett and your friend, Nathan.'

'Back to Arden House.'

Jerry nodded. 'Yes. That chap – Luc – was going to fetch the car but someone suggested it would be quicker, and less conspicuous, if we simply crossed the gardens. There were a few panels of fencing down near the shrubbery close to the house so we arrived back quite quickly.'

'Do you remember who it was who suggested that?'

'I think it was Luc. I ... can't quite remember.'

'But you all returned to the house.'

'Yes, that's right. I stayed until I was sure Faye was OK.' His voice broke as he continued, 'I didn't think the evening could possibly get any worse.'

'And you went home?' asked Pearl.

Jerry failed to reply until he appeared to reach a decision. 'I think it's time for me to take some legal advice,' he said. 'On my mother's behalf, of course.'

Having decided on this, he now got to his feet and said, 'I appreciate you coming to see me,

Pearl. It's helped to clarify my thinking. Please send me an invoice for your time and I'll make sure it's settled as quickly as possible.'

Pearl shook his outstretched hand and briefly considered accepting his offer of payment – which would clearly be a drop in the ocean to JW Holdings – but instead she said, 'That won't be necessary.' She was sure she hadn't told Jerry Wheeler anything he hadn't already known, although the meeting had apparently helped him to see a way forward.

He moved to the door with Pearl and opened it for her, before calling, 'Mandy?'

At the mention of her name, Jerry's attractive secretary got up from her desk and led the way back into the sofa-filled reception and on to the lift, which she summoned with the push of a button. Pearl stepped inside and watched the doors close slowly on Mandy's polite smile, and this snapshot of Jerry Wheeler's work environment, before she was ferried to the ground floor.

Back in the large car park, Pearl got into her Fiat and was just about to put it into reverse when she stopped. She had the feeling that she was being watched – a feeling that had come to her many times before and never let her down. She could be sitting in the car, in heavy traffic, when something made her glance across at another motorist, or a passenger on the upper deck of a parked bus, only to find them staring directly at her. Pearl figured it was nothing smart or psychic, merely a vestige of some primitive natural instinct that had once been useful to escape predators.

She heard the engine of a car before she saw it.

It reversed smartly out of a nearby parking space and drove off at speed – but not before Pearl had managed to get a good look at the driver and recognised her as Annabel Wheeler.

Chapter Eleven

'Sweetie, would you please come with me to see Barbara?' The tone of Nathan's voice on Pearl's mobile next morning was polite but firm. 'Please?'

'Why do you need *me* there?' asked Pearl.

'Why do you think? Her employer's just been murdered, she's traumatised, and it's an awkward situation. I'll probably put my foot in it and you're so much better with people than I am.'

'Flattery will get you everywhere.'

'It's true,' he said. 'Besides, she likes you.'

'How do you know?'

'I can tell.'

Pearl needed no further encouragement. She had actually warmed to Barbara too, and had been wondering how Faye's staff would be reacting to the violent death of their employer.

Judging by the warm reception Pearl and Nathan received on their arrival at Arden House, their company was welcome. Barbara led them into the drawing room, where there was no sign of sun through the rain-splashed windows. Rosine brought in a tray of tea. No longer in a state of high anxiety, the girl now seemed subdued, and even a little timid, as she deposited the

140

tray on the table, her eyes puffy and red-rimmed. She had just picked up the teapot when Barbara stopped her, saying, 'It's OK, Rosine. I will do it.' The girl gave a nod and left the room. Barbara waited until she had closed the door before confiding, 'I feel so uncomfortable being waited on. Rosine worked for Faye, not me.' She poured the tea and Pearl noted how her hand trembled slightly. 'It's going to be difficult thinking of Faye in the past tense,' Barbara went on. 'She had been part of my life for so long.'

'You mentioned that your father was her agent?' said Pearl.

Barbara nodded but it was Nathan who explained. 'Bernard looked after Faye throughout her career.'

'Until his death,' Pearl remembered.

'That's right,' Barbara said. 'I was just a young woman at the time. I had no other family. My mother had died young, and...' she trailed off.

Nathan continued in a soft and sympathetic tone, 'Faye gave Barbara the job as her Personal Assistant.'

'From pity, I'm sure,' said Barbara. 'It's no secret that my father made some extremely unwise investments. He left very little money when he died and so a job was very welcome. When Faye married Alain, I went to live with them in San Remo in Italy before they finally settled not far from Nice. I'm not sure what I would have done without Faye.'

She sipped her tea and Nathan commented, 'Nor Faye without you.'

'Well,' Barbara said, reflecting on this, 'I've

141

done my best.' She looked at them both, then went on, 'But after this ... we're all in limbo, I'm afraid. Nathan, I'm aware I need to settle with you for expenses so far, but it's difficult with the police investigation going on right now, as I'm sure you'll appreciate. They're looking at Faye's finances, her assets – and presumably, her will. We can't return to France yet, so if your friend, the house owner, Mr Chandler, returns, we'll need to find accommodation, and...' She broke off, visibly troubled by the thought of so many outstanding issues.

'Don't worry.' Nathan placed his hand supportively on hers. 'The priority right now is finding out who murdered Faye.'

'Yes,' Pearl agreed. 'The police will have interviewed you – and Rosine and Luc too?'

'Of course.' Barbara sighed heavily. 'But we could tell them no more than we told you the other morning when we discovered that Faye was missing. We've all given full statements.'

'Presumably with an interpreter for Rosine?' Pearl asked.

Barbara nodded. 'As you know, her English is limited.'

'And ... nothing more has occurred to you since then?' Pearl probed. 'To any of you?'

'About what?' Barbara looked confused.

'About how, or why, anyone would have wanted to murder Faye.'

Barbara remained motionless for a moment then shook her head, saying, 'I'm not claiming that she was perfect. Faye was my employer, not a friend, and no doubt she made enemies over the years. She had once been a star – but she was still apt to behave like one.'

'What do you mean?' asked Pearl.

'I mean that Faye was used to getting her own way. That's what happens in showbusiness. The kind of "riders" that are provided in celebrity contracts come to be expected in life: the preferred hotel, the flowers in the dressing room, the favourite brand of champagne.' She looked pointedly at Pearl. 'Hors d'oeuvre at receptions?'

Nathan broke in. 'Yes, but you could hardly call Faye demanding, compared to others. She was absolutely charming.'

Barbara mused on this. 'And that's probably the perfect word to describe Faye,' she decided. 'Charming.'

A moment's silence fell before Nathan's mobile sounded. 'Excuse me,' he apologised. 'I have to take this.'

Getting up, he moved to the far end of the room to answer his phone while Pearl was left to observe Barbara. For all the sorrow of this occasion, she seemed strangely calm, but looked pale and somewhat drawn as she put a hand to her temple.

'Are you all right?' Pearl asked, concerned. Barbara looked up, a little confused, and Pearl explained: 'I just wondered if your migraines are back with all the stress of what's happened?'

Barbara nodded slowly. 'Yes,' she said tiredly. 'If we stay much longer I may have to find a doctor for another prescription.'

'Then I'll leave you with the number of the local Health Centre.' Pearl reached into her bag for her purse in which she knew she had an old

143

appointment card, and handed it over.

'Thank you,' Barbara said, taking it from her.

Nathan returned, closing the cover of his phone as he told them, 'That was Tom, the owner of the house. I put in a call to him earlier and the police have also been in touch.' He looked at Barbara. 'He's just confirmed that it's fine for you to stay here for at least several weeks, though hopefully that won't be necessary.'

Barbara looked instantly relieved. Nathan added, 'If there's anything we can do, you will call us, won't you?

'Thank you. You've both been very kind.' Barbara got to her feet now to indicate that the meeting was over and Pearl and Nathan followed her across the thickly carpeted floor to the door. She opened it – only to find Rosine directly on the other side.

Looking guilty, the girl explained quickly, *'Excusez moi. J'allais juste vous demander, aimeriez vous autre chose?'*

'No, Rosine,' Barbara said, trying to mask her irritation. 'We don't need anything more.'

Rosine's dark eyes darted shiftily towards Pearl and Nathan before she hurried quickly upstairs. Barbara watched her go then turned again to Pearl and Nathan.

'Thank you again, for everything.'

Once outside in Nathan's Volkswagen, Pearl secured her seatbelt and then became distracted by the sight of a rather magnificent dog. As it trotted past the car, Pearl was reminded of the adage that dog-owners are said to come to re-

144

semble their pets – because the grey hair and Afghan jerkin of the man who was walking the dog certainly complemented the animal's coat. 'Is that a Husky?' she asked.

'Sorry, sweetie?' asked Nathan. Pearl indicated the man and his dog, who were now heading up the path to a house called Ravenswood, just two properties along from Arden House. 'No, that's a Malamute,' he informed her. 'Alaskan, but much larger. Look at that gorgeous double coat.'

'Yes,' Pearl agreed, watching the man open the front door with his key before disappearing inside with the dog. As the door closed after them Pearl's attention returned to the meeting with Barbara. 'Didn't I hear mention at some point that Luc and Rosine are on some temporary contract?'

'That's right,' Nathan said, as he repositioned his rearview mirror. 'I believe they're working a probationary period of some sort, at the end of which they're due a salary rise and a permanent contract.'

Pearl considered this thoughtfully. 'Except they won't be getting it now.' She turned to Nathan. 'She was standing very close to the door, wasn't she?'

'Rosine?' Picking up on Pearl's thoughtful tone, he asked, 'You ... think she'd been listening in?'

'How much would she have understood?' asked Pearl pointedly. 'As Barbara said, her English is limited – remember?' She gave him a knowing look and he started up the car.

Pearl always felt that her mother's home in Harbour Street reflected Dolly's own eccentricities.

145

The walls were covered with numerous paintings: her own work and that of other local artists, which she bought, whenever she could afford it, as a gesture of support for what she considered to be her 'creative community'. Dolly was attracted to bold colour like a bee to pollen, and today a large vase in her living room was filled with a collection of huge roses of the most striking flamingo pink, though their sweet smell was blocked by the odour of Oil of Cloves. It was one of the various remedies to which Dolly had resorted in an effort to alleviate her toothache. On the table in front of her there was also a saucer of raw garlic, some guava leaves and cotton balls soaked in bourbon. Pearl considered all this with some disapproval as Dolly lay back on her sofa, clutching her tomcat, Mojo, as she groaned in agony.

'So when was the last time you actually saw a dentist?' she asked.

Dolly held off moaning for a moment as she prodded her upper jaw with her fingertips.

'Two years,' she admitted. 'Maybe three.' She winced again with pain.

'And you wonder why you have toothache?'

'I've been busy.'

Pearl eyed her mother, feeling both sympathy and frustration for Dolly's plight. 'Scared, you mean. You may not like going to the dentist – and you wouldn't be alone in that – but if you don't want to lose your teeth...'

Dolly raised her hand. 'Don't even talk like that!' she commanded.

'Well, you can't hold on to them by sheer will-power.'

146

Dolly heaved a long sigh. 'You have no idea how hard it is to hold on to *anything* at my age: my figure, my eyesight...'

'Your marbles?' Pearl gave her a knowing look. 'I'm only saying this for your own good. You'll have to see a dentist sooner or later, so why not make it sooner and save yourself more treatment – and money?'

Her hand now clamped to her jaw, Dolly considered this ruefully. 'And ... what if they say it has to come out?'

'There are lots of other options to going toothless these days,' Pearl reminded her. 'Come on, you look fabulous for your age,' she said, adding, 'You could even think about implants.'

'And look like Charmaine?' Dolly scoffed. 'That bust of hers rounds corners before she does.'

Pearl admonished, 'I *meant* for your teeth,' hoping to get Dolly off the subject of Whitstable's cosmetic surgery queen, Charmaine Hillcroft, the owner of beauty salon Whitstabelle. Dolly reacted to a sharp pang and Pearl tried again. 'Look, you have a good track record for keeping yourself well with all this homoeopathy and the herbal remedies, but you simply can't go on like this. At least have a check-up. Please?'

Dolly took her hand away from her jaw and saw that even Mojo, otherwise known as her 'familiar', was looking beadily at her. She finally capitulated. 'Very well, if I must. Make the appointment for me,' she ordered, much like a defeated officer finally sounding a retreat.

That afternoon, Pearl had just paid her window

cleaner for his work and was waving him off through her garden gate when she saw someone approaching on the prom. It was Purdy. The girl appeared to have come from Starboard Light Alley. On seeing Pearl she looked taken aback for a moment, her expression changing to one of embarrassment. It was left to Pearl to break the ice.

'Good to see you, Purdy,' she said kindly. 'Care to come in for a coffee?'

'I'm afraid I can't,' the girl said. 'I've just been to see Nathan and now I'm heading to Tankerton.'

'Along the beach?'

Purdy gave a quick nod.

'Then wait for me to get a coat and I'll walk part of the way with you – if that's OK?'

Purdy brightened. 'Of course.'

Pearl quickly disappeared into the cottage, emerging with a jacket before she joined Purdy on the prom. The wind had dropped and the tide was coming in, washing up on to the beach in a steady rhythm. It seemed to calm Purdy as she walked with Pearl and explained. 'I'm sorry about the other day. What happened with Daddy, I mean...' She paused before clarifying. 'He really shouldn't have asked you to leave like that, but he was concerned about me. They're my parents, after all, and they love me.'

Some dog-walkers passed by on the prom and Pearl allowed a space before she commented, 'It can be difficult sometimes being an only child, can't it?'

Purdy looked at Pearl as she realised. 'Yes. You know that too.' She smiled, clearly feeling a little more comfortable. 'People always say that only children are spoiled but it doesn't seem that way to me. I mean, we have to shoulder all our parents' expectations, don't we? I would have liked brothers and sisters and I know Mummy would have loved a larger family, but ... well, it just wasn't to be.' She looked directly at Pearl. 'Daddy was right, you know. I was upset – but how could I not be? Up until the reception, everything had been going so well. Faye had actually told me how pleased she was about everything, how grateful she was to have met me, and ... and how she knew she could trust me to arrange everything so that May Day would all work out perfectly. And then, just as we'd had the most wonderful screening, Mrs Wheeler had to gate-crash the reception and spoil it all. Those terrible things she said to Faye – and in front of everyone like that! How could she possibly think that anything was going on between Faye and Jerry Wheeler?' Purdy looked incredulous.

'You don't think there was?'

'Of course not,' Purdy said, emphatically.

'They *were* seen out in public together, you know.'

Purdy frowned at this. 'Well, that proves it, because surely if something *was* going on, they wouldn't have gone out openly together.'

Pearl had to concede it was a good point. 'And you don't think Faye was flirting with him at the reception?'

'No,' Purdy protested. 'It's just ... well, Faye had a certain way of giving you her undivided attention, didn't she? Of making you feel special?'

'Yes,' agreed Pearl. 'And she certainly managed

to make Jerry feel special.' She eyed Purdy, who didn't seem to spot the irony in her remark. 'Had you been in touch with Faye for some time?'

The girl nodded. 'Weeks,' she said. 'Nathan was the first person to write and Barbara replied, but then Faye began corresponding directly with me and we decided on all the details to do with the screening. She was really looking forward to coming back for the festival.'

'She told you that?'

'Oh yes. Whitstable was her home town.'

'Though she left it all those years ago,' mused Pearl.

'Does that matter?' asked Purdy. 'You can never really leave your roots behind, can you? We're all a product of where and how we've been brought up, aren't we?'

Looking at Purdy's innocent expression, Pearl recognised that the girl had said something that was quite prescient. From time to time through-out the years, Pearl herself had contemplated leaving Whitstable – but for what and for whom? Instead, she had stayed put and had come to realise that the town was her home, not simply in a geographical sense but as a community to which she belonged. Equally, she now considered that perhaps Purdy's father, Oliver Hewett, might have been offered a much wider concept of home through his work and because of his in-volvement with it. Archaeology had taken him all over the world and would surely continue to do so, but nevertheless, it was clear he loved his wife and daughter – and if Purdy had ever desired a job that took her away from home, her protective

150

parents would surely miss her.

Having walked as far as the Horsebridge together, Purdy suddenly said: 'It really doesn't seem possible this could have happened, especially here, of all places. Does no one at all have any idea who may have done this?'

Pearl shook her head. 'Not yet,' she said. 'But you can be sure of one thing, Purdy. Whoever did this murder will not get away with it.'

Purdy seemed stung by the baldness of Pearl's remark, but she recovered sufficiently to give a small smile, saying merely, 'I'm sure you're right.'

Dolly's dental surgery was situated at the top of Borstal Hill in a swanky new health centre that also offered treatment for minor injuries. She had managed to get an appointment – a cancellation – and had made the trip on the bus. Feeling sorry for her mother, Pearl had decided to surprise her with an unexpected lift home. Parking her car, she imagined that she too might feel as nervous as Dolly had felt on her arrival, and she hoped the dentist would not file assault charges should Dolly have lashed out in self-defence. In the packed waiting room sat patients of all ages, united by painful dental problems, judging by the expressions, which resembled Dolly's own in the past few days. Having informed the receptionist that she was here to meet a relative, Pearl was offered a seat but, before she could take it, a door opened and a dental nurse appeared, followed quickly by Dolly. Unexpectedly garrulous in the circumstances, Pearl's mother was chatting away merrily while dabbing a tissue against her mouth.

151

'Thank you!' she exclaimed finally. The nurse smiled goodbye and after filing some notes in a drawer, disappeared back into the treatment room. Dolly then turned – and saw Pearl. 'What're you doing here?' she spluttered, her mouth lop-sided due to local anaesthetic.

'I came to see how you were, of course,' Pearl led the way outside.

'I'm fine,' said Dolly rather extravagantly.

'And ... the dentist?'

'The man's a genius! I can honestly say I didn't feel a thing – thanks to Dr Fang.'

'Dr...?'

'Yes, I know. I'm sure he's sick of everyone reacting like that to his name. I did too, but apparently it's a very common name in China and in any case it's pronounced *Fong* in Cantonese.' She gave a sniff. 'We had a fascinating conversation about it all – well, *he* did. I just listened, not being in a position to respond.' She thought for a moment. 'Nominative determinism.'

'Eh?' asked Pearl, confused.

'That's what they call the phenomenon whereby people's names seem to influence their choice of jobs. There's been lots of research done and Dr Fang knows of at least two other dentists to reference this – they're called Paine and Spittle. Do you know there was even a urological report once written by a Mr Weedon?' She grinned unevenly.

Pearl gave her mother a sidelong glance. 'I don't believe it.'

'It's true,' said Dolly. 'Dr Fang says you can check for yourself on a computer. Well, if you think about it, there are plenty more examples, aren't there?'

'Are there?'

'Well yes,' continued Dolly confidently. 'There's the footballer, Alan Ball. The gardener, Bob Flowerdew, and how about the poet – Wordsworth?'

Pearl noted that Dolly had clearly forgotten all about her tooth. 'So ... Dr Fang has a fan?' she asked, amused.

'He does indeed,' Dolly replied. 'Not only can he save my tooth, he said I have the gums of a woman half my age.' She preened for a moment. 'So I've promised him a good table at the restaurant and a bottle of wine on the house.'

'Oh really?' asked Pearl, reacting to Dolly's largesse, though it was a small price to pay to have Dolly on form again and out of pain.

After Pearl had deposited her mother at the local chemists where she was keen, on Dr Fang's recommendation, to buy a good supply of mouthwash and floss, Dolly said she wanted to walk the short distance home afterwards so Pearl drove alone to Island Wall where she noted that Nathan's car was in place outside his cottage. Killing her engine, Pearl had just decided she would call on him to check if he had heard from either Barbara or Purdy about any progress on the murder, when her mobile rang. The caller's voice was clipped and to the point.

'Pearl? It's Annabel Wheeler. I'd like to make an appointment to see you – in your capacity as detective. As soon as possible – and in the strictest of confidence.'

Pearl rushed home to manage a cursory tidy of

her office, clearing a few more cobwebs away, before Annabel's arrival. It wasn't long before she placed a cup of instant coffee before Jerry Wheeler's wife and asked: 'So what can I do for you?'

Annabel was sitting across the desk from Pearl wearing a pale cream jacket and a string of natural pearls. They took on a glow from a shaft of afternoon sunlight, matching what appeared to be a newly acquired fake suntan. She said nothing for a moment but simply stirred her coffee, all the while keeping her gaze fixed on Pearl, before saying, 'You saw me leaving Jerry's office yesterday, didn't you? No doubt you wondered why I drove off as I did.'

Pearl shrugged. 'I'm sure you had your reasons.'

'Yes,' said Annabel, and she looked tense. 'Your website states you offer an efficient and discreet service, Pearl. So I trust what I have to say to you now will remain within these walls?'

'Of course.'

'Good,' said Annabel briskly. 'Because I believe my husband is having an affair.'

Pearl said nothing. Annabel took a sip of coffee. 'I was in the car park because I've actually been keeping an eye on Jerry. I take it you've met his secretary, Mandy Prosser?'

Pearl gave a nod and Annabel continued. 'I think my husband is sleeping with her. Jerry is never really satisfied – with anything, not even the size of his bank balance – and certainly no one woman will ever be enough for him. Perhaps that was the fault of Faye Marlow. Dumping him as she did all these years ago may have given him a desperate need to prove himself, but I have no interest in exploring his psychological motivations because this has gone on for long enough. Frankly, if he hasn't got over that by now, I know he never will. I've been keeping an eye on Jerry and Mandy for some time, trying to gain evidence of his adultery. When I saw you leaving the office yesterday, it occurred to me that he might be keeping an eye on me, while I've been keeping my eye on him. If so, I'm here to tell you that whatever he's paying you, I'm willing to pay double.'

'That won't be necessary,' Pearl said finally. Annabel looked surprised but Pearl went on, choosing her words carefully to preserve Jerry's confidentiality, 'I was at your husband's office on another matter. Jean has been questioned by the police...'

'And he thinks she may be arrested for Faye's murder,' Annabel said impatiently. 'I've told him it's all nonsense. Jean couldn't possibly have had anything to do with it. I told the police myself how I took her home and made sure she was quite calm before I left. She had managed to get a good bit of trifle over herself, so I ran a bath for her and when I left she was wearing a nightdress and was ready for bed.'

'She was no longer angry?' asked Pearl.

'No.' Annabel shrugged. 'If anything, she looked happier than I've seen her for some time. In fact, I think the incident with your dessert was very cathartic. She'd clearly been furious with Faye for years, so humiliating her as she did at the Castle was a major release. Why on earth would she then decide to go back and murder the

155

woman? I mean, there must be plenty of others who had good reason to want to see the back of Ms Marlow.' She paused as she noted Pearl's look. 'Me?' asked Annabel, incredulous.

Pearl explained. 'Jean thought you'd be very upset when you discovered that Jerry had been out with Faye the other day.'

'Posing in the Duesenberg, you mean? Look, whatever the stupid old fool is up to, I really don't care. Whether it was Faye or Mandy Prosser, I've had enough. Twenty years is a long time. A prison sentence. That's how it's beginning to feel – though I've no chance of parole.'

Pearl took this in. 'And how can you be so sure he's having an affair?'

Annabel gave a snort. 'How else? The usual signs, of course. Forgive me if I don't go into too many details about our married life, but needless to say, we are not living the closest of existences. When Jerry put on weight he began snoring, which was a good enough reason for me to move out of our shared bedroom, but now he seems to have slimmed down I'm not tempted to move back in. There was a time he disliked me going away to see friends or family or even to Hove last week, but now he positively encourages me. I've done some checks on social media and I see Ms Prosser is on Facebook, but I can't gain access without putting in a Friend request, though I doubt if she's been stupid enough to post photos or anything else too incriminating on there, though you never know. She may be a dab hand at shorthand and typing but I don't think she'd qualify for *Mastermind*. So...' Annabel Wheeler

156

raked a hand through her newly coloured hair. 'If you really aren't acting for Jerry, can you please act for me?'

Chapter Twelve

McGuire had arrived early and was sitting at a table by the window in Jo-Jo's restaurant. A friendly young waitress had initially seated him close to the open-plan cooking area but after only a few moments he had decided he didn't want to observe the busy chef and her assistants all evening. He was feeling stressed and needed to relax so opted instead for a sea view.

The restaurant had moved away from the general style of the more traditional grand eateries in Whitstable and had a certain fun feel to the place, a bit like The Whitstable Pearl, though it was several times larger. McGuire had gone through the menu twice already. There were plenty of mouth-watering meat dishes on offer such as Spanish cured pork loin and Italian *fiocco di spalla* – he was grateful for the translation 'air-cured lean pork rolled in ground pepper'. There was also mutton, lamb and a special venison dish, but thankfully for McGuire – no oysters. He hadn't eaten since lunchtime, and then only a sandwich on the hoof, so the vivid descriptions of the dishes on offer were making him feel ravenous. When the waitress returned and asked if she could get him a drink, although he would have liked an oyster stout he thought he had better choose wine instead – then decided he should wait until Pearl arrived in case he made the wrong choice. So now he had a menu and the wine list to peruse.

He realised that he hadn't actually asked a woman out for a meal for some time. He'd had lunch with a good-looking WPC in London during a recent court case, but she'd wanted to talk shop, and he'd invited her out purely to forget about it, so he had glazed over after the first course. Tonight, he hadn't even been too sure of what to wear. He thought it was important to be seen to have made an effort so he had put on a new shirt, but now the collar felt stiff and the fabric tended to rise up above the waistline of his trousers whenever he raised his arms. He glanced around, and when he saw that other guys in the restaurant wore casual linen shirts, he wished he could take off his own shirt and simply wear the white T-shirt he had on beneath it – but that would mean a quick costume change in the toilets or risk looking as though he was about to strip off in the restaurant. Instead, he ran a finger under his shirt collar in an effort to loosen it up then decided to at least take off his black jacket. Getting to his feet, he hung it on the back of his chair. When he turned to take his seat again, she was there.

Pearl was standing before him dressed in a light blue crêpe dress. At first, McGuire thought its pattern was made up of white dots before he noticed that they were, in fact, tiny swallows. The dress's sharp 'V' neckline exposed the silver locket she wore. Her dark hair was loose and fell around her shoulders, shiny and still slightly damp from the shower. Her only make-up was a slick of red lipstick but as she smiled, the effect on McGuire was as though he had been stunned. He was used to noticing small details, storing them up in his memory in case he should need to relate them for a court appearance or to reconstruct a Photo-fit likeness. It was an essential part of his job. But tonight, he took in every detail of Pearl's appearance simply for pleasure.

He smiled, said 'Hi,' and was about to lean over and kiss her cheek when the bubbly young waitress came back and did it for him. She welcomed Pearl warmly.

Before McGuire could follow suit Pearl told him, 'I promise I'll be right back.'

She had caught sight of the busy chef waving to her from the open-plan kitchen and hurried across to chat to her for a moment. McGuire might have felt awkward at being so swiftly abandoned but instead he was intrigued, because as Pearl returned to him, it became clear that she knew almost everyone in the restaurant – both members of staff *and* customers. The interesting thing for McGuire was that everyone seemed pleased to see her. Sitting back down at the table, she explained, 'I hope you don't mind but I just ordered some calamari to start. You simply have to try it.'

'Because it rivals yours?'

'I did say that once, didn't I?' she remembered. 'But "equals" is probably a better word because there's no rivalry between me and Mikki, the chef.'

The waitress brought across a bottle of chilled Pinot Grigio. 'Compliments of Mikki,' she beamed as she poured them both a glass.

'That's kind of her,' said Pearl, nodding across at the chef before she looked back at McGuire. 'Is wine all right or would you prefer beer? They have oyster stout.'

'Wine's fine,' he said, lifting his glass. 'You *can* have too much of a good thing.'

'Can you?' asked Pearl. He looked at her and touched her glass with his own. It was the nearest he'd got to her so far. 'So, how's your new flat?' she asked. 'I guess you've had time to settle in by now.'

'Yeah, I have. And it suits me.'

'In the city,' she noted.

McGuire recognised that Canterbury was indeed, technically a city, though it failed to resemble the only city he really knew – London. 'It's just a small apartment on Best Lane. Overlooking the river.'

'Nice,' she acknowledged, part of her hoping that he might suggest she should come over and visit some time. But the invitation failed to materialise and she glanced out of the window towards the sea. There were no signs of the usual ships or boats but the sails of the wind farm turned on the horizon.

'We got the autopsy results,' he said.

She looked back at him. 'That's quick. You'll have a more accurate time of death now, won't you. What about the murder weapon?'

'A fifteen-centimetre all-purpose chef's knife.'

Pearl reacted with surprise. 'It could have come from the Castle kitchen.'

'It did,' said McGuire. 'The inventory shows a professional knife-block – but one knife is missing from it.' He waited. 'I understand the kitchen was

160

open and accessible to anyone on the night of the reception?'

'That's right. I was in and out of it all evening, as were Luc and Rosine. Barbara came in to chat to me at one point, but I'm sure she didn't take any knife. Marty used the kitchen too...' She suddenly realised something.

'What is it?'

'The knife-block. It was in the marquee.' She looked at him. 'Marty had needed it to chop fruit for his smoothies.'

'Your friend, Mr Cornucopia?'

'He's a good man. He just has a problem with you.'

'As does your mother.'

'Yes,' Pearl agreed. 'So perhaps you need to work harder on your public liaising skills.'

Before he could respond, the waitress returned with a green-leaf salad and a bowl of calamari, glistening with fresh lemon juice and sprinkled with finely chopped Continental parsley.

'You must try this,' said Pearl to McGuire. 'Here.' She took a piece for herself, dipped it in some garlic mayonnaise and pushed the bowl towards him. He tried it and found it was as good as she had promised. Allowing himself to savour the food, and Pearl's company, he once more picked up his thread. 'So the murderer didn't need access to the kitchen because the knives were in the marquee.'

'That's right. And I don't remember them being taken back into the kitchen.'

Pearl took a last mouthful of calamari and caught him staring at her. 'What else would you

161

like?' she asked.

'Why don't you choose?'

'Don't tell me – anything but oysters?'

'You're a mind-reader.' The wine had begun to work its magic and he relaxed and allowed her to order a variety of dishes: the *fiocco di spalla,* lamb cannon, roasted cherry tomatoes with goat's cheese and red onions, flat bread, Verdale olives and various cheeses. She did so expertly, comfortable in her element, and the dishes were brought to the table as soon as they became ready, as though it were a professional tasting. McGuire forgot all about his stiff shirt as he focused on Pearl.

There was never an embarrassing gap in the conversation, which drifted from good food and wine to something Pearl clearly valued – good friends. 'Nathan is devastated about this,' she said. 'As is Purdy, of course, who was his partner in crime.' She smiled, admitting: 'Unfortunate turn of phrase. I know. If I'd used that about anyone else I might be tempted to say that it was my subconscious talking. But I know Nathan had no reason to kill Faye. He was a fan – as was Purdy. Besides, he was looking forward to an interview which he'll never get now.'

As she sipped her wine, McGuire asked, 'And Purdy?'

'To be honest, I find her a little intriguing,' Pearl admitted. 'I know her parents only from the restaurant. Oliver is a brilliant archaeologist and his wife, Maria, is a kind woman. She's the antithesis of Faye – she isn't glamorous but she's never prettier than when she's in the company of

162

her own family. She lights up. Literally.' She paused to put an olive to her lips.

'I could say the same for you.'

'Really?' asked Pearl. 'Well ... I've always thought there was something special about Maria, something almost self-sacrificing – supporting Oliver, bringing up Purdy. She only has her charity work now that her daughter's grown up, but...' She looked pensive.

'What is it?'

'I'm not sure Purdy really has grown up,' she said frankly. 'In many ways she appears very child-like, but she's also very capable and she certainly had the confidence to organise the screening as well as liaising with Faye and Barbara when they were still in France.'

McGuire said softly, 'We all need to find the confidence to go after what we want. Or we let opportunities slip by.'

'Yes,' Pearl agreed, wondering if his invitation to her for supper was part of that same thinking. Aloud, she said only: 'That's precisely what I thought when I started up the agency. I've waited twenty years to become a detective.'

'A private detective,' McGuire qualified. 'So ... do you actually enjoy catching cheating partners?'

'I enjoy solving crime,' she said. 'And I think I'm good at it. No, I *know* I am. And private detectives do have a role to play in solving crime – just like the police.'

He picked up his wine. 'You've already got a successful business with your restaurant, Pearl.'

'Well, life isn't all about business,' she said. 'It's

about taking up new challenges.'

'Chasing dreams?'

'Can you think of anything better to chase? Dreams show us the way. If you can dream it, you can make it happen.' She sliced a small piece of cheese and handed it across to him on the knife. He took it from her and tasted it.

'That's great,' he said. 'What is it?'

'Manchego. Made from the milk of a breed of sheep from La Mancha in Spain.' Then she added: 'That's where Don Quixote came from. Remember him?'

'The guy who fought windmills, thinking they were giants?'

'That's the one.'

'But he never got the girl,' said McGuire.

'No,' said Pearl, sipping her wine. 'He never did.'

She smiled mischievously, leaving him in no doubt that this might be the perfect moment for him to make a move – to reach across the table and maybe put his hand on hers. The light was just fading outside the window and the waitress was lighting candles for the tables. McGuire waited until Pearl had set down her glass but she was startled by a squeaking noise outside the window. It stopped as quickly as it had started, but Mc-Guire followed her gaze and saw a face staring in on them from the other side. Dressed in his signature Cornucopia T-shirt and baseball cap, Marty's hands were still firmly clasped to the hand-rail of a shopping trolley he had been pushing. He was frowning as though having some difficulty processing the image before him.

'Mr Cornucopia,' said McGuire, decidedly un-impressed.

'Looks like he's just made an "out of hours" delivery,' Pearl explained. 'His trolley always squeaks when it's empty.' She raised her hand and offered Marty a small wave but the greengrocer's gaze shifted from Pearl to McGuire and to the wine bottle between them before finally settling on the candle that the young waitress had just lit for their table. His mouth clamped shut like a snapping turtle and raising his cap as the smallest acknowledgement he could possibly muster, he beetled off, the wheels of his trolley squeaking and grinding into the distance.

Later that evening, McGuire pulled up outside Seaspray Cottage, got out of his car and went round to open the passenger door for Pearl. She stretched and looked up at a clear night sky, just in time to witness a shooting star. 'Would you ... like to come in for a coffee?'

She half expected him to decline the offer but instead he smiled and locked his car. 'Thanks.'

At the front door she fumbled slightly for her keys but covered any nerves by commenting: 'I really must get a light for this porch.' She entered, and McGuire followed. Usually she would have put on the overhead lights but tonight she opted for the softer glow of a table lamp. Having slipped out of her coat, she took McGuire's jacket from him and placed both on the banister. Pilchard and Sprat, huddled on the sofa, raised sleepy but suspicious glances at McGuire while Pearl moved to put on some music, suddenly aware that she hadn't a clue about his tastes. 'What kind of music do you like?' she asked.

McGuire gave a casual shrug. He was a fan of country rock, which he always played at loud volume when he was driving alone, but he wasn't about to admit that to Pearl for fear of being thought sentimental. 'Whatever you want to hear will be fine.'

Pearl selected some Norah Jones then instantly wondered if the sultry track was too obviously seductive. 'I'll make the coffee,' she said. 'Or would you prefer a liqueur? I have some delicious limoncello.'

McGuire thought back to the last time he had drunk limoncello – in Venice with Donna – but instead of opting for coffee, he told Pearl, 'Just a small one. I'm driving.' He followed her into the kitchen where she efficiently crushed some ice and placed it in two small glasses before tipping over it the bright yellow liqueur.

She handed the drink to him. *'Salute.'* Their glasses touched before they took a sip. The taste and smell of lemons lured McGuire back to the Piazza San Marco in Venice but he willed himself to stay in the moment with Pearl. She closed her eyes, savouring the taste. 'I can't wait for summer,' she said softly.

'Will you go away?'

She shook her head. 'It's the restaurant's busiest time, and one drawback of living in Whitstable is that everything you could possibly want is here – apart from guaranteed sunny weather, of course.'

She sipped her drink and McGuire had to admit, if only to himself; that the area had charms that were difficult to resist – like Pearl. A short drive east, away from Whitstable's pebbled beach, lay the sandy coastlines of Broadstairs and Ramsgate, while to the south, there was countryside with cherry fields and orchards and the Great Stour River.

'If the weather's fine,' Pearl said, 'why would I go anywhere else?'

It was a question McGuire now asked himself as he became locked in her gaze, remembering another time when there had been mistletoe above them ... but right now he needed no excuse to kiss her. After all the distractions of the evening, he set down his glass and moved forward while Pearl remained rooted to the spot, her eyes slowly closing before she suddenly pushed him away.

'What was that?' she said, her nerves alert.

'I didn't hear anything.'

'It sounded like my gate closing.'

He frowned. 'Are you expecting anyone?'

She shook her head.

Switching off the light, McGuire moved to one of the kitchen blinds and peered from behind it, only to find his view of the sea gate was blocked by Pearl's office. He let the blind drop and pressed his back against the wall, listening carefully. Footsteps could be heard in the garden, then a faint rustling near the lavender bushes close to her office. McGuire looked back at Pearl and she began to whisper urgently but he quickly silenced her by pressing a finger gently to her lips. The footsteps seemed to stop, then began once more, treading softly on the pea gravel immediately outside. Slowly, noiselessly, McGuire turned the key in the lock of the kitchen door then waited before choosing his moment. Throwing open the door, he dragged the intruder inside while Pearl fumbled for the light.

'Charlie!'

Pearl's son looked totally bewildered in McGuire's grasp, blinking as he stared between them while labouring under the weight of a heavy backpack.

'What on earth are you doing here?' Pearl asked.

'Trying to surprise you?' he offered lamely.

McGuire immediately helped Charlie shrug off the backpack and then Pearl pulled her son towards her and held him close. 'What a stupid thing to do. You could've been hurt.'

'You're telling me. Is this the kind of welcome you give to all your surprise visitors?'

'I'm really sorry, Charlie.' said McGuire. 'But you do a great impression of a housebreaker.'

Charlie smiled but his mother remained concerned. 'Has something happened?' she demanded. 'Is that why you came home early?'

'No,' the boy said wearily. 'No dramas. No disasters.' He helped himself to a large shot of limoncello. 'I just fancied being here for the summer, that's all.' He downed his drink and sighed with satisfaction before suddenly looking awkward. 'I ... wasn't interrupting anything, was I?'

Pearl and McGuire exchanged a look.

'Nothing at all,' said McGuire. 'In fact,' he made a quick and tactical decision, 'I was just leaving.' He gave the boy a smile. 'See you around, Charlie.'

The young man responded with a mock salute and McGuire's eyes met Pearl's as he moved to the door, saying, 'Don't worry, I'll see myself out.'

Once the front door had closed, Charlie noted how his mother was still staring after McGuire. 'You sure I wasn't interrupting?'

She quickly took in her son's appearance, noting that he looked well, but slightly pale – though she knew a few days on the beach would fix that.

'What could you possibly have interrupted?' she asked innocently.

Chapter Thirteen

The next morning brought more rain but it had almost stopped by the time Pearl was ferrying Charlie back to his flat in Canterbury. He had been scanning a front-page story about Faye Marlow's murder in the local *Courier* and said: 'OK. So now I can see why McGuire overreacted last night.' Pearl concentrated on taking a sharp right turn into the Street where Charlie's apartment block was situated. 'There's got to be a psychopath on the loose, right?'

He waited for a response but as Pearl killed her engine, she felt the need to move the conversation on. Charlie had been away for several months, with only a brief flying visit at Christmas, and she had no wish for his return home to be tarnished by a brutal murder. 'Come on,' she smiled. 'Let's get inside.'

Charlie had travelled light, apart from the presents he had brought over from Berlin and left with Pearl: a bottle of corn schnapps and some of her favourite marzipan from a shop in Charlottenburg, while Dolly received some delicious Pannkuchen and a book of photographs of the toppling of the Berlin Wall. Having spent his first term at college, sharing digs, Pearl's son had surprised her by finding a suitable place to rent at a very reasonable price and he had managed to keep the flat going with minimal contributions from his mother. Although she was glad to have him home, she wished she had been given some notice of his return so she could at least have come up and made the flat more welcoming for him.

The block was no more than a decade old and well maintained in its communal areas with a clean stair-carpet and newly painted walls, but the main hallway always seemed to Pearl to lack one of the signs of a real home: the smell of freshly made coffee or, better still, some baking. Instead, an odour more akin to fly-spray was emanating from the car air-freshener that dangled from a hook on the back of the main front door. Once inside Charlie's own flat, however, she was relieved to find it surprisingly clean and tidy.

Charlie dumped his backpack on the floor and took a quick look around. 'No major disasters,' he said, looking relieved. 'I sub-let the place for the past few weeks to Jake's sisters.'

'Jake?'

'A mate from Kent Uni,' he explained. 'Looks like they took care of the place OK.' He checked, in turn, to see that the bedroom and bathroom had been left in good order before he moved on to the kitchen, carrying a fresh container of milk.

Pearl followed behind to see him filling the kettle. Witnessing Charlie in his own environment was always a bittersweet experience for her, because while it was good to see that he was confidently negotiating an adult world, he did so increasingly without her help – and each step taken on his own path was one he now made without her.

After making a pot of tea, he handed a cup to Pearl, who asked, 'Do you want some cake to go with that?'

Somewhere inside the two bags of food she had brought with them was some homemade lemon sponge, but Charlie reminded her, 'I've only just finished a mega-breakfast, Mum.' It was true that Pearl had served him up a huge plate of ham and eggs, so the cake would be saved until later, along with all the many other items of food she now began unpacking. Olives, mozzarella and prawns all went into the fridge with a few tinned goods stored in the cupboard and some freshly baked ciabatta in the breadbin.

'You've given me more than just a care package,' he noted as Pearl now tipped some pomegranates into one of Dolly's oyster bowls. Sipping his tea, Charlie then returned to the subject that was uppermost in his mind. 'So ... McGuire's on the hunt for the murderer?'

'That's right,' said Pearl, though she was still hankering after changing the subject and thought of a suitable comment to divert her son's attention. 'You know he's got a flat in Best Street, don't you, so you're bound to see each other around.'

'I guess he sees a bit of you too?' Charlie probed.

Pearl set the bowl of pomegranates down on the

kitchen table as her son continued quickly: 'I really don't mind, Mum. He seems like an OK guy.'

Pearl appreciated that this was some compliment from her son. In all the years he had been growing up, there had been a handful of men who had appeared on Pearl's horizon, never to remain more than a very temporary flirtation for her.

'Try telling your gran that,' she said.

'Well, Gran's always gonna be hard to please and she probably thinks you've chosen a policeman just to annoy her.'

'I haven't "chosen" anyone.'

'No?' Charlie looked more than a little sceptical at this. 'Then maybe McGuire has.'

Pearl looked at him. 'I hadn't heard from McGuire since Christmas and he's only in touch now because of the murder. For all I know, he could be seeing someone.'

'Yeah, I guess he could,' said Charlie. 'But I don't think he is.'

'And what makes you think that?' Pearl was keen to know.

'Because of the way he looks at you.' Charlie said nothing more on the subject and sipped his tea before asking, 'So, are there any leads?'

'Not that I can see,' Pearl said honestly. 'But it's early days.' An idea suddenly came to mind and she asked her son. 'What do you know about Purdy Hewett?' Charlie looked blank so she offered some more details. 'Tall girl. Lives on Marine Parade in Haversham House.'

'Oh, I know. The daughter of that historian guy.'

'Archaeologist,' said Pearl. 'Oliver Hewett.'

'Yeah, that's right,' Charlie said. 'She went to

school with a mate's girlfriend. She ... can be a bit intense. I don't think she gets out much.'

'Maybe not,' said Pearl, grateful for Charlie's point of view. 'And if she does, she probably doesn't mix with your crowd. She's a few years older than you.'

'Yeah,' Charlie agreed. 'But in lots of ways she's younger. I mean, she hasn't even left home yet, has she?'

'Not yet,' said Pearl, musing on this. Charlie took Pearl's thoughtfulness for suspicion.

'Has she got something to do with the murder?' Selecting an apple, he inspected it before biting into it.

'I doubt it. But she'd been helping Nathan to organise the visit. She was a fan of Faye's.'

Charlie frowned at this. 'Well, there you go,' he said. 'I've never even heard of this actress, but Purdy's a "fan"?' He pulled a face. 'She's a bit of a geek, Mum.'

'A film buff,' Pearl corrected.

'Whatever,' said Charlie. 'But all the girls *I* know are into Robert Pattinson – not Faye Martin.'

'Marlow.' But as she said it, Pearl realised that Charlie had a point – and one she hadn't quite registered until now. There *was* something old-fashioned about Purdy, perhaps something that feared growing up and finding her place in the world. That wasn't so surprising, considering her parents continued to treat her like a teenager. Pearl looked at Charlie and smiled.

'What is it?' he asked, curious.

At that moment, she actually wanted to ask him for a few more details about the way McGuire looked at her – but she decided against it.

'Nothing,' she said, suddenly feeling all the more comfortable about her son's growing independence – and his view of McGuire.

Before she left, half an hour later, Pearl had made Charlie promise that he would come over to Whitstable for a family meal just as soon as he had settled in. Unlocking the door to her car, she then re-locked it, deciding she would use the visit to Canterbury to head on foot to a wholefoods store in Jewry Lane that stocked some speciality cooking ingredients that were hard to find in Whitstable. Wandering around the store, she soon located some Moroccan harissa paste and the Himalayan pink salt that she now used at the restaurant. She had begun to do so on Dolly's recommendation, having heard from her mother how the crystallised sea-salt beds that lay deep within the Himalayas had once been covered by lava, which had kept them in pristine condition. Use of the salt reduced signs of aging, Dolly insisted, and though it had clearly yet to preserve Dolly's teeth, she now had Dr Fang to help with that.

Pearl recalled her mother's comments about names influencing jobs and professions, and remembered now that Jerry Wheeler had actually started off in the car business. Dolly's remarks had sparked another idea for Pearl, although for the time being it appeared buried, much like Oliver Hewett's archaeological treasures.

Setting off for busy St Peter's Street, the main pedestrian thoroughfare from the old Westgate Tower, she found herself caught up in the usual current of shoppers and tourists. The old pilgrims' city was a veritable maze of history and Pearl never tired of uncovering it with her visits, but the place now had an extra attraction as McGuire lived here too. She knew little more about his home other than the fact it was situated on Best Lane and near to the river but, never one to resist a mystery, she decided to investigate.

Passing a popular Italian restaurant and pizzeria situated on the site of an old pub on the banks of the Great Stour, Pearl remembered that some major archaeological work had taken place a few years ago at number 10, Best Lane, after the property – an old music shop – had changed hands. In the course of some repairs, an important discovery had been made of a fine medieval crown post roof, leading to a dig revealing examples of twelfth-century pottery and the remains of an early timber-framed building. The latter had undergone many transformations, all charted by the members of the Trust that'd conducted the excavation as they peeled back centuries of history.

It occurred to Pearl now that in some ways both she and McGuire had the same task before them as Oliver Hewett encountered in his own work: sifting for the truth amongst buried clues – only now she was sifting for clues about McGuire, or at least, where he lived. In many ways the man was a conundrum, but for the first time in almost a year, she felt she was getting closer to him – especially after last night.

Approaching the Tudor Guest House that lay on the river side of Best Lane, Pearl came across a wrought-iron gate. Its mailboxes indicated that it was the entrance to two separate dwellings, divided into apartments, with courtyard gardens that overlooked the river and the pizzeria with its vine-covered trellised patio and a small jetty from which tourists could make river trips on the Stour. Window boxes filled with red geraniums completed the impression of a residential area that had far more in common with a small town in Italy than a traditional English city. Pearl tried the wrought-iron gate but found it was firmly locked. The series of doorbells on the wall beside it failed to show McGuire's name and, for a moment, Pearl remained staring beyond the bars of the gate, wondering if this was an indication of how her relationship with McGuire might continue – with Pearl forever on the outside of his life, looking in.

Giving up, she moved further along Best Lane, taking a quick peek in the window of a second-hand bookshop across the road. She'd just turned back towards St Peter's Street when she saw two figures at the metal gates through which she had been peering only moments before. A tall blonde woman was blocking Pearl's view of a man who appeared to be locking the gate behind him. She was dressed in a taupe linen trouser suit, her long hair falling halfway down her back, a large designer handbag hitched over her shoulder. As the man straightened after locking the gate, Pearl saw that it was McGuire. Still engaged in conversation with the woman, he failed to notice Pearl as he headed on towards St Peter's Street with his companion. Pearl stood motionless, watching the couple walk away from her to disappear into the crowds of shoppers until, instinctively, she decided to follow.

Back on St Peter's Street the buskers were all in position, strumming guitars or playing cellos, their music cases open on the ground before them begging contributions. Pearl caught sight again of McGuire, still giving his undivided attention to the blonde, close to where a group of young men wearing straw boaters were trying to interest passers-by in taking a punt along the river. McGuire was wearing a lightweight suit with the collar of his white shirt undone. His hair was ruffled and he looked as though he could do with a good night's sleep. Pearl could now see that the blonde woman was in her early thirties, attractive with a fine bone structure and a beautiful smile with which she left McGuire. She walked on in the direction of Whitefriars leaving McGuire staring after her for a moment before he checked his watch and headed quickly off in the opposite direction. He had taken only a few steps, however, when he caught sight of Pearl. For a moment, she remained frozen, unsure quite what to do, then she hurried off away from him. McGuire quickly followed and caught up with her.

'Pearl?' He caught hold of her arm – his expression one of startled confusion. 'What's going on?'

'I ... just dropped Charlie home,' she replied. 'I'm sorry, but I need to get back to Whitstable.'

She tried to move on but at that moment, a commotion started up in the street. Two police constables were questioning a young busker about his sound system. It hadn't been too noisy but nevertheless the constables were taking note of it, and the boy's protests were starting to attract the attention of passers-by. As a loose crowd began to

177

form, one of the constables stepped forward to take control and McGuire clasped hold of Pearl's arm again and pushed her gently, but forcefully, into a nearby doorway.

Her protests were silenced as soon as she found herself having to clumsily negotiate two stone steps down into the building. A Gothic door led into a flagstone vestibule that was set almost a metre lower than the height of the street pavement, and Pearl recognised that she was now in the old Eastbridge Hospital of St Thomas the Martyr – a hospital in the old sense of the word – a place of hospitality. The historic building had been in place since the twelfth century to accommodate visiting pilgrims following the murder of Thomas à Becket, and a small group of sightseers was just about to enter its Chantry Chapel.

Pearl swung round to McGuire and asked fiercely: 'What on earth do you think you're doing?'

Her raised voice caused the tourists to stare across and McGuire made a quick decision, taking out his wallet to pay the entrance fee to an admission assistant who was offering brochures and information. She handed him two tickets and a smile. 'Enjoy your visit.'

'We shall,' McGuire replied pointedly. He took Pearl's arm again, and this time ushered her on towards an old refectory, where a German tour guide was confidently instructing a dozen sightseers about the details of an old mural showing Christ with the symbols of the Four Evangelists.

Pearl turned to McGuire, saying tightly, 'You haven't answered my question.'

At this, the tour guide gave her an admonishing look as members of his group began to take more interest in Pearl than the lecture.

'Carry on like this and you'll get us thrown out,' warned McGuire.

'Good,' she snapped. The tourists were still observing her but McGuire merely smiled at them politely before pushing Pearl on towards a further set of steps at the very top of which lay the Pilgrims' Chapel. On entering, they found themselves looking up at a complex structure of oak beams in the high ceiling – all the more unusual because it contained an elaborate cage to hold a bell. Pale sunlight streamed through three windows on the north side, and though the distant sounds of St Peter's Street could be heard outside, the chapel was still and peaceful. Two elderly ladies who had been investigating the altar turned to acknowledge them as McGuire and Pearl entered. McGuire indicated for Pearl to take a seat on a nearby pew and, trapped under the gaze of the elderly tourists, she did so.

McGuire picked up a leaflet from his seat and feigned interest in it. 'Are you spying on me?' he whispered.

'*Me?*' Pearl was outraged at the suggestion – even though it was deserved. She noted the elderly women look across and lowered her voice. 'I just told you,' she said. 'I came to drop Charlie home.' She eyed him. 'I would have expected you to be working.'

'I am,' McGuire said. 'I have a murder case on my hands, remember?'

He looked sidelong at her but she failed to hold

his gaze. She was feeling guilty, not for having investigated his new accommodation but for having been caught observing him with the blonde. 'Was she a suspect?' she asked, looking back at him. 'If so, I'm surprised you didn't take her in for questioning.'

McGuire said nothing.

Pearl went on, 'She's very attractive.'

'Yes, she is,' he agreed. Pearl felt stung but failed to show it. McGuire continued, 'And as the managing agent for my apartment, she's also very efficient. I need some repairs done and she's agreed to contact the freeholder for me.'

Pearl took this in. Then: 'You could have told me that outside,' she said. 'Why did we have to come in here?'

McGuire waited until the elderly tourists had gone to light some candles. He lowered his voice. 'I'm feeling under pressure.'

'From me?' she asked defensively.

'From my superintendent.'

'Welch.'

McGuire gave a nod. 'He's been on my case for a while. I would be too, in his shoes.'

Pearl frowned. 'Why?' Then she realised. 'You mean because of me.'

'You're a private detective, Pearl. There are protocols to be observed.' He reflected on how Welch had surely recognised that Pearl was his Achilles' heel. If at one time, McGuire had harboured a plan to use Pearl as an informant in the pursuit of his investigations, there were strict procedures in place and he had never once declared her as such. For a senior officer, trained to rely on procedure,

180

he had made himself vulnerable by trusting Pearl with important information and collaborating with her in an effort to gain results – results he had used to try to establish himself at Canterbury. However, this had backfired. All he had done was make enemies for himself – with Welch fast proving to be his nemesis. McGuire was aware that he had to tread carefully but as ever, Pearl's contribution could be vital to his new case, particularly with her local knowledge and her instinct for people.

'Is that the reason why you haven't been in touch for so long?' she asked.

McGuire offered a sad smile. 'Why else?'

Pearl reflected on this, as she observed the candles the two other visitors had just lit. 'And ... what about last night?'

'I said I owed you supper.'

'So you did.'

'The only person likely to be keeping tabs on us last night was your friend, the fruit and veg man.'

Pearl smiled. 'And Charlie.'

McGuire returned her smile, relaxing for a moment as the tourists now left the chapel.

'Are there any new leads?' she asked.

McGuire shrugged. 'House-to-house enquiries have drawn a blank. Apart from a dog barking in the early hours of the morning, no one heard a thing. It's possible that the dog may have been reacting to the sound of someone gaining access to the grounds – or to the murder itself.'

'Do you have a time of death?'

'Not later than two a.m. But two night cleaners left the Castle at one thirty after tidying up the kitchen – and they reported nothing suspicious, which gives a narrow thirty-minute window in which the murder could have taken place.'

Pearl considered this. 'Barbara mentioned hearing a dog too.' She thought it through and made a connection. 'There's a Malamute two doors down from Arden House. That's what Nathan said the breed's called. Like a Husky – only larger. We saw it being taken for a walk by its owner, and he must be a neighbour rather than a visitor as he let himself in with a door key. The house is called Ravenswood.' She paused. 'We know that Faye returned straight after the reception with Jerry Wheeler, Barbara, Luc, Rosine and Nathan. Luc appears to be the last person to have seen Faye alive, just shortly after midnight – apart from the murderer, of course. But where was everyone else?'

'Everyone?' asked McGuire.

'The guests who were known to Faye at the reception. We both know that a high percentage of murders are committed by people known to the victim.'

'The families seem to be corroborating their own alibis,' McGuire said. 'The Hewetts, for example – Oliver, Maria and their daughter, Purdy – all swear they went home together, but as they live only a stone's throw from the Castle it really wouldn't take very long for one of them to slip away from Haversham House, arrive inside the Castle grounds and then return home, without anyone noticing their absence. The same goes for the Wheelers...'

'Jerry and Annabel live in Northwood Road – in the opposite direction to the Hewetts, but...'

182

'...the same distance from the Castle,' McGuire said.

'One must assume that Jean would not have risked arrest for gate-crashing the reception and assaulting Faye if she had secretly planned to return later to finish Faye off with a knife. The earlier incident puts her under scrutiny for the crime but makes her too much of an obvious suspect,' Pearl decided.

'Which is what she may be counting on,' said McGuire, 'in order to be discounted as a suspect. The fact is: she has no alibi.'

'From midnight,' said Pearl. 'That's the time Annabel said she left her.'

'She told you that too?' McGuire looked at her in exasperation. 'Have you already begun some parallel investigation? Because if you have...'

'I'm acting for a client in another matter. I'm bound by confidentiality and I can't say any more.'

McGuire tried to compute this. He considered that if Pearl had only remained a restaurant-owner, their relationship might have progressed beyond bumping heads about murder cases, but as it was, running two businesses left her about as much free time as he managed to get himself. When they did finally come together, somehow she always managed to tread on his professional toes. Right now, he would really have liked to have underlined for her that while crime seemed to be little more than a hobby for her, for himself it was his entire life. Instead, he said only, 'There's too much at stake here.'

He expected her to take issue with this, but to his surprise she replied: 'I agree. Especially with you and Welch.' She looked at him. 'Perhaps we should keep our distance for a while. Charlie's home now and I'm going to need to spend some time with him.'

McGuire's heart sank at the thought of not seeing her, but he knew that some degree of separation on the case would be the sensible answer to his dilemma.

Pearl continued. 'The important thing now is finding the murderer. It's a case of putting all the pieces of this jigsaw together.'

'The ingredients?' he said, remembering the analogy she often used about cooking and crime.

She smiled, and in that moment he realised he could have kissed her but her smile suddenly faded as her interest moved away from him to a painting on the wall of the chapel above the lit candles. It featured the Madonna wearing a black veil, adorned with gold stars, her right arm supporting the infant Christ while her left hand reached out to the child who gently touched her cheek. Pearl picked up the leaflet that McGuire had been pretending to read and stared up again at the painting.

'What is it?' he asked.

'This leaflet,' she began. 'It identifies this painting as a copy of a medieval icon – *Our Lady Vladimir*.' She continued reading. '"Originally painted in Constantinople and regarded as the patron of Russia ... this is an example of a Hodegetria, which means: *The one who shows us the way*".' Pearl moved closer to the icon. 'Look, the veil she wears...'

'What about it?'

'Well, it's a little like the shawl Faye wore during the screening of her film the other evening. It was dark blue, not black, but there's something about this painting...' She trailed off.

'What?' asked McGuire, impatient.

For a moment Pearl couldn't be sure if she had simply been struck by the force of such a captivating image of motherly love. Mary's face looked out to the world but she remained physically connected to the child in her arms who was tenderly nestled against her cheek. Then suddenly it came to her.

'The Madonna's left hand,' she said. 'Her fingers are long and tapering, just like Faye's. But there's no ring.'

'What do you mean?' McGuire was confused.

'When Faye and I were introduced, at Arden House, the first thing I noticed as she offered me her hand was the ring she wore. It had a large, rectangular diamond. I think the stone is called an emerald cut.' Pearl looked up again at the icon, remembering. 'It went missing. But only temporarily. Nathan told me how Faye had been in a complete panic about it. According to him, she swore she had locked it away in the safe at Arden House, but when she opened it the next morning, the ring was nowhere to be found. She must have been worried that it had been stolen, but...'

'But what?' prompted McGuire.

'Well, it wasn't – stolen, I mean. Nathan mentioned that Faye had probably just been overtired from the journey and after a search of the house, Rosine, the maid, found it caught up in Faye's bedding.'

'So she didn't take it off. She must have gone to sleep wearing it.'

Pearl nodded. 'It looked that way – but wouldn't you expect her to have taken more care of something so precious?' And then she remembered something else. 'She was wearing it on the night of the reception–'

McGuire broke in. 'It was collated by our Forensics officer, along with a wedding ring.'

'So, she was wearing it when she was killed. I was too shocked to notice when we came across the body.' Pearl looked at McGuire. 'Don't you think it's strange that whoever killed Faye didn't take the ring? I was looking at a photograph of her wearing it just the other day. Her husband bought it for her.'

'Sentimental value.'

'And the rest,' said Pearl. 'Nathan told me it was a five-carat diamond, mounted in gold, and I'm guessing that the added provenance of having Faye as its owner would have increased its value for collectors?'

McGuire thought about this. 'So this would seem to exclude financial gain as a possible motive for her murder.'

'Yes,' said Pearl, 'but in that case, what *was* the motive? And what was Faye doing at the Castle at that hour of the morning, dressed only in her nightclothes and dressing gown?' As one of the chapel candles guttered on the breeze from the open window, McGuire's eyes met Pearl's. Neither of them had the answer.

An hour later, Pearl was still concentrating on the

icon but this time as an image on her laptop screen at home. She had attempted to do some research on the painting and learned that *The Lady of Vladimir*, as it was also known, was a truly famous icon that had been copied repeatedly throughout the centuries, with each copy thought to have a significance of its own. Its artistic quality was beyond doubt and it was widely accepted to be one of the finest Byzantine icons surviving from its period. Pearl had also learned that icons were considered to be 'windows into heaven'. Having managed to resist the distraction of Pilchard and Sprat trying to remind her that it was almost their feeding time, it was the ringing telephone that finally got her attention. Still concentrating on the image on her computer, she reached for the phone and answered the call, but without putting on her glasses to check who the caller might be.

'Pearl speaking,' she said automatically.

McGuire spoke softly on the other end of the line, giving her the impression that he was at the police station in Canterbury. 'I checked it out,' he said.

'And?' asked Pearl, now fully concentrating on the call.

'The ring that was found on the body was just as you described, and it exactly fitted the description in an insurance policy. Apart from one thing.' He paused now.

'So tell me,' said Pearl, in suspense.

'It was a cubic zirconia.'

Pearl frowned. 'A what?'

'The stone in the ring that was found on Faye Marlow's body was a fake.'

187

Chapter Fourteen

At midday on Saturday morning, McGuire came out of the police interview room and headed directly to his office. He opened a window to take in some air and looked out on to the view beyond. It consisted of the high glass wall of the St Augustine's building of Canterbury Christ Church University, through which, at different times of the day, he could witness – on a series of floor levels – students engaged in a variety of activities: reading at desks, studying in the library or chatting together over coffee. From time to time, the students would glance back at him and in those moments, McGuire often wondered how they might consider him, assuming it would be little more than as a tired man captive in a police building. The students were young and had their futures all ahead of them while McGuire had, long ago, chosen his own.

Now, moving away from the window, he gave his attention once more to the case in hand. He had arrested three people for questioning: Barbara March, Rosine Palomer and Luc Mercier, but the clock was ticking for him. He had exactly thirty-six hours in which to hold them, but the final twelve hours would be dependent upon agreement from his superintendent – and he didn't much fancy relying on Welch for that. Officers were busily conducting a search of Arden House for the missing diamond because without it, McGuire knew that the chances of bringing a charge were slim. It was true that sometimes in a murder case the investigation could be hampered by the absence of a body, but he now had a murder case *and* a body – and what appeared to be a diamond theft – but no stone.

Barbara March had stated that she had no prior knowledge of a replica ring. The other two members of staff concurred with this. The man, Luc, spoke English well, with a Provençal accent, and was co-operative, but there was something edgy about the girl, Rosine. Due to her limited English, she had answered her questions through an interpreter, which, in turn, had given McGuire extra time to check out her body language. She had spoken quickly and fidgeted constantly, her hands flapping like the wings of a delicate bird. At times she became heated and McGuire thought she might completely boil over, like the milk he watched in the Gaggia coffee machine at the café he stopped by most mornings. He had tried to keep up the pressure but it was now time for a break – something he needed too.

He took a deep breath of air out of his office window. It wasn't that fresh as the traffic was always heavy along Longport at this time of day. He knew that he had very little on his detained suspects other than the fact that they had all shared an opportunity to steal the ring belonging to their employer. But how and when had they managed to do so – if at all? That the same employer had been murdered didn't alter the fact that McGuire needed much more to detain them further – or to charge them. Closing the window, he took out his phone and dialled a number.

Pearl replied after only a few rings. 'McGuire?' She sounded suitably taken aback to receive his call since she was in the busy restaurant and about to serve a table.

'Don't say anything,' he ordered. 'Just let me ask you something. The girl, Rosine.'

On the other end of the line, Pearl wiped her hands on her apron and asked, 'What about her?'

'She was Faye's maid...'

'And Luc's girlfriend.'

'Hear me out,' said McGuire, not wanting to become side-tracked. 'Tell me what else you know of her – what you've seen her do. Her duties.'

'Well, you just said yourself, she was Faye's maid...'

'That's not what I asked,' said McGuire quickly. 'Tell me what you saw her do.'

Pearl considered his question. 'She answered the front door to visitors – and to me, that first day I went to the house.'

'What else?'

'She announced guests to Faye.' Then Pearl remembered something else. 'She looked after Faye's wardrobe too. I noticed that Faye's clothes were immaculately pressed, and Rosine must also have been in charge of repairs.'

'Why?'

'Barbara mentioned that Rosine had been a seamstress in the theatre and I saw her with a sewing box that first day at the house.' Pearl broke off in frustration. 'Look, why are you asking me all this?'

There was only silence on the end of the line. 'McGuire...?'

'Thanks,' he said finally, and was gone.

Pearl looked at her phone, further frustrated as she realised he had hung up. She picked up her dishes and moved on to serve them – to Nathan, who registered her mood as she set down a seafood risotto and salad before him.

'What is it?' he asked, but as Pearl sat down with him, he quickly guessed. 'Don't tell me – your detective.'

'How many times do I have to explain? He's not "mine".'

She helped herself to a glass of wine from Nathan's carafe and he leaned across the table towards her, lowering his voice so that other customers would not hear. 'It's appalling, Pearl. Dolly's quite right about the police, you know, because after everything that's happened, there they were this morning at Arden House, tearing up the place, clearly looking for this missing diamond you told me about – your detective included.' He quickly noted Pearl's look and apologised. 'OK, sorry. He's *not* yours – which is a good thing, if you ask me, because I don't think he has the first clue what he's doing with this case. He carted them off to the police station in full view of all the neighbours. Can you believe that? Luc, Rosine – even Barbara?'

Pearl would have expected nothing less of McGuire than to arrest all the main suspects for questioning but kept her thoughts to herself.

'He won't find anything, of course,' Nathan said dismissively.

191

'And if he does?'

'Well that would, of course, imply that one of them had something to do with the missing diamond.'

'One? Or all of them?' asked Pearl.

Nathan looked at her searchingly. 'Some sort of conspiracy, you mean?' He pondered on this for a moment before saying, 'But it doesn't make sense. I mean, Faye was wearing the ring.'

'Correction: she was wearing *a* ring. But the one found on her body was not the same ring bought for her by her late husband. If it had been, it would have been worth £100,000 at least.'

'How do you know?'

'How do you think?' she asked sharply. 'I'm a detective, remember?' In fact, Pearl had sat at her computer until the early hours of the morning, researching diamond prices and the various cuts used by the industry. She had also learned about cubic zirconia, ashamed that she hadn't known more when McGuire had alerted her to the fake diamond yesterday. In fact, she now knew that spotting the difference between a naturally formed diamond and the man-made stone that it so resembled was not quite as simple as might be imagined. It was always possible to try checking the surface of the stone because, as the hardest naturally occurring surface, a diamond should never show scratches. There was also the more commonly known method of trying to scratch glass with the diamond. Although a genuine stone would achieve this, there were now some fake diamonds that were capable of doing it too. In fact, recent advances in the manufacture of 'faux' diamonds meant that some high-quality cubic zirconias could easily pass some of these tried and tested methods, even that which gemologists still considered one of the most effective: trying to read text through the stone. This, because it was now actually possible to make out lettering through a cubic zirconia.

Flaws might suggest a man-made stone, along with colour, since the light of a diamond should refract grey and, as diamonds do not retain heat, another test might consist of breathing upon the stone to see if it instantly clears. However, what Pearl had learned was that the most reliable way to tell the difference was with an electronic device that gave a reading of electrical and thermal conductivity; and McGuire had duly confirmed that when examined under a black light, the stone in the ring found on Faye's body had failed to reflect the blue fluorescence that a real diamond would have produced.

'Tell me,' Pearl asked Nathan. 'What happened that morning when Faye thought she had lost the ring?'

'I already told you...'

'Tell me again.'

Nathan heaved a sigh. 'Faye raised the alarm and everyone went into panic mode. Apart from Barbara, of course. She's a "coper", in case you hadn't noticed.'

'And it was Barbara's idea not to call the police?'

'That's right – not before we had made a proper search for it, which was perfectly reasonable. I mean, we only had Faye's word for it that she had put the ring into the safe the night before.'

'And it was Faye, not Rosine, who had done so?'

'Right,' said Nathan. 'Rosine couldn't have done it because she didn't have the combination. Tom Chandler had given that to Faye.'

'How?'

'Over the phone before she left France. It was one of the things that Purdy reminded me to get from him. To be honest, he didn't want anyone else to know it. Why would he? It's his safe. Faye was just using it for this visit to protect her jewellery – not that it helped, did it? Although,' he thought aloud, 'if the real ring was switched, there's nothing to say that it didn't happen *before* Faye arrived here. It could have occurred in France, right?'

'Perhaps,' Pearl conceded.

Nathan looked encouraged by this. 'And what if Faye had done this herself? Perhaps she got a copy made with a faux diamond and sold the real thing?'

'For cash?' asked Pearl. 'McGuire would have known if there was evidence of a bank transaction having taken place. But admittedly, she could have got a copy made for security reasons.'

'Yes,' said Nathan brightly. 'People do that with paintings. Collectors buy a priceless work of art and then commission a replica that they can safely display in its place. Museums do it too, don't they?'

'Do they?'

'Sure. If the original item risks damage they'll show a replica or even get one specially made to see how the original was put together.' He paused. 'Archaeologists sometimes do it too, in order to see what skills were needed to create the artefact.'

'Interesting,' said Pearl, thinking of Oliver Hewett.

'In fact, come to think of it, there's a replica of Stephenson's Rocket, the train engine, at the Science Museum, and I believe it follows exactly the original design.' Nathan looked positively pleased with himself for a moment, then suddenly confused, as though finding it a challenge to link a famous train engine with Faye Marlow's diamond ring. 'Well,' he resumed hastily, 'my point is: people do get these replicas made – and maybe Faye did just that.'

'And did she give you any idea that that was what you were looking for the other morning?'

'Sorry?'

'You said she was upset and in a panic about losing the ring, but did she give you, or anyone else, the impression that it might not be the original ring given to her by her husband?'

Nathan frowned. 'No. In fact, she said quite the opposite. In French – to Rosine.'

'Can you remember exactly *what* she said?'

Nathan set down his glass of wine as he made an effort to recall.

'Rosine was flapping around like a butterfly, and I think Faye was just taking out her irritation on the girl. Like I say, she was panicking and wailing, "It's gone. *C'est disparu!*"' He recalled something more. 'She said, *"Mon cadeau précieux d'Alain."*'

Pearl frowned as she tried to make sense of this. 'My precious...?'

'Gift,' Nathan translated. 'From Alain. Her husband.'

'Well, that's not exactly the way you'd describe a replica, is it?'

'I guess not,' Nathan agreed.

'Which suggests that, at that moment in time, Faye believed she had been wearing the original ring – and not a copy. So the question is: when was the ring switched?'

'After she was killed?' Nathan wondered aloud.

'If so, why go to all the trouble of creating a replica? Why not simply murder Faye and steal the ring?' Pearl shook her head. 'No. Forensics confirmed that the same ring was on her body at the time of death, so the ring was switched without her knowing.'

'It could even have been sold?'

'Yes, quite possibly.'

'But when?' asked Nathan. 'And by whom?'

'Well, that's clearly what McGuire is investigating right now,' Pearl replied, articulating the one thing she could be sure about.

As soon as the restaurant had closed, Pearl identified an address for Mandy Prosser. It hadn't been too difficult to find. She was listed on the electoral register as Amanda, and a cross-reference with an online business directory showed that she lived in an apartment block in Canterbury. Pearl could have tailed Jerry Wheeler but she had decided to keep tabs on his secretary instead so, having bought a burrito from the Mexican restaurant on St Dunstans, she drove the short distance back on to Roper Road where she parked a little ahead of a distinctive building. It was called The Maltings, a modern conversion of what had once been an old Malt House, and it boasted gated under-ground parking but had tiny windows – presumably, Pearl thought, to meet some conservation guidelines.

As she settled down to eat her burrito, she began listening to a programme on the radio about butterflies. An expert was explaining how various cultures had related or compared them to the human soul. One Russian dialect was said to refer to them as *dushuchka,* derived from *dusha,* meaning 'soul' – and Aristotle had given the name *psyche* to the butterfly – Psyche being also the name of the lover of Eros as well as the Ancient Greek word for 'soul'. The Aztec Indians related the morning star to the butterfly, which they also believed represented the souls of the dead, so that the appearance of beautiful butterflies was considered by grieving relatives to be a reassuring sign that all was well with their dearly departed. The presenter went on to explain that during Mexico's famous Day of the Dead festival, the annual migration of millions of Monarch butterflies is still viewed as the physical manifestation of liberated souls.

Listening to this, Pearl was prompted to recall the single butterfly that had flitted in the conservatory at Arden House on the day she had served lunch for Faye and which, with hindsight, might well have been viewed as a possible omen. And with the mention of Mexico came another memory – of Oliver Hewett's study of the Mayan murals, which Dolly had found so fascinating. Pearl decided there and then that the archaeologist's upcoming lecture was an event she should definitely attend. In fact, she would even try to tempt Charlie along and make it something of a family occasion.

At around 6.30 p.m., Roper Road was quiet, apart from the occasional sign of someone entering or emerging from the small business complex situated in Roper Close. Some carried bags that revealed they had just visited Marlowe Costumes and Canterbury Fancy Dress – a hire company whose selection was so extensive it had been used for local theatre productions. The famous Canterbury Marlowe Theatre shared its name. Thinking about this, it suddenly occurred to Pearl that while Dolly might well have been correct about Faye changing her surname in order to disassociate herself from a family history of whelks, she had chosen another that had surely been inspired by the theatrical connection between the actor and dramatist, Christopher Marlowe, and the celebrated Marlowe Theatre. All that was missing was an 'e' at the end of Faye's own professional surname. In fact, it now seemed as obvious as it had perhaps appeared to Dolly's dentist, Dr Fang, to become a dentist. Nominative determinism might well have influenced Dr Fang's choice of career, but what if Faye's choice of career had determined her choice of name?

Pearl was still thinking this through when she noted a car turning into the street from St Dunstans. She immediately recognised it as belonging to Jerry Wheeler – not his Duesenberg '38 but a far less conspicuous silver E-type Jaguar. It drew up outside The Maltings and Pearl observed through her rear- and side-view mirrors, that there were two people inside it. Jerry was driving, while Mandy Prosser sat beside him in the passenger seat. Pearl was immediately surprised by what she saw, though she couldn't be sure why this pairing should have been so unexpected. To make sure she wasn't imagining things, she took out a small camera from her glove compartment and snapped a few photos using the reflection of her side-view mirror.

Jerry and Mandy remained seated in the car, chatting together before eventually the young woman opened the passenger door and got out. She had walked halfway to the entrance door to the apartment block when she suddenly hurried back and spoke to Jerry through the open passenger window. They continued to chat for a few moments more before the car window was finally closed, as was the conversation. Mandy then walked back to The Maltings, gave a quick wave to Jerry and let herself into the front door of the block. The E-type's engine started up and Pearl sank lower in the driver's seat of her Fiat as she realised Jerry might well drive the car beyond her in order to execute a three-point turn. Instead, to Pearl's relief, he managed to effect the turn closer to where he had been parked, before heading back on to St Dunstans.

On the second storey of The Maltings, Pearl noticed that one of the small windows was now open. Inside, Mandy Prosser was clearly visible, talking on a mobile phone. Moments later, she moved away and a light went on in another window. It was Saturday evening and if Pearl's instincts were correct, her surveillance would soon be rewarded.

On the other side of Canterbury, McGuire was on his way back to work, heading along the walkway of the ancient city wall that overlooked, on one side, the busy Longport road, and Dane John Gardens on the other. Although the police station lay outside the city wall McGuire often felt trapped within it. He could have sent out for food but he had needed a break and hated the smell of stale fat that always hung on the air in the offices belonging to burger eaters. McGuire tried to eat well but it wasn't always possible with the hours he kept. Deadlines meant that food was snatched and eaten on the hoof: never fruit, always carbs for energy, which tended to hang around the waistline these days.

People always seemed to think of a police officer's job as being an active one, but as McGuire was pretty much desk-bound these days, he tried to find some time for exercise wherever he could. Due to the pressure of work he was never able to venture far from the station, but he liked to seek refuge, and some privacy, by crossing traffic-filled Longport by the subway to enter the gardens. At one time, their main entrance would have attracted more attention, but the original gates had long been lost to the commission for metal during the last war and McGuire had stumbled upon the area quite by accident one day. The most popular local park in Canterbury, Dane John Gardens appeared like an oasis in a desert, offering respite from the bustling city. Laid out as lawns and gardens with fountains and a bandstand where concerts took place on summer weekends, one edge of the gardens was bounded by the city wall while the main attraction for tourists seemed always to be the grass-covered tumescence known as the Dane John burial mound – which marked the area as a former Roman cemetery.

For McGuire, however, a new appeal was a small cabin that had once dispensed weak tea and packet soups, but which now, in its new guise as the Don Juan café, offered South American food served by a duo of young guys from Uruguay and Venezuela. There was paella on offer or barbecued short ribs, but usually McGuire opted for *choripán*, if he was in a hurry, or a cornbread *arepa* if he could spare the ten minutes required for it to be cooked. He liked the place, feeling he could engage the two chefs in conversation if he was in need of company, but otherwise he would simply sit beneath a lime tree and enjoy his food while contemplating a problem. The café had been busy today and there was an apology by one of the chefs for the wait before McGuire was brought a plate of home-made paella with seafood and chicken.

'Don't worry,' said McGuire. 'All the best things are worth waiting for,' to which the guy replied, 'Sure. My wife had to wait thirty years for me to come along!' He smiled and pushed some salsa McGuire's way, leaving the remark to echo for McGuire.

He had known Pearl for less than a year but in that time the principal thing he had learned about her was that they were opposites. She was a family person – he was a sociable loner. She was for instinct – he trusted procedure. She was small-town – he was city. She was also, in his eyes, a cook with a hobby for snooping while he was a professional, an experienced detective who lived for his job. But, increasingly, he longed for something else in his life too, not the few brief physical encounters he had had with women since Donna had died, but something that resembled more of a partnership. In spite of the usual sparring, this was something he had enjoyed with Pearl on the cases they had shared, but on a personal level, there always seemed to be obstacles in the way, of one sort or another. Pearl's mother could be spiky with him, though knowing Pearl's independent spirit he didn't consider that to be too much of a problem. But on an emotional level there was something separating them.

McGuire sensed that Pearl sometimes pulled up a drawbridge to emotional closeness – but he was guilty of this too, though for his own part, he simply didn't want to put a foot wrong with Pearl. Clearly she was used to being in control of her own life and her emotions: it was one of the things that had first attracted him to her, like the colour of her pale grey eyes. But right then he wished he was sitting with her in this quiet spot with only the sound of a nearby fountain and the strains of a lazy *milonga* coming from the cabin. Beyond the city wall, his work still waited, but here, for a short while, he felt buffered from its pressure.

Finishing his last bite of food he had thanked the guys at the cabin and headed off towards the city wall-walk. The music from the Don Juan grew fainter as he found himself back on the street, and as he looked across at the grey flint wall of the police station he braced himself, preparing to frame more questions for the three people he still held in custody. It was a contest of wills but he knew he was capable of winning it. The one thing against him was a ticking clock.

As McGuire entered the bowel of the subway, a bundle of rags suddenly moved as he passed by. A young lad and a mongrel terrier seemed to be relying on one another for company – and heat. McGuire failed to identify himself as a police officer but instead tipped a pocketful of loose change into the young boy's denim cap and continued on. Emerging from the subway on the other side of Riding Gate roundabout, he crossed the road towards the police station. It was open from 9 a.m. until 5 p.m. from Monday to Sunday, with an intercom for use outside these hours. A yellow phone receiver was attached to the exterior wall with an instruction to dial 123, from top to bottom, or to press any button to call the Control Room. Any moment now, McGuire would enter and pass the semi-circular reception desk, watching himself on the CCTV screen before taking a lift up to the interview room for another bout of questioning. Before his hand had even reached the door, however, his mobile rang and he found himself speaking to the sergeant engaged in a search at Arden House.

McGuire stopped dead in his tracks, brought up short by what he had just heard. 'Are you sure about that?' He listened again to what the officer had to say, acknowledging to himself that he had Pearl to thank for some progress.

Still sitting at the wheel of her Fiat outside The Maltings, Pearl was surfing radio channels trying to find something new to listen to. The programme on butterflies had ended and a burst of Cuban music seemed like a good contrast, something that was guaranteed, at least, to raise her mood. No sooner had she fine-tuned the channel, however, than another sound drowned out the song. The engine of a powerful motorbike was roaring into Roper Road. It braked right outside The Maltings.

Pearl wasn't well up on identifying motorbikes though she knew quite a bit about her son's scooter, since she'd had to fork out a few times for its repairs. Compared to Charlie's Piaggio, the bike parked on the other side of the road was a brute. Sleek but solid, it appeared to be a cruiser of some kind, with lots of steel and some red on show – presumably to denote danger. The rider slung a long leg over the saddle and took off his crash helmet, on which a dragon was painted. His blond hair spilled down on to his shoulders, suddenly reminding Pearl of Charlie's father, Carl, but the biker across the road was far taller and in some ways more handsome, with regular features and a chiselled jaw. In fact, he was beautiful, like an actor from a Hollywood film – resembling a young Brad Pitt.

He strode across to The Maltings, but before he could select one of the apartment bells, the front door opened and there stood Mandy Prosser, no longer wearing her office uniform but a tight red leather biker suit instead. Her hair was down and she carried her own crash helmet. Looking at the

204

young man, her face broke into a slow smile and she took a small jump towards him as he caught her in his arms. She wrapped her legs tightly around his hips and he kissed her hard on the lips. Viewing this from the rear-view mirror of her car, Pearl couldn't help but feel like a voyeur, spying on a couple who were not only in love – but in lust. Then, holding hands, they returned to the kerb where they put on their crash helmets and mounted the bike. Mandy took her place on the pillion as her lover revved the engine back into life. Turning in a neat circle, the bike roared off back towards St Dunstans, with Mandy clinging to its driver not for security but from passion – reminding Pearl what it was like to be young and in love.

Chapter Fifteen

'I could stay on the case, but in all honesty I believe it would be a waste of your money and my time.' Pearl waited for Annabel Wheeler's reaction.

'Why?' Annabel asked, mystified.

'Because I honestly don't believe your husband is having an affair with Mandy Prosser.'

Sitting opposite Pearl in her office, Annabel's face screwed into a tight ball of frustration. 'How can you say that? I only hired you a few days ago.'

'Despite everything you told me, I didn't detect any of the usual signs of a cheating husband.'

'And how would *you* know?' Annabel blurted

out in exasperation. 'You've never even *been* married!'

It was hard for Pearl not to take this as an affront. Annabel, however, was quite right, so Pearl adopted a professional tone in order to assert herself. 'Admittedly, no two cases are ever the same,' she began. 'But ... aftershave is a usual indication.'

'Aftershave?' echoed Annabel.

'Yes. Something out of the ordinary,' Pearl continued. 'Young, sweet, overpowering? Often it's a brand bought by the other woman – just to lay claim on him.'

Annabel's eyes widened.

Pearl went on, 'Have you noticed if Jerry's been guarding his mobile phone lately? Taking it into the bathroom with him, perhaps? Does he switch it off when you're together?'

'No,' Annabel muttered, more subdued now.

'Well,' Pearl continued, 'that's usually a surefire sign, because no cheating husband would ever risk the other woman calling in front of his wife.' She paused. 'You could check to see if he's taken out new credit cards. Though, for sure, he would arrange for the bills to go to his office and not to your home. But I still think you'd be wasting your time.'

'Why?' asked Annabel.

'Because Mandy Prosser is in love,' said Pearl. 'But not with your husband.' She allowed this news to settle before going on. 'Jerry gave her a lift home but I saw no signs of anything other than a good working relationship between them. Besides, it would seem Mandy's leading something of a dual existence.'

Annabel looked up at this.

'Efficient secretary by day,' explained Pearl. 'Biker by night.'

'What!' Annabel exclaimed, increasingly disconcerted by what she was hearing.

'Her very handsome young boyfriend runs a powerful motorbike. I think they share a love of life in the fast lane – and leather. But your husband's taste in the latter seems to extend only to comfortable office sofas.'

Annabel looked away, defeated, at this news.

'I would add,' said Pearl gently, 'that in my experience, the partners who are most likely to suspect their spouses of cheating, do so because they have something to hide themselves.' At this, Annabel's head jerked up, but before she could say a word, Pearl delivered her *coup de grâce:* 'The talk on Suffragettes? It was cancelled. There's a notice on the Hove W.I. website to that effect.'

Annabel Wheeler visibly slumped. 'Oh God,' she said. 'Have you told Jerry?'

Pearl shook her head.

'Well, I suppose I should, at least, thank you for that.'

'No,' said Pearl. 'You're my client and I have a duty to observe confidentiality.'

'And I can still rely on that?'

Pearl nodded.

Annabel took a deep breath and made a weary admission. 'You're right, of course. I wasn't at a Women's Institute event last week. I was at the Malmesbury Hotel in Wiltshire. I'm seeing someone. But not just anyone, you understand. His name is Mark Boyle and he's an ex-boyfriend of mine. A remarkable man. I ditched him many years ago for Jerry, which is the biggest mistake I have ever made. But mistakes can sometimes be rectified, and that's what I've been trying to do – ever since Mark's divorce came through.' She looked unrepentant. 'So that's why I was hoping you could find some evidence of Jerry's adultery.'

'And was it Mark you were texting at the reception the other evening?'

Annabel gave a slight smile. 'You're rather good at this, aren't you, Pearl? Yes, it was. Not that Jerry noticed. He may not be having an affair, but he *is* having a mid-life crisis. A young secretary like Mandy? The Duesenberg? Ferrying Faye around like he did? I was so looking forward to finding out that he was cheating – with Mandy, with Faye – with *anyone*.' She calmed herself for a moment. 'You might well know all the signs of a cheating husband, Pearl, but if you've never been married, you can't possibly know how very dull it can be after decades of marriage to the same person.'

'The wrong person?' said Pearl pointedly.

'Perhaps,' Annabel said dully.

'Have you talked to Jerry?'

'Jerry and I do not talk,' Annabel snapped. 'At least, not about the things that matter. We've become rather like a business partnership.'

'Partnerships can be dissolved.'

'Not without good reason.'

'And what better reason could there be than love?'

Annabel stared at Pearl. 'Oh my God. You haven't been married, Pearl, and you certainly haven't been divorced, have you? It might sound easy but it's not. Mark's wife divorced him after his business failed. If I went to Jerry now and asked for a divorce ... if I explained why...' She sighed heavily. 'He'd make sure I was left with nothing.'

'You'd still have Mark.'

'Yes,' Annabel agreed, 'and he's a brilliant man – an inventor, fill of ideas. But he's now penniless. And what kind of life can you have without money?'

For a moment, Pearl assumed that Annabel's question was merely rhetorical but she now saw that Jerry's wife was, in fact, waiting for a reply.

'What kind of life do you have *with* it?' Pearl replied.

Annabel Wheeler looked away to the window. For a moment, Pearl imagined that she might be using the sea view to help her to reflect, as she herself was apt to do when faced with a dilemma, but instead Jerry Wheeler's wife merely commented, 'You have cobwebs in your windows, do you know that?' She got to her feet. 'Send me your bill and you can use the money to pay for a spring-clean.'

Annabel picked up her handbag and left the beach-hut office without once looking back. As the door closed after her, Pearl calmly glanced away to the window and saw that Annabel Wheeler was quite right: the cobwebs were back. Unperturbed, however, Pearl chose to look beyond them and enjoy the sea view.

After the meeting with Annabel, Pearl decided she needed some air. The shops in Harbour Street had already closed for the day though a small newsagent's was still open, as was the adjoining bar to a delicatessen where a few local men were sitting at a table outside, drinking coffee and chatting. There was a Mediterranean feel about the scene, complemented by the spring flowers on the table that sat in a colourful can that had once contained Greek olives. The breeze that blew in off the sea was cool, but the air felt heavy and slightly oppressive. Pearl bought a few magazines and some biscuits from the newsagent and decided to take them to Dolly just to make sure that Dr Fang's work was still holding up. An earlier text from Pearl to her mother had gone unanswered, which wasn't at all unusual since Dolly disliked using a mobile phone and often neglected to recharge her battery.

In no time Pearl stood outside Dolly's Pots, investigating the shop's new window display. It featured a selection of her mother's latest creations: tea-light holders, mugs and some newly designed decorative plates, all arranged in Dolly's own inimitable and eye-catching style. Pearl rang the doorbell and Dolly quickly ushered her inside.

'Come in,' she said impatiently, as though Pearl was interrupting something. 'I have a visitor.' Following Dolly into the sitting room, Pearl was taken aback to find Jean Wheeler on the sofa, a cup of tea in her hand and Dolly's temperamental tomcat sleeping close beside her.

'It's only Pearl,' Dolly said as a cursory announcement.

It was a challenge for Pearl to cover her surprise at coming face-to-face with Jean so soon after her daughter-in-law's revelations, but Jean mistook

Pearl's reaction, saying, 'I know what you must be thinking, dear, and I know how it must look to everyone. I may have attacked Faye Marlow with your dessert but I swear it wasn't me who killed her.'

'Pearl knows that,' said Dolly, taking a seat beside Jean, seemingly in a show of solidarity: She reached out a hand to stroke Mojo but he instantly lashed his tail in disapproval so she picked up her cup instead.

'To be perfectly honest,' Jean said, 'if I had really wanted to kill Faye I would've done it, there and then, and not cared about the consequences. There was plenty of cutlery around, as I recall.'

'But you chose Pearl's trifle,' Dolly reminded everyone. 'Hardly a deadly weapon,' she sniffed.

'It was actually a summer pudding trifle,' Pearl corrected her, feeling a need for accuracy.

'Don't be pedantic, Pearl,' her mother reprimanded her.

'Well, whatever it was,' Jean continued patiently, 'I'm sure it was delicious and I'm only sorry for wasting it.'

'I wouldn't say it was wasted,' argued Dolly. 'It played an important part in helping you to express your long-buried anger.'

'Yes,' Jean conceded wistfully. 'I really thought I'd put a lid on that, but Faye's return just brought it bubbling to the surface again. Nevertheless, I really should have shown more control and I didn't.' She looked at them both. 'The thing is, Faye did little more than use my son all those years ago. She was only ever interested in him for his prospects, and ditched him when something better came along. But he did go on to marry Annabel and, while I'm not saying they haven't had their problems, it's been a good marriage and I really didn't want to see it jeopardised by Faye.'

'Problems?' asked Pearl innocently.

Dolly looked up quickly. 'Don't pry.'

'No, it's fine,' Jean sighed. 'I meant – and it's no secret, of course – that Jerry and Annabel haven't been blessed with children. It's a little late now, so I shan't ever expect to be a grandmother.' She pulled out a handkerchief from her bag and dabbed her nose before clearing her throat and popping the hanky back in the bag. 'The truth is, I've got used to the idea and I dare say, if Jerry had married Faye, the outcome would have been just the same – as she had no children either.'

Pearl began to sympathise with Jean, not just because of her lack of grandchildren, but because she clearly had no idea whatsoever about Annabel's adultery.

'At least I'm a mother,' Jean said. 'And you both understand about that. We're all mothers of a single child, aren't we?'

'So we are,' said Dolly, looking at Pearl.

'And it's true I've been a little over-protective of Jerry,' Jean conceded. 'But in the circumstances, that's only to be expected.' She looked at Pearl and Dolly, as if for confirmation.

'Yes,' said Pearl. 'I can totally understand how Faye's return must have opened old wounds...'

At that moment, Jean sneezed, rather powerfully, although Mojo remained firmly fixed to the sofa. Jean looked at the cat then at Dolly – who suddenly got the message.

'Oh, I'm so sorry. Jean. You should've said: you don't deal with cat fur very well, do you?' She began to lift Mojo from the sofa, which wasn't easy as he was reluctant to move. 'Why they are always drawn to those they don't agree with, I will never know. Contrary creatures, eh?' Dolly finally released Mojo's tenacious claws from the sofa and moved off with him. 'Come on, fella. I'll give you some biscuits and you can go outside.'

She disappeared with the cat in her arms while Jean brushed down her skirt. 'You were saying, dear?'

'I was just sympathising,' Pearl replied. 'It must have been difficult for you – but also for Jerry, having been abandoned, as you mentioned, when Faye's film role came along.'

'Oh, but I wasn't referring to the film role,' Jean told her. 'Sadly, Faye had tired of Jerry before that – in fact, as soon as Oliver Hewett came along.'

'Oliver?' asked Pearl, innocently, keen to hear more.

'Yes, that was around the time her interest in poor Jerry waned and, to be honest, I can see why. Oliver's always had some Hollywood glamour about him, don't you think? But especially back then. Anyone could see there was a spark between them – including Maria. She and Oliver were engaged, but that wouldn't have stopped Faye. After all, she was still engaged to Jerry – and sporting a rather beautiful ring to prove it, though she never returned it when she left him – not that I would have expected her to.'

Jean sipped her tea then set down her cup. 'I remember being at a cocktail party at Faye's, one

213

evening,' she reminisced. 'At that time, she was living in a house on Borstal Hill. It was summer and she'd organised the evening beautifully – lights strung in the garden – and she was always one for the very best hors d'oeuvre. But she invited Oliver and Maria, and I swear she got him rather drunk. We are, of course, talking about nearly twenty-five years ago and he was only a young man then but ... well, it was all rather embarrassing – for Jerry *and* for Maria, of course. She went home alone, and after what I think were a few tense words in the gazebo. I persuaded Jerry to take me home. There were plenty of other guests still there so we were hardly missed – and Faye didn't give a damn. What I'm saying is, Faye was ambitious even then – for money, for fame, for men. And if it hadn't been for feisty little Maria, she might even have stolen away poor Oliver too.'

'But instead they went to Mexico?'

'That's right.'

'And it was after they'd left Whitstable that Faye went to America to audition for a role?'

'Yes,' said Jean, 'though she didn't get the part. Still, she clearly saw where her bread was buttered and stayed on in America. The rest is history.'

'What is?' asked Dolly, returning.

'Jean's just been filling me in about Faye's ambition,' Pearl said.

'It won't get her far now,' Dolly said ruefully.

A hush fell, broken suddenly by the sound of Mojo scratching at the door of Dolly's conservatory. As they turned to view him, he issued a silent cry on the other side of the glass.

'Oh, and I've just fed him too,' Dolly grumbled.

'Don't worry,' said Jean. 'I'd better get myself home.' She picked up her handbag and got to her feet. 'Nice to see you, Pearl.'

'And you,' she replied honestly.

Dolly stood up to follow, but Jean protested. 'No, please. I can see myself out.' She gave Dolly a peck on the cheek. 'See you tomorrow.'

Once the front door had closed after Jean, Pearl turned to her mother and asked, 'Tomorrow?'

'Yes,' smiled Dolly. 'I went out today and bought tickets for us all for Oliver's talk at the library tomorrow night. I hope you can make it because Charlie can.'

'Really?' asked Pearl, surprised.

'Yes. I told him all about the murals and he's as fascinated as I am. Remember he did that Maya project in his History of Art studies?'

'So he did,' Pearl recalled.

'So, if you can come too, I promise I'll buy us all supper afterwards. My treat. How's that?'

Pearl felt warmed by the thought. It wasn't often that her mother made such extravagant gestures, and another invitation, coming so soon after McGuire's, to sample someone else's cooking, was certainly something to look forward to.

Pearl called Charlie as soon as she arrived home. 'So is it true you can make it to this talk tomorrow?' she asked.

'Sure,' he said, but his next words were swallowed up in the loud music that was playing in the background.

'What was that?' asked Pearl, straining to hear.

'I said, I'm looking forward to it,' repeated

215

Charlie. 'I've heard about the Bonampak murals.'

'Then maybe I'm the only person who hasn't,' Pearl realised.

'Don't worry. Gran says Professor Hewett'll be talking about the copperas site too. I guess that's what most people in Whitstable will be interested in.' The music soared again in the background.

'Where are you?'

'A bar called Los Locos.'

'In Canterbury?'

'Where else? Don't worry, I haven't flown off to Mexico. I'm just catching up with some friends.'

'OK, I'll let you do that,' Pearl said, recognising that she was holding him up – then she suddenly remembered. 'Charlie?'

'Yeah?'

'When you did History of Art, did you happen to study anything about icons?'

'Not much. Why?'

'Because there's an icon known as *The Lady of Vladimir...*'

Charlie stopped her immediately. 'Mum. That's not *an* icon – it's *the* icon.'

'What d'you mean?'

'It's considered to be one of the best surviving examples of Byzantine icons from that period.'

'And it's called a ... Hedegetria?' asked Pearl. 'A Virgin Mary icon?'

'Hodegetria,' he corrected her. 'Madonna and child. There's a story, and I don't know how true it is, but it's said that when the icon was being transported somewhere, the horses suddenly stopped near Vladimir and refused to go on, so people took this to be a sign that the icon should

216

stay there – and so they built a cathedral.'

Pearl reflected on this then smiled. 'I'm glad to see all those tuition fees weren't wasted.'

'See you tomorrow, Mum.'

'See you then, sweetheart.'

Once the line went dead, Pearl allowed herself to savour a moment of pride in her son's education, until the phone rang. Thinking it was Charlie again, she found herself talking instead to McGuire.

'OK,' she began. 'What can be so important that you're calling me at this time of–'

'I have to be quick,' McGuire said tersely. 'You'll hear about this soon enough tomorrow. She broke down under questioning.'

'Who did?' asked Pearl, suddenly focusing her attention.

'Rosine. She's confessed.'

'To the murder?' gasped Pearl. For a moment there was silence, then several voices could be heard in the background. 'McGuire?'

He returned to the line, and delivered the following succinct message: 'To the theft of the diamond.'

Chapter Sixteen

Nathan was finding it a challenge to keep up with Pearl as she hurried along Island Wall. She was on her way to The Whitstable Pearl but he was urging her to take notice of the online news story on the tablet in his hand. 'Look,' he said. 'It's all about Luc and Rosine having been charged with the theft of Faye's ring.'

'I will,' Pearl said a little breathlessly. 'Just as soon as I get to the restaurant.' As she disappeared around the corner into Terry's Lane, Nathan followed quickly after her.

'Aren't you even a bit curious?' he asked. 'It says here they made a full confession.'

'To the theft, but not to the murder,' said Pearl.

Nathan eyed her suspiciously. 'Ah, I see,' he realised. 'You already knew, didn't you?' He looked back at his tablet. 'This story's only just gone online, so you must have had some insider information.' He frowned and asked petulantly, 'Why didn't you tell *me?*'

'I'm trying to get to the restaurant, Nathan...'

'Well, in the circumstances, I'm surprised you're not on a stake-out or whatever it is you do. How can you possibly juggle molluscs and murder?'

Pearl was about to explain, but having just turned into the High Street, she stopped dead, her attention drawn to something.

'What is it?' Nathan saw that she was eyeing something in the charity shop behind him. There were numerous posters attached to the shop's window but one in particular had caught her eye; it advertised the talk that Oliver Hewett was due to give at the local library, the title of which was 'Simply Stones'.

'Are you going to that?' she asked.

'Why? Are you?'

'Yes. A family outing.'

'Then I guess I should come along too,' Nathan

218

decided. 'In the words of the old fridge magnet: "Friends are the family you make for yourself".' He smiled and then demanded: 'Are you going to fill me in about Luc and Rosine or not?'

'Later.' Pearl unlocked the door to the restaurant, and as she stepped inside, Nathan put his hand out to prevent her from closing it. He tried one last time.

'One quick coffee while you give me the gist in bullet-points?'

'I said – later.'

'Well, at least tell me if you think Luc and Rosine murdered Faye?'

'To be perfectly honest,' she said, 'I really don't know. And I'm not sure anybody else does either – apart from the murderer.'

She gave him a quick peck on the cheek then entered the restaurant and locked the door behind her. Through the glass, she saw Nathan heading off up the High Street, looking defeated. Pearl went into the kitchen, but hadn't even got her jacket off before her mobile rang.

McGuire was heading down a flight of stairs in Canterbury police station, having decided not to take the lift. He had discovered it was a good place to make a private call while stretching his legs after he had sat for far too long in an interview room.

Pearl spoke first after seeing the caller ID. 'Is it true Luc and Rosine are still denying the murder?'

'I've just given a statement to the press...'

'I know – the story's up online already. But they've confessed only to the theft of the ring?'

'Yes,' McGuire confirmed. 'Look, I'm sorry I had to cut you off last night but I had to go and see Welch.'

'Is he still being a problem?'

'Not since we found the diamond ring sewn into the shoulder-pad of a dress.'

Pearl paused to take this in, then said: 'So that was a good tip-off I gave you about Rosine having been a seamstress?'

'Good thing I happened to ask you too,' he pointedly reminded her.

'So what now?' She took off her jacket and hung it by the door in the kitchen.

'They'll be released.'

'What? You're letting them go?' she asked, shocked.

'On bail,' he explained. 'With conditions to report to the station.'

'I see. So, you're going to keep them under surveillance?'

McGuire remained silent as another officer passed by quickly on the stairs.

'McGuire?'

'I'm still here.'

'What do you think about this? I mean, it's perfectly possible that Faye may have discovered about the ring, confronted Luc and Rosine and they resorted to murder to silence her?'

'Forensics say it's unlikely Rosine could have inflicted the stab wound.'

'Due to her height and stature, you mean?'

'The force required and the angle of entry indicate that the killer was much taller.'

'And stronger,' mused Pearl. 'Like Luc? If he

had murdered Faye, Rosine would still be guilty of conspiracy to murder.'

'Yes. Except he now has an alibi,' McGuire informed her. 'During questioning, Barbara March suddenly remembered that she had heard him coughing around one-thirty-five a.m. So he was still in the house.'

'How can she be so sure about the time?'

'Because she says it was shortly after the dog had begun barking.'

'Ah yes...' said Pearl thoughtfully. 'The dog.'

'It seems possible that the barking woke Luc, though not Rosine. He said he got up to get a drink of water.'

'From the kitchen?'

'No, the en-suite bathroom. Then he insists he returned to bed.' McGuire had just reached the ground floor where he leaned back against the wall. 'Barbara March had always remembered the dog barking – but nothing more until now.'

'Until it became important,' Pearl commented.

'Well, that's often the way it goes,' said McGuire. 'A witness swears they don't remember...'

'But they do,' Pearl went on. 'It's just faulty recall. The memories are still there, but the challenge is coming up with a way to retrieve them.'

'Finding the right trigger,' said McGuire. 'Which seems to be the case here.'

'Unless Barbara is lying, of course.'

'Yes. It's possible she's involved in the theft – *and* the murder.'

Pearl paused on the other end of the line. 'But if Rosine broke down in questioning and implicated Luc, why would she protect Barbara?'

McGuire thought about this. 'Maybe to offer Luc an alibi that only Barbara could provide for him?'

'Intriguing,' murmured Pearl.

The ground-floor door to the police station opened and a young constable acknowledged McGuire as he passed by to take the stairs.

'I'm sorry, Pearl, but I have to go,' McGuire decided.

'Me too.' Pearl glanced at the clock on the kitchen wall, then bit her lip before asking, 'I ... don't suppose you're fond of archaeology, are you?'

'Why?'

'It doesn't matter,' she said hurriedly. 'Let's talk later.' The call ended and she slipped on her Whitstable Pearl apron.

After the lunchtime service was over, Pearl sat across the marble table from Barbara March in the conservatory in Arden House.

'I just can't believe it,' said Barbara, shaking her head, 'that Luc and Rosine could possibly have done something so stupid. What on earth were they thinking?'

'I'm not sure "stupid" is the right word,' said Pearl. 'It was an audacious plan – quite brilliant, in fact – and had it not been for Faye's murder, the theft might have taken a very long time to discover, well after their probationary period was up. They could have left Faye's employment and gone anywhere – and there would have been nothing to incriminate them. The real diamond ring could have been passed on here, in the UK.

222

There may even have been a buyer already in place. It was a well-thought-out plan, not a rash, opportunistic action on their part, but ... Faye's murder changed everything.'

Barbara reflected on this. 'I'm relieved you don't think they're capable of murder.'

'You don't think they are either?'

'To be perfectly honest – no.' Barbara paused. 'I've thought about it, of course, but the answer still has to be no. I think they're young and foolish and possibly tired of ministering to others.'

'To Faye?'

'Perhaps. They had both been in service previously. Maybe in Monaco, Luc caught a glimpse of the life he would rather be leading.'

'And Rosine?'

'She seems a simple girl, uncomplicated – easily led, maybe?' Barbara frowned. 'Isn't there something called a *folie à deux*? A form of madness that can affect two people in a close relationship and cause them to commit crime – like, say, Bonnie and Clyde.'

'Bonnie and Clyde did commit murder,' said Pearl. 'But it would seem Luc and Rosine did *not* kill Faye.' As Barbara looked up at her, Pearl went on: 'You remembered something of the night of Faye's murder?'

'Yes. I heard Luc coughing soon after that dog began barking.'

'So now Luc has an alibi,' said Pearl starkly. 'Lucky for him.'

'If you think there's more to it than my memory being jogged, I can assure you that you're wrong. That police inspector is very thorough. He went

223

over every detail of the evening and that helped me to remember.' She took a deep breath and sighed lengthily. 'So what now?'

'No doubt that's a question for Inspector Mc-Guire.'

Barbara leaned forward and pinched the bridge of her nose. 'I'm sorry. I feel so very tired.' Pearl saw how true this was. Barbara actually looked a ghost of the woman she had met only a few days ago. On her arrival in Whitstable, she had appeared businesslike, savvy and in control, but now, in contrast, she seemed lost and directionless.

Pearl heard herself say, 'If there's anything I can do, you will let me know?'

Barbara looked back at Pearl, her eyes filled with grief and confusion, but they conveyed something else – an entreaty of some kind, thought Pearl, though for what, she couldn't say, as Barbara did not enlighten her.

'Thank you,' was all she said.

A few minutes later, Pearl left, and once back on the pavement, she looked up at Arden House. The white plantation blinds were almost down so that the windows appeared like heavily lidded eyes, laden with sorrow like those of Barbara March. Pearl headed immediately right, as though returning to town, but then deftly took the side-turning adjoining the property and found herself on the access path that separated the Tankerton Road properties from the Castle.

Counting the rear gates along from Arden House, Pearl finally stood facing that of Ravenswood, its garden fenced off from the access path by some pine-slat panelling. Pearl put her eye close to a knot in the wood and through it obtained a view of a fairly large, attractive garden that was somewhat bohemian in appearance. A Buddha statue overlooked a pond and a day-bed strewn with large Moroccan cushions. Several batik shirts hung on a carousel dryer on the lawn that was spinning gently on the warm breeze but, much closer to Pearl, on the other side of the fence from the access path, she spied a small, simple structure and recognised immediately what it was. Taking her mobile phone from her bag, she dialled a stored number.

'Which room did Luc and Rosine occupy at Arden House?' she asked.

McGuire replied, 'First floor at the back of the house.'

'Facing the garden?'

'That's right.'

'How about the en-suite?'

'Same. Why?'

Pearl glanced across at the rear of Arden house, its windows clearly visible above the fence.

'Pearl?' he asked cagily.

'I think I may have an important question for you to ask someone,' she replied.

That evening, Pearl stepped out of the shower and searched for something to wear. She hadn't quite sorted out a proper spring wardrobe and the weather was proving to be too unpredictable to go out in a summer dress without a shawl or jacket in reserve. As she flicked through several items on hangers, part of her began to wish that she had invited McGuire along for the talk this evening, but she was torn because the other, greater part of her was looking forward to spending time with Charlie and hearing what her son had been up to, in Berlin, and since his return. It was also a rare thing to receive an invitation from Dolly to dinner – one that Pearl was not likely to reject. Regarding her choice of clothes, she opted for comfort with a pretty white top and some loose blue trousers.

Beyond her bedroom window the tide was fully out, revealing a landscape that might appear desolate to some, if they had missed the bait-diggers at work on the mudflats, soon to be followed by flocks of gulls. Pearl swept up her dark hair then let it fall again. Over the years, she had sometimes thought of cutting it much shorter and then thought again, since it was an intrinsic part of her image. She wasn't vain and had little time for clothes shopping or even putting on much make-up, but sometimes she wished she could be a little better groomed. She found herself wondering what kind of woman McGuire was really attracted to and reflected on her reaction to seeing him with the elegant managing agent in Canterbury. It hadn't been jealousy that she had felt that day but instead something more akin to a mixture of embarrassment and disappointment on discovering him with a beautiful woman.

Trying not to think any more about this, she looked on her dressing table and found some pink nail polish. She hadn't used it for months as she wasn't able to wear it when preparing food at the restaurant and it chipped too easily when she was gardening. That thought made her consider her neglected allotment, realising how there would be little time to visit it until Faye's murder was finally solved. She worked quickly and had just finished painting her last nail when her mobile sounded. It was bad timing but she managed to take the call, only realising, once she held the phone to her ear, that the fresh nail polish had stuck to her hair.

'Damn.'

'What?' McGuire sounded confused on the other end of the line.

'Me – not you,' she said quickly. 'Why're you calling?'

'To tell you that you were right.'

She smiled. 'You've spoken to the dog-owner?'

'Mr Loman. A saxophonist.'

'Jazz, I'll bet,' said Pearl. 'That's what his shirts say.'

'I didn't ask,' McGuire replied. 'It's not relevant.'

'Everything's relevant until we find the murderer.'

McGuire continued on, 'He keeps late hours – and has a Malamute called Alaska.'

'And the dog sleeps in the kennel in the garden on the other side of the fence from the rear access path?'

'That's right. Gets too warm for her in the house, apparently.'

'And that's definitely the same dog that was heard barking on the night of the murder?'

'Almost certainly. It went on for a while. From around just after one-thirty a.m.'

'And possibly as a reaction to something taking place in the Castle grounds,' said Pearl, 'or just across from the shrubbery on Gatehouse Walk.'

'Well, whatever the dog heard,' McGuire said, 'the owner checked his watch at one-forty-five, realised he couldn't leave the animal to continue barking and finally came out to quieten her. He'd already told my officers a few days ago that he had heard nothing more that night.'

'But he did *see* something?' asked Pearl, in anticipation.

McGuire left her in suspense a moment longer, before replying, 'In the garden, on his way back into the house, he happened to look up, and saw a light go off in a first-floor window.'

'At Arden House?

'Yes – the window to the bathroom. A moment or two later, Loman says a man appeared at another window – this time the one belonging to the adjoining bedroom – and closed it. Loman identified the man as Luc Mercier.'

'So,' Pearl said thoughtfully, 'Barbara was telling the truth. Luc couldn't have been at the Castle at the time the murder was taking place.' She paused. 'So he couldn't possibly have murdered Faye Marlow.'

Chapter Seventeen

The conference room at the local library held almost a hundred people and promised to be filled to capacity for Oliver Hewett's talk. Dolly had made sure to arrive early in order to save good seats for Pearl, Charlie and Jean Wheeler, who, in turn, had each told many others about the evening's event.

As people began to arrive, Pearl was surprised to see Jerry and Annabel Wheeler among them. The couple managed to find seats in a nearby row and Annabel exchanged only the briefest glance with Pearl – nothing more to reveal their recent meeting. For a moment, Pearl considered the story that Jean had relayed about the cocktail party thrown by Faye Marlow all those years ago. Faye may have flirted with Oliver Hewett – just as she had flirted with Jerry on the night of her death – but Oliver was no longer a rival for Jerry, if indeed he had ever been one. The last two decades had revealed him only to be a respected archaeologist and a devoted family man. His conduct had been impeccable.

Pearl glanced around the room at the number of people taking their seats in readiness to hear what Oliver was about to impart. If only she had lived, Faye could have been one of them but, instead, her body now lay in a chilled drawer at the police morgue. An impressive banner on the stage showed the title of the lecture: *Simply Stones*. Pearl imagined that Purdy might have arranged that for her father's event but, as she was reflecting on this, someone came up beside her and broke her train of thought.

'Made it,' said Nathan. He held up two tickets. 'These are like gold dust.'

'You were lucky then,' said Pearl. 'Who's the other one for?'

'I invited Barbara,' he whispered. 'She's not been feeling too well lately, which is hardly surprising in the circumstances – and I didn't think she would be recognised here tonight, apart from by anyone who came along to the reception. It'll do her good to be out, and besides, you said this was going to be interesting.'

'Yes,' said Pearl thoughtfully. 'I'm sure it will be.'

At that moment the lights in the lecture hall dimmed and some spotlights were thrown onto the stage. It was only now that Pearl noticed Purdy, seated at the side of the stage, operating a laptop for her father's presentation. The first image showed the beach at Tankerton Slopes. The young woman was dressed soberly in black tonight, perhaps out of respect to Faye's passing. Maria then emerged from a door next to the stage and whispered something to her daughter. Purdy listened carefully before nodding and Maria took another seat offstage, characteristically out of the spotlight. She was clutching a clipboard, attached to which were numerous sheets of paper, giving Pearl the impression that Maria was taking on the role of prompt for her husband. She was dressed in a pretty floral smock and linen trousers, and her hair was tied up into a neat ponytail. She had also applied a touch of pink lipstick and, overall, her appearance and solemn expression showed that she was conscious of the responsible role she had to play in tonight's event.

As the lights dimmed further, Pearl spotted a figure entering, almost unnoticed. Nathan stood up as Barbara approached and offered a polite kiss to her cheek, gesturing to the empty seat beside him. Pearl then caught sight of another familiar face. It was Marty Smith, who raised a hand in what Pearl took to be a conciliatory salute following his display of temper the other evening. He then gave her a wink and a cheerful nod, indicating that someone was approaching to take a seat beside her. To Marty's obvious relief it was Charlie and not McGuire.

Pearl barely had time to greet her son before a ripple of applause announced the entry of Oliver Hewett into the room. Dressed in a smart black suit, he climbed the stage and took a seat there while his companion, a middle-aged man attired less formally in a beige linen jacket and corduroy trousers, addressed the audience with a hand-held microphone, introducing himself as Dr Terence Rodgers of Whitstable's Archaeological Trust. Dr Rodgers thanked everyone for coming and announced that he was there to explain a little about the Trust's work before he would hand over to the special guest for the evening – Professor Oliver Hewett.

Another ripple of applause went around the room and Dr Rodgers continued, 'The Trust is immensely grateful to Professor Hewett for all the important work he has done in contributing, not only to local archaeological knowledge, but regarding sites on the other side of the world.'

The mere suggestion of Bonampak had Dolly chomping at the bit. 'Get on with it,' she uttered under her breath as Rodgers continued with his introduction. Pearl gave her mother an admonishing look but Dolly, unrepentant, hissed: 'I paid to see the organ-grinder, not the monkey.' Pearl then gave her full attention to Dr Rodgers in an effort to disassociate herself from any further comments

231

from Dolly, but thankfully, the man soon began to wind up his opening speech.

'So, without any further delay, please welcome ... Professor Oliver Hewett.' As if echoing Dolly's own impatience, the hall now erupted with loud applause.

As Oliver Hewett came forward to take the microphone, Pearl was surprised to see Purdy rise to her feet too. Oliver began, 'As a short prelude to what I have to say this evening, I'd like to invite my daughter to read a poem, the words of which have resonated powerfully for me in connection with my work throughout the years. Purdy?'

Purdy now joined her father centre-stage. Taking a piece of paper from her pocket, she carefully unfolded it as though it contained a precious item, then she cleared her throat slightly before announcing into the microphone, '"The Barrow". By Anthony Thwaite.' She glanced towards her mother, who gently nodded, and like a child reading at a school assembly, Purdy began to recite.

'In this high field strewn with stones
I walk by a green mound,
Its edges sheared by the plough.
Crumbs of animal bone
Lie smashed and scattered round
Under the clover leaves
And slivers of flint seem to grow
Like white leaves among green.
In the wind, the chestnut heaves
Where a man's grave has been.'

Purdy's face clouded for a moment and she

looked up, as though fearful, but on recognising that she now had the full attention of everyone in the hall, she summoned some confidence and continued with the second verse.

'Whatever the barrow held
Once, has been taken away:
A hollow of nettles and dock
Lies at the centre, filled
With rain from a sky so grey
It reflects nothing at all.'

She paused again, and Pearl now imagined that with those words, the girl might have been taken back to last Monday, when they had come upon Faye's body in the driving rain ... but once again Purdy composed herself and went on with the poem. This time, she did so not as a simple recital, but as though she was intimately connected to the words themselves – as though they spoke for – and through – her.

'I poke in the crumbled rock
For something they left behind
But after that funeral
There is nothing at all to find.

On the map in front of me
The gothic letters pick out
Dozens of tombs like this,
Breached, plundered, left empty,
No fragments littered about
Of a dead and buried race
In the margins of histories.'

233

She looked up once more and glanced towards her father, but Oliver reassured her with a smile. And so she read on.

'No fragments: these splintered bones
Construct no human face,
These stones are simply stones.
In museums their urns lie
Behind glass, and their shaped flints
Are labelled like butterflies.
All that they did was die,
And all that has happened since
Means nothing to this place.
Above long clouds, the skies
Turn to a brilliant red
And show in the water's face
One living, and not these dead.'

A silence fell during what appeared to be a time-less moment ... until Purdy released her attention from the words in her hands and Oliver began clapping. The audience quickly followed suit and Maria too, radiant with pride, began applauding her daughter. Oliver came forward and Purdy handed the microphone back to him before taking up her place once more at the laptop.

'Thank you, Purdy,' he said, then turned his attention once more to the audience. 'You'll no doubt have noted that the title of this talk is taken from some of the words of that poem – *Simply Stones* – and the reason for this is that while many of us consider them to be nothing more, to an archaeologist, the stones we find – the fragments,

234

the splintered bones and the many tombs we have the fortune to investigate – are so much more. They are our clues to the past.'

He nodded to Purdy. 'I'd like to begin with slides from the upper foreshore on the western part of Tankerton Bay where, in 1995, members of the Oyster Coast Fossil Society noticed that some erosion from the sea had exposed the first important clues of what had once been the first industrial-scale chemical production in this country.'

As Purdy obliged with a slide, Oliver Hewett began to speak in a way Pearl had never heard him do before – with true passion. Slide after slide was produced, extraordinary images of a buried landscape on Whitstable's shores, but it was Oliver's enthusiasm and respect for his subject that brought this particular project alive – along with a vibrant picture of the men, women and children who had once powered this long-forgotten industry with their labour. He charted the archaeological finds: the lead seals from the Tudor period, iron nails, the tooth of a wool comb and the fragments of a wooden vessel that had survived centuries of a seawater environment.

In due course, he moved on to speak about the Mayan murals at Bonampak, and as he did so, Pearl noted that Dolly was lost in rapt attention – as were many others, Marty included. Oliver Hewett, the man generally considered to be a dry academic was, in fact, an inspiring storyteller resurrecting for a brief time the lives of those who had gone before. All at once, it became clear to Pearl why Oliver's wife and daughter should be so obviously devoted to him and why colleagues at the Archaeological Trust, and all over the world, should have held him in such high esteem. He was an academic – and one among many – but what separated him from others was his gift of communicating a complex subject in the most brilliant but accessible way.

One thing alone was hard for Pearl to grasp: the unanswered question of how Faye Marlow could ever have hoped to hold the attention of a man like this. Only a partner like Maria, a woman willing to accept a role in her husband's life that would surely remain secondary to his subject, could ever gain a proper place in his heart. The picture of Faye Marlow in Pearl's mind, constructed from every statement she had gathered in the past few days, was of someone who needed to remain centre-stage – especially where men were concerned. Many years ago she may have chased after Oliver Hewett, but it was evident that Oliver, at least, had recognised that a long-term relationship between them would never work. He had gone on to marry Maria and had made a perfect match for himself, while Faye had married Alain Severin, a film producer who would have been aware that he had captured a star – and had signalled this with the extravagant gift of a precious but ostentatious diamond ring.

Pearl glanced around the room to see Nathan, sitting bolt upright, focusing on the story Oliver was relaying of how an American photographer and explorer by the name of Giles Healey had been led to the Bonampak ruins by the local Lacandon Maya, who still prayed in the ancient temples. It was a tale that bore all the hallmarks of an Indiana Jones film – and yet it was true.

Beside Nathan, Barbara sat motionless, but her expression was tense, leading Pearl to wonder if she was suffering from one of her headaches. Jerry Wheeler was listening intently but with his arms folded across his chest, perhaps as a subconscious sign of hostility towards Oliver, while Annabel was engaged in the talk, but sitting with her crossed legs pointing away from her husband as though they might have been complete strangers. Marty's jaw had dropped slightly open, a sure sign that he was caught up in Oliver's story, while Dolly and Charlie's gazes remained fixed on the stage, fully engrossed in a slide showing a stunning Mayan mural – until the rustle of a sweet wrapper caused them to glance accusingly at Jean Wheeler. She looked guilty for a moment then popped the sweet in her mouth and hid the wrapper in her pocket as she concentrated once more on the talk.

Oliver was reaching his conclusion now, conveying a summation of all that he had said so far. 'And so, while it may be something of a cliché to say that we cannot know where we are going until we know where we have been, our lives and the landscape we occupy are inextricably linked with those who have gone before us. Perhaps by acknowledging those antecedents with true respect for the clues they have left behind, we can build on what went before us and so make a better future for those who are sure to follow us.' He signalled to Purdy, who clicked off the final slide before applause began to ring out.

In that moment, Pearl found herself suddenly

and instinctively aware that somewhere within this room, buried among the many small observations she had made in the past few days, the answer to Faye's murder lay waiting for her to uncover it – just as the fragments left by others throughout the centuries had led Oliver Hewett to his own buried truth.

After the event was over, Pearl, Dolly and Charlie were heading towards Harbour Street but making slow progress as Dolly kept pausing to study images from the book she had bought straight after the lecture. Oliver Hewett had signed it for her, in a general and simple way, but she insisted on re-reading the inscription several times as she had been so impressed with the lecture.

'Absolutely riveting,' she enthused.

'Yes,' Pearl agreed. 'But you have mentioned that several times.'

'Have I?' asked Dolly, dawdling again as she looked down at Oliver's book. *'Simply Stones,'* she said. 'Good title. For the book – and the lecture.'

'Yes Gran,' Charlie agreed, exchanging a look with Pearl before attempting to divert Dolly's attention by saying, 'So ... where are we going for supper?'

'I told you. It's a surprise.'

'Any chance we could get a move on, then?' suggested Pearl. 'We don't want them giving our table to someone else.'

'Oh, there's no chance of that,' Dolly said with conviction.

'Good,' said Charlie. 'But gee up, Gran. I'm starving.'

'You're always starving,' Dolly told him. 'I don't know where you put it. If I ate half of what you do I would be the size of the Taj Mahal – and no comments!' she added quickly. 'But I promised you dinner, and dinner I shall provide. Come on. Look lively!' Slipping Oliver's book into the huge carpet bag she carried over her shoulder, she marched on ahead, leaving Charlie and Pearl to catch her up.

At the Horsebridge, Dolly took a sharp left turn and beckoned to Pearl and Charlie before barrelling onwards. For a moment, her daughter and grandson were left with the impression that Dolly's choice of restaurant might be one of the fine establishments facing seawards but, curiously, she continued on as if heading towards the Old Neptune pub, which was situated on the beach itself. This made no sense since there would have been a quicker route from the High Street via two of the alleys on offer – Bonners followed by Squeeze Gut – but Dolly trundled on, with Pearl and Charlie following in her wake. It was almost sunset and the sky looked beautiful, streaked with red, though a single dark cloud speared the lowering sun. The tide had turned and Dolly finally halted near a bench on the beach.

'What a perfect spot,' she decided.

'Yes,' Pearl agreed, 'it is. But what about our dinner?'

Dolly turned to her. 'You know, I really should have called you Patience,' she said. 'Because you could certainly do with some. Just relax, will you?' She took the carpet bag from her shoulder and pulled from it Oliver's book, which she gave

239

Charlie to hold, followed by a brightly coloured blanket, which she spread on the beach. Using the bag much as a magician might use a top hat, she now proceeded to produce from it: three beakers, napkins, cutlery and a bottle of wine around which was wrapped a silver cooler. She then sat down and looked up at Pearl and Charlie as though bewildered. 'Well, what are you waiting for?' She made a large expansive gesture with her arms as she announced: 'The table is laid.'

Before Charlie or Pearl could utter a word, a bell sounded loudly and heads turned to see a young man cycling along the prom. He drew up, leaned his bike against the prom wall then took something from the basket attached to the handlebars and brought it across.

'Here you go, Dolly,' he smiled. 'Jimmy said to tell you that's only,' he checked his watch, 'three minutes from the fryer.' He handed a plastic bag to her, but before it could even be opened, Pearl and Charlie knew exactly what it was.

'Fish and chips,' said Charlie. 'Fantastic! I haven't had any for months.'

'Don't you think I guessed that?' said Dolly proudly. She unwrapped the packages as though they were gifts to open on Christmas morning. 'Cod for me, rock salmon for you, Charlie, and skate for you, Pearl.' She rummaged in the bag. 'There's salt and vinegar here and Jimmy's even put in some lemon too, and ... three *wallies*.' She beamed, victorious, as she brandished a trio of pickled cucumbers. 'Now Pearl, pass the wine, will you?' She poured three beakers of white wine and gave one to Charlie and Pearl in turn before raising her own. The setting sun fell upon it as she said warmly: 'Welcome home, Charlie.' He leaned across to give her a kiss. 'Thanks, Gran. It's really good to be here.'

Pearl remained silent, simply treasuring the moment. Dolly's supper had indeed been a surprise; in her mother's own unique style she had chosen the most idyllic venue and, for the occasion, the perfect menu. Pearl was now convinced she had been right not to invite McGuire to what was essentially a family reunion. Charlie tucked into his meal, eating chips with his fingers as Dolly used her cutlery on her cod. The bench close by had been installed on the beach to commemorate the peace campaigner, Brian Haw. Dolly had helped with a local campaign to fund it and the message carved into its side panel seemed to echo the serenity of the moment: *Wage Peace.*

Charlie asked: 'So how's your tooth now, Gran?'

With a mouthful of food, Dolly was unable to reply so Pearl did it for her.

'Much better after a visit to Dr Fang.'

'Dr Fang?' echoed Charlie. 'You've got to be kidding me.'

Dolly shook her head. 'Not at all. That is, indeed, his name though pronounced "Fong" in Cantonese.'

'Cool,' said Charlie.

'Which reminds me,' Dolly went on. 'I found some more.'

'More what?' asked Pearl.

'Dentists?' Charlie wondered, confused.

'Names that reflect professions. How about these for a few more examples: Brenda Song, the

241

singer. Bob Rock...'

'The music producer!' said Charlie. 'Yeah, he produced albums for Bon Jovi and Metallica.'

'Anna Smashnova?'

'The tennis player,' Pearl remembered.

'Peter Bowler?'

Pearl looked foxed but Charlie explained, 'Cricketer – but he was in fact mainly a batsman.'

'Don't split hairs,' ordered Dolly, continuing on. 'Lord Brain – neurologist. Igor Judge – Lord Chief Justice of England and Wales. And how about Margaret Court?'

'Yes,' said Pearl, a little wearily. 'Another tennis player.'

'How's this?' said Charlie. 'Usain Bolt – world record sprinter!'

'And my favourite,' said Dolly. 'A book on the Polar regions written by ... Daniel Snowman.' She giggled to herself, then looked down at their supper plates. 'You might even consider this meal, you know.'

Pearl and Charlie looked blank for a moment before the penny dropped for Charlie. 'Cooked by Jimmy Fryar. Of course! Wow. That's amazing, Gran.'

'Yes,' said Dolly proudly. 'A rose by any other name would smell as sweet. But if you think about it, the names we attach to things are usually very important, which is why I named my darling daughter Pearl.' She took another large gulp of wine and gazed at Pearl with a certain squiffy bonhomie. 'It was a wonderful talk tonight, wasn't it?' she said once again.

'Yeah,' said Charlie. 'I'm really glad I made it

along. The whole thing was pretty magical.' He looked up. 'I never realised Oliver Hewett was such a cool guy. And that poem ... what was it called?

'"The Barrow",' Pearl remembered.

'Yes,' said Dolly. 'Young Purdy gave a great performance reading it, don't you think?'

Pearl had heard her mother's words but she was busy imagining the thrill of finding a piece of half-buried treasure. She felt she could almost see it – and yet she couldn't be sure quite what it was.

'Mum?'

Pearl's attention snapped back with Charlie's voice.

'You OK?' he asked, seeing she was miles away.

'I'm absolutely fine,' she replied, losing herself in her son's beautiful blue eyes, so like those of his father, Carl.

It was almost 10.30 before Pearl arrived home. Charlie had headed back to Canterbury on his scooter and Pearl had walked Dolly home. It was true that working together sometimes created a spiky quality to their relationship but nevertheless it was built on an unshakable foundation of love. Closing her front door behind her, Pearl experienced the warm glow of satisfaction she always felt after spending some quality time with family, particularly with her son. During the evening, she had managed to forget about the restaurant, her unfinished plans for the allotment and even about Faye's murder for a while, though something still gnawed.

Moving over to her laptop, she switched it on,

243

gazing for a moment at the new screensaver she had recently selected by mistake. It consisted of a dark-blue night sky, studded with numerous planets. Staring into the cosmos for a moment, she allowed herself to imagine that she was truly travelling back in space before she decided to search for an image. It took a few seconds for the icon to fill her screen: and then The Lady of Vladimir appeared, wearing her dark veil sprinkled with gold stars. There was something haunting about the image – something that Pearl felt the Madonna had yet to communicate to her. The icon was symbolic of a mother's love: the Infant Christ nestled against Mary's cheek reminded Pearl of the vulnerability of her own child as well as the close relationship she had with her own mother – but the ring-less hand kept drawing her mind back to Faye and the way Luc and Rosine had abused her trust.

Pearl now searched for the poem whose words still echoed in her mind from the earlier lecture. She found it. 'The Barrow' by Anthony Thwaite – and read the poem through now, at her own pace, dwelling over certain lines. She came to: *These stones are simply stones./In museums their urns lie/Behind glass, and their shaped flints/Are labelled like butterflies. All that they did was die...*'The words succeeded in expressing the inexpressible and brought Pearl back to that first day in the conservatory at Arden House, when a white butterfly had flitted between orchids on the warm air. Something significant had happened that day but she couldn't quite pin down what it was.

Waves were sounding gently outside the window with the returning tide, restful, meditative – until

244

Pilchard suddenly jumped up on to her lap. For a three-legged cat, he was surprisingly agile, and was soon joined by his brother, Sprat, who decided to position himself by the computer screen, trying to rival it for Pearl's attention. She stroked each cat in turn, thinking about their names, which had been given to them by their previous owner to reflect their love of fish. Then, suddenly, it came to Pearl – the half-buried piece of treasure now seemed almost within her grasp. A link to the past. To everything. It was there before her – but now she knew it had been there all along.

She reached for her mobile, which had remained switched off all evening – since the beginning of Oliver Hewett's talk, in fact. Scanning her voice-mail she found no new messages from McGuire or, for that matter, from anyone else. She then checked her contacts for a name and a number and, in spite of the late hour, made a call. The dial tone sounded several times and Pearl was about to give up when the call finally connected.

'I know it's late,' she said, 'but I wonder if I could possibly talk to you tomorrow?' She paused. 'It's about something extremely important.'

Chapter Eighteen

The Tuesday-morning sky was finally clearing of cloud, which seemed fitting as it reflected Pearl's clarity of thinking as she climbed Tower Hill to the Tea Gardens. The old servery was not yet open and the lawn was empty of visitors and families but she spied a figure, dressed in a light beige raincoat, sitting on the bench just beyond the boundary, staring out to sea.

'Thanks so much for coming,' Pearl said as she approached. Barbara March was about to get to her feet but Pearl pressed her to stay seated and took a place beside her.

'Your message sounded urgent,' Barbara said.

'It was,' Pearl replied. 'It suddenly occurred to me last night that something Oliver Hewett had said during his talk was exactly right. That the clues to the past are all around us, but once we've completed the search we need to put them together correctly.'

'Like the right ingredients to make the perfect meal?'

Pearl smiled. 'You remembered.'

'Yes. You said that on the first day we met at the house. Faye had asked what you could possibly find to investigate in a small town like this.' Barbara broke off for a moment. 'If we'd only known then.' A chill seemed to go through her and she shivered and looked out to sea again. 'You know, in spite of everything that's happened, I still find this place to be very calming.'

Pearl nodded. 'I know,' she said. 'I feel the same way.'

Barbara offered up the ghost of a smile. 'I think you and I are alike in many ways, Pearl. We work hard, we take pride in what we do and, while everyone else might be floundering, we're the ones who offer a safe haven – just like that harbour down there.' She glanced towards the masts of fishing boats swaying in the distance, then her smile faded. 'Since Faye's death, I've come here most days – just to sit and watch.'

'Watch?' asked Pearl, trying to see what it was that was holding Barbara's attention.

'The sea,' she said simply. 'I spent a long time looking after Faye and I realise now how I forgot that the world still turns without my help. As does the tide. It's reassuring, don't you think? And humbling – to be reminded how unimportant our lives really are. We say we know it. We think we know it.' She raised a finger and tapped her temple very lightly. 'Here. But not here. Not where it counts.' She had placed the palm of her hand firmly against her chest and kept it there as though feeling the beating of her own heart, then she thrust both hands deep into her coat pockets. 'What was it you wanted to ask me?'

Pearl began. 'Oliver's talk last night included details about his study of the murals in Bonampak.'

'Yes. Fascinating, wasn't it?'

'He spent some time there with Maria,' Pearl went on. 'She's been such a support to him and they're a very close-knit family. I find it rather inspiring to watch them together, like last night, with Maria helping him in his work and Purdy contributing by reading that poem. When I got home, I looked for a copy of it on my laptop and I reread it.' She paused, reflecting on the words. 'Then, I thought back to the night of the reception and I began to retrace events. Do you remember that, at one point, Faye disappeared from the marquee? I thought she might be outside with others or having some photographs taken. But the press had left ... and I then remembered Maria asking me if I had seen Oliver. If he had been outside, she wouldn't have needed to ask because she would have seen him. But, in fact, she asked me just as I came out of the Castle, which tells me now that she must have known he was inside.' She paused before she went on: 'I think Faye knew that too.'

Barbara looked at Pearl. 'What are you trying to say?'

'I found it quite difficult to believe but many years ago, Faye and Oliver Hewett had been attracted to one another. There were other relationships for her to come, no doubt, and finally a happy marriage, but after all these years Faye was still able to lead poor, rich Jerry Wheeler by the nose – and he was allowing her to do so – because of his mid-life crisis. But Oliver – he was the one who had got away: the man who had not only rejected Faye, but had left her completely behind – unless, of course, it was Maria who had managed to do that for him? Maria, with her homely looks and figure, was no rival for Faye, but she had given Oliver all that he had needed: dedicated support so he could pursue his career, and her undying love – two things he would never have got from Faye, who was perhaps too vain and possibly too selfish for such love. When Alain Severin died, I presume Faye came to rely on you even more.'

'You are right,' said Barbara. 'In many ways, she and I were like an old married couple who are stuck together, for better or worse.'

Pearl smiled at this, thinking for a moment of

Annabel and Jerry Wheeler before continuing, 'You know, Nathan had told me that Faye was charming, and indeed she certainly could be, but she was an actress and I recognised something of the way she could manipulate others on that day she persuaded Purdy to insist on her parents coming to the screening, and to the reception. Faye was indeed used to getting her own way. She was a star – but somebody once said that a star is someone people pay money to see – and people had stopped paying to see Faye a long time ago.'

When Barbara made no comment, Pearl went on. 'In fact, Faye had been out of the public eye for a long time, but then she suddenly won an award – for Best-Dressed Woman Over Fifty. And then she was offered another chance for more attention, for her fans to see her again – even though they didn't have to pay. At the reception she was fêted by the press – if only by our local papers – but I think the real prize, the real attraction and purpose of this visit for Faye was something else. Or someone else. She was to see Oliver Hewett again – and how crushing it must have been for her to witness his indifference. He was caught up in his work and then he ignored her throughout the screening and spent most of the reception with his wife and daughter. That must have infuriated Faye. So instead she made use of her old fiancé – faithful Jerry Wheeler – to satisfy her need for attention, and to assuage her injured pride. And then, when she was having the last of her photographs taken outside the marquee, she suddenly saw something: Oliver entering the Castle. She followed him inside.'

Pearl turned to Barbara. 'She must have been inside because, if you remember, you came into the kitchen and asked if I needed help with the dessert – and you wouldn't have done that if you'd had to be on hand for Faye. You, too, must have noticed that she was no longer in the marquee. Can you think back, Barbara? I'm sure I can jog your memory as Inspector McGuire did about Luc.'

Barbara nodded. 'OK. Go ahead.'

'This is very important, but that night in the kitchen, my attention was fixed on getting the dessert off the table, although I did hear your footsteps on the Castle's wooden staircase, heading upstairs, and I naturally assumed that you were going to the powder room. I wasn't aware of who else might have been upstairs at that moment. It was only when I returned to the marquee that I noticed that neither Oliver nor Faye were there. But I now believe they may have been in the Holmes Room upstairs in the Castle. If so, could you have heard something?'

'Like what?' Barbara, frowned, lost.

'I'm sorry. I know this must be stressful for you. You mentioned how Luc and Rosine might have grown tired of ministering to Faye, but you had twenty years of doing the same thing, and I know you suffer from migraines.'

'Yes,' said Barbara honestly. 'I admit it wasn't always easy having Faye as an employer but as I've told you: I was grateful for a job and I have travelled all over the world, seen places I would never have got to see and met people I will never forget. I've lived in comfort in the South of France for two decades. It's been a good life.'

250

Pearl acknowledged this. 'But with all due respect, it wasn't really your life, was it? I mean, you never married, never had children of your own. But then neither did Faye, so perhaps you all became your own family? You, Faye...'

'Luc and Rosine?' finished Barbara. 'A rather dysfunctional family, wouldn't you say? My family is dead.'

'Yes, and I'm sorry,' said Pearl. 'Your father died when you were a young woman, didn't he, and your mother when you were even younger?'

'Yes, so I was grateful for Faye and Alain. But after Alain died...'

'There was only Faye,' said Pearl. 'And something Jean Wheeler said, about Faye being childless, just like her son and daughter-in-law, set me thinking. An old Russian icon put an image in my mind of another kind of truth.' She broke off, then continued. 'It showed me the way.'

'I don't understand.' Barbara confessed.

Pearl enlightened her. 'Oliver Hewett may have fallen under Faye's spell – but only briefly. He and Maria were engaged but she forgave him and she made sure that, afterwards, they went as far away as possible, to Mexico – the Chiapas state on the Guatemala border. When they returned, they had a daughter, but Maria never had another child.'

'And you have only one son,' Barbara reminded her.

'True,' said Pearl. 'But Purdy told me how her mother had always wanted more children but that it was not to be. Then something my mother said made me think about the importance of names:

251

how they might shape what we do and what we become. Some names are given for special significance. Purdy, short for Perdita, is not a common name and no doubt most people would associate it with the character in the Shakespeare play *The Winter's Tale*. I thought about this last night but it made no sense to me, then I realised I was looking too deeply. The simple meaning of the name, Perdita, is the "lost girl". And that's precisely what Purdy is – a lost child. The very first day she walked into Arden House, Faye's exact words to her were: *"Enfin, mon enfant."* I only have schoolgirl French and I thought, at the time, that she was simply using a fairly common and affectionate term – but it was more than that. *"Enfin, mon enfant."* – I believe Faye was greeting her long-lost child.'

Barbara said nothing and Pearl continued on. 'Purdy told me she had spoken to Faye over the phone many times. She liked to think that she and Faye were friends, but Faye was actually cultivating a relationship with the daughter she had given away all those years ago ... in exchange for her career. Who better to bring up that child than her own father, the man Purdy resembles so closely – Oliver Hewett.'

At this, Barbara got up and turned away, but Pearl demanded: 'It's true, isn't it? Did Faye arrive in Hollywood for her audition, only to discover she was pregnant with Oliver's child? But he had left her – he had gone to Mexico with Maria. So what happened? Tell me, Barbara. Because I'm sure you know.'

After a moment spent struggling with this

question, Barbara nodded very slowly. 'Faye took it badly,' she said quietly. 'She was distraught. It was the reason she couldn't take the part. She knew the child was Oliver's and she tried to contact him but it was difficult: he wouldn't return her calls and she couldn't write to him, as he was travelling around Guatemala. Faye talked about an abortion, but then my father stepped in. Dad felt that Oliver had a right to know. My father was a great "coper" – we always had that in common. He flew to Guatemala and arranged a meeting with Oliver and Maria. Together, the three of them came up with a plan.'

'For Oliver and Maria to adopt Faye's child?'

Barbara shook her head. 'Not exactly. A legal adoption would have left a trail and Faye was always terrified of a scandal, so she went to Mexico where she gave birth, and where the paperwork was "fixed". She asked only one thing: that her daughter should be called Perdita – Spanish for "the lost girl".'

'Which is what Purdy was,' Pearl sighed. 'Lost to Faye ... while Maria and Oliver brought her up as their own child.'

'Yes. It was agreed there would be no contact with Faye – and indeed, there was none.'

'Until Faye's career was finally over – and a young girl from her home town got in touch with her about the May Day celebrations. Fate at work, perhaps.' Pearl murmured, 'I always wondered why Faye had agreed to come back to Whitstable after all this time.' She paused. 'Did Purdy know? Did she suspect something?'

'Of course not. You might call it Fate, Pearl, but

253

I believe it's something more complicated than that.'

'So, Faye accepted the invitation. Not because of Nathan's persuasion but because she knew she would be meeting her long-lost daughter – *and* Oliver.'

Barbara replied reluctantly, 'The truth is, Purdy was always just a means to an end. And that end was Oliver – *not* Purdy.'

Barbara's words were damning. Pearl shook her head. 'You can't know that for sure.'

'No one knew Faye better than I did,' said Barbara. 'And you're right: Faye *had* cultivated a relationship with Purdy, on the phone and via emails. But ask yourself if she had really cared about her, would she have come back here to turn the poor girl's world upside down? Purdy is an innocent. She was dazzled by Faye, flattered by her attention, her charm. She would have gone anywhere with Faye. If she had been asked.'

'And is that what you heard Faye telling Oliver, that night in the Castle? That he risked losing his daughter to her?'

'He also risked Purdy finding out the truth – that she wasn't Maria's natural child,' said Barbara.

'And so he threatened Faye.' It was a statement, not a question. Barbara said nothing, but she didn't need to.

'Of course he did,' Pearl went on. 'What parent wouldn't go to any lengths to protect their child? Even murder?' She looked at Barbara. 'What else did you overhear him say to Faye in the Castle that night? That he would kill her if she tried to take his daughter away?'

'I didn't hear a thing,' said Barbara stoically.

'Why are you protecting him?' asked Pearl in frustration.

But as Barbara turned back to face her, the grief-filled look in her eyes confirmed to Pearl all she needed to know.

'He didn't kill her, did he?' Pearl said. 'Oliver didn't kill Faye because he didn't need to.' She moved closer. 'That night, after the reception, you came home to Arden House and found a way of luring Faye back to the Castle. Perhaps a message – a note – claiming to be from Oliver.' It then came to her. 'Of course ... Luc said that Faye was staring from the conservatory into the garden, but in fact she must have been planning to head off to the Castle. She thought she was meeting Oliver, so she would have been surprised to find he wasn't there. But you were, Barbara, and you didn't even give her time to cry out.'

As Barbara stood motionless before her, denying nothing, Pearl asked her, 'Was she standing with her back to the maypole when you stabbed her with the knife you had taken from the marquee table earlier? It would have been easy enough for you to have slipped that into your bag during the drama with Jean Wheeler at the reception. Everyone was distracted. No one would have noticed. And having stabbed Faye through the heart you were strong enough to support the body while you tied it to the maypole. Why? Was it to make it look as though this was the work of a maniac – a psychopath – as everyone had assumed? But instead ... it was an execution. You must have hated Faye very much, to go to those lengths.'

Barbara gave a deep sigh. 'No. I didn't hate Faye at all, but I knew her too well. I would have put up with her to my dying days or until she got tired of putting up with me, but why should others have their future destroyed because of mistakes they made in the past? Oliver had threatened Faye – and though I had no way of knowing if he would ever go through with murder, I knew that Maria had even more to lose. Purdy would always be her father's daughter, but Maria...' She turned to face Pearl and said passionately, 'Why would I stand by and allow a family to be torn apart?'

'And *that's* the reason you killed Faye?' asked Pearl, incredulous.

'What better reason could I have?' Barbara asked, her voice calm – showing that she was once more in control. 'Pearl, I always hoped that you and I would one day find time for a proper conversation, but I never dreamed for one moment it would be this one.'

'With you admitting to murder?'

Barbara shook her head slowly. 'No. I haven't admitted to anything. We're simply discussing an hypothesis of yours. There's no evidence ... no proof at all that I committed any crime.'

'The Criminal Prosecution Service will have to decide that.'

'Based on what?' Barbara asked. 'These ... suggestions? That's all they are, and they amount to no more than circumstantial evidence. You cannot prove a thing, Pearl, and if you choose to go to the police with this story, you'll achieve exactly what Faye had wanted – *and* what Oliver was so adamant he could never allow. Right now, Purdy believes she is the daughter of loving parents. True, she felt a link to Faye. And they were indeed linked. By blood. By genes. *But nothing else.* Last night, when she was reading the poem for her father, for a moment, I could see Faye, standing on stage again, keeping an audience in thrall. The girl has her mother's skill for performance. But do you really want to shatter her world?'

'You can't possibly believe I could keep this to myself,' said Pearl. 'What if someone else were to come under suspicion?'

'Luc? Rosine? No. Rosine would not have been physically capable of Faye's murder, and Luc has an alibi.' She held Pearl's look.

'Given to him by you,' said Pearl, light dawning. 'But you didn't hear him, did you?'

'No,' Barbara admitted. 'Luc and Rosine may be guilty of stealing a diamond but they're innocent of Faye's murder, so it caused me a dilemma, knowing they might be charged by the police.'

'And why would you have worried?' Pearl demanded. 'You hardly have respect for the truth!'

'I do,' said Barbara. 'But I respect some things more: such as the love of a child for her family. That's something I know. Something that I understand. And I believe you know it too. I have lived and worked in Hollywood, Pearl, where the one thing we believe in ... is pretence.'

'And now you want *me* to pretend.' said Pearl. 'To allow you to get away with murder.'

'I promise you, Pearl, I shan't get away with a thing. If you believe in karma, you'll know that life has its own way of righting wrongs.' She slipped her hand into her pocket and pulled out a small bottle of pills, which she passed to Pearl. 'Dia-morphine. A palliative – not a cure. And for something more serious than migraine. I am eight weeks into a six-month sentence – what you'd call a hopeless case. And I know that, because my mother died of the same form of cancer.'

Pearl looked again at the bottle then handed it back to Barbara, asking. 'Who else knows about this?'

'My doctor in France – and the doctor you referred me to, who kindly prescribed these for me. And you, of course.'

A silence fell and an unexpected wave of sympathy washed over Pearl. 'I'm sorry,' she said truthfully.

'It's all right,' Barbara responded. 'The prospect of death has given me great clarity. It unclouded my mind, stripped away all the unimportant things, and people, that we allow to waste our time and ... our lives. Confronting this lack of time has given me a curious sense of liberation. In this vulnerable state of health, I am, in other ways, invincible. Unless, of course, you think otherwise?'

In a gentle voice she went on: 'I'm sorry, Pearl. I've confronted *you* with a moral choice. It's a great responsibility and whatever you choose to do, I want you to know that I shan't blame you.' She added finally, 'I just wish you hadn't been such a good detective.'

After those words, Barbara March began to walk slowly back towards the Tea Gardens in the direction of Arden House. Left alone, Pearl could hear the soft clink of bowls being played on the Castle green, but she looked down the slopes to where the full tide was washing against the shore, and she moved towards it, drawn in the direction of her home and her family – two things that seemed all she could count on and be sure of now.

In spite of Oliver's lecture, it was still hard to imagine that an industry had once flourished on the shore beneath her feet, vanishing as easily as the lives of those who had worked within it. Only traces had remained, revealed finally by the tide, for someone as dogged as Oliver Hewett to find: someone who recognised that the clues left behind would always be more than simply stones – although, as Pearl now realised, there would be truths that even he would rather remained buried.

Chapter Nineteen

On Wednesday – the day that always signalled the delivery of the local *Courier* to homes in Whitstable – a teenaged newspaper-boy, with waxed hair and a mountain bike, dropped a copy of the paper through Pearl's letterbox and headed on along Island Wall to complete his round.

On the other side of the front door to Seaspray Cottage, Pearl picked up her copy from the mat. She was wet from the shower and wrapped in a towel, a cup of coffee in her hand, but she took a few moments to scan the newspaper from page to page. It held no further news about Faye's murder and no stories charting progress with the case. Instead, a front-page headline reported on

WhitLit, a new local literary festival that promised the arrival of some celebrity authors to the Horsebridge Cultural Centre.

Pearl asked herself how something as important as the murder of a once high-profile figure could be relegated so quickly to yesterday's news, but life moved on – even in Whitstable. Soon, the town's annual timetable of events would revolve once more through the calendar, turning in due course from May Day to the annual Oyster Festival, the Regatta, Harbour Day and the town's Carnival until finally, Christmas would again be looming. Pearl remembered the words she had used to Barbara at their last meeting: 'a star is someone people pay money to see'. That had been true enough of Faye, at one time, but now it seemed that Faye Marlow would drop out of memory just as easily as had Frankie Marshall – the granddaughter of a local whelk merchant. There were no surviving family members to keep Faye's star alive – only a young faithful fan – a lost child called Perdita who might never know how connected she really was to the actress, but who had been lucky to find a home filled with love.

Pearl reflected on this as she finished her coffee and fed the cats. Outside her window, the sky melded seamlessly into the grey incoming tide as gulls scavenged on the shoreline. She washed up her cup and was heading upstairs to get dressed for the day when her mobile phone beeped. McGuire's text was short and sweet, asking only if she could meet him as soon as possible before The Whitstable Pearl opened. She hesitated – and then responded, unsure why he had suggested the meeting but aware that she still carried the weight of truth around with her like a heavy burden she found impossible to share.

McGuire had asked Pearl to meet him at Dane John Gardens in Canterbury and she arrived in only fifteen minutes, finding a parking space for her Fiat in Watling Street before the shoppers descended on the Whitefriars precinct. Pearl hadn't visited the gardens for some considerable time, but the place still held memories. At one time, the local Register Office had been situated in an elegant building that looked out on to the lawns, where happy couples had posed for their wedding photos near an avenue of lime trees. She also recalled enjoying an outdoor performance there of *Romeo and Juliet* with a friend who had gone on to find her own Romeo and was now long married with children.

As Pearl reflected on this, she began to realise that her own life over the past twenty years had been inextricably linked to the stages of her son's development. Her diaries and calendars had marked dates of school terms, reports and exams, but now that Charlie was living independently of her, she wondered if time might slip away, un-detected, without any markers – without her even noticing. Nevertheless, in her heart there would always remain an image of the bond between mother and son – like that of a precious icon, con-stantly showing the way.

Pearl knew that being busy prevented her from contemplating the big questions that life was apt to pose, about purpose and direction, but at this moment, as she caught sight of McGuire standing near a fountain, facing away from her, she felt burdened not only by the moral dilemma she had been set by Barbara March, but by the fact that she had failed to share this with McGuire. She approached tentatively, noting that he was staring down into the fountain as though he might be counting the coins that lay scattered beneath the shallow, rippled water. She was almost standing in front of him before McGuire became aware of her presence. Allowing him to speak first, she felt uncomfortable, as though something lay between them – and knew that it was the truth.

McGuire was slightly taken aback to see that Pearl looked altered somehow, more serious than usual – the mischief gone from her eyes. 'Are you OK?' he asked. She nodded and managed a smile, still pleased to see him despite the burden she carried. In the pale morning light he looked weary, but the tension had gone from his face and his blue eyes had a certain sparkle to them, like sun on the sea. 'Thanks for coming,' he said. 'Would you like to get a coffee? There's a little place over there.'

But Pearl replied quickly, 'No, I'm fine.'

McGuire experienced a pang of disappointment: the Don Juan was opening and he felt like ordering some breakfast. He also felt like showing her off to the guys at the cabin – allowing them to see that he wasn't a complete loner – but he saw she was looking up at him, still waiting to hear what he had to say. Finally he explained, 'I thought you'd like to know that the case is pretty much sewn up.'

Pearl frowned. 'What do you mean?'

'Late last night...' McGuire broke off suddenly to ask again, 'Are you absolutely sure you don't want a coffee?'

'*No,*' she snapped. 'Just tell me what happened.'

'Well,' he began again. 'Last night, at around midnight, Barbara March walked into the station and made a full confession.'

'A confession?' Pearl echoed.

McGuire took note of her reaction, then went on. 'The whole story. How, and why, she murdered Faye Marlow.'

For a moment, Pearl felt an enormous sense of relief, and gratitude, to Barbara March for having lifted the burden from her shoulders, but then a seed of suspicion took root. 'What exactly did she say?'

McGuire shrugged. 'She claimed Faye was threatening to sack her and employ somebody younger. Possibly the Hewett girl.'

'Purdy?'

McGuire nodded but Pearl could see he was unconvinced. 'I think it ran deeper than that.'

'Why?' asked Pearl, guardedly.

'Because she seemed too calm when giving her statement. Resigned, almost.'

Pearl looked away as she tried to assimilate this news. 'And ... did she say *why* she came forward?'

'No – and that's another mystery. Because if she hadn't done so, I wouldn't have had a thing on her. And I'm betting she knew that too.' He was watching Pearl closely, but she still failed to meet his gaze. 'Do you have any idea why she'd do that?'

At this, Pearl summoned up the confidence to

look back at him. 'Why does anyone ever confess to a crime? Conscience? Guilt?'

McGuire wondered why she hadn't suggested another reason that he now put to her. 'She might also have expected a lighter sentence for pleading guilty.'

'Yes, of course,' Pearl said hastily, recognising her omission.

'And she might be right,' he continued. 'But she'll still go down for a very long time.'

In the next moment, he took a coin from his pocket and began to toy with it in his palm before running it across the back of his fingers. Pearl watched him, then heard herself murmur, 'Perhaps not as long as you think.'

McGuire stopped toying with the coin and looked back at her. 'What do you mean?' She opened her mouth to explain – then thought better of it. McGuire came closer. 'You don't exactly seem surprised by this news.'

'And is that why you invited me here?' she asked. 'To judge my reaction? You could have told me this on the phone.' She moved away from him, walking to the other side of the fountain, finding some welcome distraction in a sign that informed visitors that any coins found in the fountain would go towards a charity of the Lord Mayor's choosing.

McGuire joined her, but instead of taking up the thread of their conversation, Pearl pointed beyond him towards the city wall, saying, 'Did you know that you can climb that burial mound for a view of the city? It's been there since the Roman occupation. And the name, Dane John, is said to be a corruption of the Norman word *donjon*. I think it means fortification.' She paused. 'I learned all that at school. We came here one afternoon on a study trip. When you're a child and you look up at that burial mound ... it looks so big.'

McGuire gazed over at it, thinking about what she had said, then noticed that she was now staring straight up at the sky where the clouds were finally parting to allow the sun to burn through. Tilting her face to its warmth she closed her eyes before asking, 'I suppose you're going to be very busy later?'

Her eyes were still closed and McGuire took advantage of this to scan her features: the upturn of her nose, her long dark eyelashes, her full lips. 'Why d'you ask?'

'Because whatever happens, this evening I'm planning to go to the allotment. And you're welcome to come too.'

McGuire looked suitably confused by her invitation. 'Gardening?'

'I know,' she said with a smile. 'You're a city slicker, right? The nearest you've ever got to a plant is opening a supermarket salad. But the weather's being kind to us and you've seen for yourself how special it is there, so ... I was thinking of taking a picnic – some good food, wine, Manchego cheese, maybe even an oyster stout or two? If it does rain, well, there's always the shed for shelter.' As she looked at him, he saw the mischief was back in her expression. She finally admitted, 'To be honest, McGuire, I'm tired of digging.'

He gazed into her beautiful grey eyes and finally confessed, 'So am I.'

Then, in an effort to further lighten her mood,

265

he said: 'Here.' He was holding out a coin to her and as soon as she took it, he quickly tossed another into the fountain.

'You're meant to make a wish first!' she admonished him.

'I did,' he said. 'Now it's your turn.'

Closing her eyes again, Pearl tossed her own coin. Afterwards she was just about to say something but he spoke first. 'You know, this has got to be the first time that nothing's going to get in the way.'

'Of what?' she asked, puzzled.

'Of this.'

She felt his warm lips upon her own. As he held her close, she instantly responded, hearing only the soft trickle of water falling from the fountain upon their wishes. It was a moment she always knew would come – though not quite like this. The timing was unexpected, but had McGuire left it a moment later, something else would inevitably have intervened.

Sure enough, just then a group of young schoolchildren ran up to the fountain, chattering away as though they hadn't even noticed the two kissing strangers whom they now surrounded. McGuire smiled and offered Pearl his hand. 'Come on.'

Pearl paused, but only for a second, before she took McGuire's hand, aware that it had been a very long time since she had walked hand in hand with any man. But as they moved on together, leaving behind the old burial mound and crossing the gardens in which she had once watched *Romeo and Juliet*, it felt good to be with McGuire.

Good to be alive.

Acknowledgements

I would very much like to thank Tim Allen, Director of Kent Archaeological Projects, and also Canterbury Archaeological Trust, for the fascinating information and research given to me on the early copperas industry in Whitstable.

I'm also very grateful to John and Rosine Clandillon-Baker for their help with French translation and to Anthony Thwaite for his kind permission for the use of his beautiful poem, 'The Barrow'.

Continued thanks go to Krystyna Green, Clive Hebard, Florence Partridge and Kate Doran at Little, Brown and to Joan Deitch for her editing skills – and last but never least: Alex Holley, Michelle Kass, Taran Baker and Nicola O'Connell for their continued support in representing me.

The publishers hope that this book has given you enjoyable reading. Large Print Books are especially designed to be as easy to see and hold as possible. If you wish a complete list of our books please ask at your local library or write directly to:

Magna Large Print Books
Magna House, Long Preston,
Skipton, North Yorkshire.
BD23 4ND

This Large Print Book for the partially sighted, who cannot read normal print, is published under the auspices of

THE ULVERSCROFT FOUNDATION

THE ULVERSCROFT FOUNDATION

... we hope that you have enjoyed this Large Print Book. Please think for a moment about those people who have worse eyesight problems than you ... and are unable to even read or enjoy Large Print, without great difficulty.

You can help them by sending a donation, large or small to:

**The Ulverscroft Foundation,
1, The Green, Bradgate Road,
Anstey, Leicestershire, LE7 7FU,
England.**
or request a copy of our brochure for more details.

The Foundation will use all your help to assist those people who are handicapped by various sight problems and need special attention.

Thank you very much for your help.